Steamy Jailbird Romance Collection

Just Bae

Contents

McKenzie

Chapter 1 3
Chapter 2 19
Chapter 3 34
Chapter 4 55
Chapter 5 73
Chapter 6 94
Chapter 7 116
Chapter 8 134
Chapter 9 155
Chapter 10 176
Chapter 11 200
Chapter 12 212

Jennifer

Chapter 1 223
Chapter 2 247
Chapter 3 261
Chapter 4 275
Chapter 5 300
Chapter 6 319
Chapter 7 331
Chapter 8 350

McKenzie

Chapter One

It's a brown and orange sticky mess, and I wonder if it's even legal to call it food. Then again, the law doesn't apply here - we're all criminals. It doesn't matter if you're actually guilty of the crime you're convicted of because, as soon as you're on the other side of the fence, you're a felon in everyone's eyes. They could feed us dog food, and no one would care.

If you close your eyes, you can almost imagine this being a cafeteria bustling with people. But it's a difficult task - since we're only allowed plastic trays and cutlery, the sound isn't the same. Not to mention the stench. I try to block out the odor by imagining the sweet smell of freshly baked cinnamon... No, I can't go there. That was another time, another life. I've made a new one here. Besides, I can't show any signs of weakness.

I push the tray in front of me and stand up, heading for the exit.

"McKenzie!" a familiar voice barks behind me. I stop and turn around to look at Brad, one of the guards. His smile is smug, his stance wide, and he's holding his belt with both of his hands, trying to look intimidating. Like he's trying to make up for that tiny dick of his. "You know where the tray goes," he says, giving me a stern look.

"So do you. Why don't you put it there?" I challenge, not breaking eye contact.

"I'm not your servant, McKenzie! Now take your fucking tray and put it where it belongs." He's losing his patience. Good. It allows me to make a statement.

I walk back to the table, pick up the tray and walk to him slowly, dropping the tray on his feet. "Go fuck yourself," I say and saunter away, not bothering to look back. I know exactly what's in store for me after this, but it's worth it. I must assert my authority here. I've worked my ass off for almost eight years to build myself a reputation - sucking dicks, licking pussies, taking beatings, etc. And a prick like Brad will not take it away. The people in here are like wolves - they can smell fear. And the moment you show any type of weakness they will rip you to pieces. *Kill or be killed.*

On my way back to my cell I pass a couple of guards sneering at me. I just glare back. *Pieces of shit.* To be able to climb to the top of the food chain, whether you like it or not, you'll have to suck *a lot of* dicks. The new ones usually settle for a handjob, but once you've given them an inch, they want a mile.

I've never liked my cellmate. I can't put my finger on what it is, but she gives me a bad vibe. Rumors say she's an axe murderer, but I don't know how much of that is true. I find it hard to believe that she would end up in a medium-security prison if that were the case. She doesn't like me either, but at least she's not sucking up to me, which I can respect. We have a mutual understanding - I don't mess with her, and she doesn't mess with me.

She's reading a book from the prison library as I walk in. "Heard you told Brad to go fuck himself," she says without lifting her gaze. "You know that's going to cost you."

"Yeah, it's nothing I haven't done before. Where did you hear that anyway?"

"You know I won't tell you that. You've got your ways to stay on top, I've got mine."

That's the longest conversation we've had in a week, so I leave it at that.

I should be used to the blaring horn at night, but I still jerk at the sound.

"Twenty minutes before lights-out!" a robotic voice

shouts through the speaker. I drag my tongue across my front teeth, feeling their ragged surface. I grab my bag with toiletries and walk toward the communal bathroom. I'm not surprised when I meet Brad in the hallway on the way back.

"I think you have a problem with authority, inmate," he says, pointing his baton at me.

"I don't. Because you don't *have* any authority over me." I try to keep a condescending tone - fear or weakness will get me nowhere.

Brad approaches me with long strides and grabs the collar of my shirt, pulling my face toward his. "We'll see about that," he hisses in my ear, roughly shoving me into a nearby closet - a closet I'm more familiar with than I would care to admit. As soon as he's closed the door, he grabs my left hand, cuffs it, and locks it above my head on one of the metal shelves. I close my eyes and hear the familiar sound of pants unzipping. Pulling out a knife, he presses it to my throat. Guards aren't allowed to carry knives, but I guess he's found a way to smuggle one in. It's not that difficult.

"Grab it," he growls into my ear. I take his dick in my hand and start stroking it, making sure to squeeze the head the way I know he likes. He's already hard, and I hope I can finish him off as soon as possible, so I speed up the motion with my hand. "Not so fast, Laura." There's a hiss at the last syllable, and I cringe at the sound. I prefer if they don't use my first name - it makes it too personal. "Do you think a simple handjob is gonna make up for that stunt you pulled?"

He puts both hands on the waistband of my pants and pulls them down along with my panties, leaving me completely naked from the waist down.

"What's the matter, inmate? Don't know where to put it?" he mocks. I stay silent, not wanting to give in. "I think you do. It's not our first time," he groans in my ear, his breath on my skin disgusting me. "Why don't you put it there?" he taunts, mimicking my words from earlier. I could refuse to do it, but he's got the upper hand, and I know there's no way of escaping. So, I might as well get it over with.

Reluctantly, I bring his cock to my pussy, and when he pushes it in, I try not to show the pain that he's causing. He can feel that I'm not wet enough for this not to hurt, but I think the fucker thrives on that.

Instead of fighting it, I put my head against the wall and try to imagine someone else. Someone who never would have been this rough without my permission. I remember him moving above me, inside me, showing me what real pleasure was. How his gentle touch always made a warm, fuzzy feeling spread throughout my body. *No.* I won't go there.

"That's right. Right there," Brad pants, breaking me from my thoughts. For a second it didn't hurt, but with his words, the pain comes back in full force. He seems to be close, pushing into me faster and faster. He puts one of his hands on my breast, squeezing it hard, and this time I can't hold back a cry. I curse myself for letting him know much this hurts. I can't be weak - not in here. But he seems to be too wrapped up in his pleasure to notice. He's pressing himself into me with such roughness that my back is starting to hurt too. I'm relieved when I feel his grunting get louder, and I finally feel his semen filling me and then seeping out as he pulls out.

He tucks himself back into his pants, staring at my naked legs the entire time. "You little cunt. Don't you think you can give me that crap again? *I* rule this place, not you. Or we will find ourselves in this closet again. And next time, I won't be so gentle."

It's not the first time I've heard it, and it won't be the last. He looks me up and down. My pants are still at my ankles, and my hand is above my head. It's degrading, standing like this, completely at Brad's disposal, but giving him blowjobs and the occasional fuck is worth it. No inmate here dares to cross me, and the fishes are terrified of me. Exactly the way I want it. I guess my murder conviction doesn't hurt either. Well, technically it's not a murder conviction, but that's what everyone thinks. It works to my advantage, so I don't bother clearing up that misunderstanding.

"I would love to just leave you here, like this. But I need the handcuffs." He unceremoniously unlocks me and leaves without another word. Good. I have to wash his fucking cum off me.

There is no risk of pregnancy. Not anymore. After a year here it was discovered that I was pregnant. I have no idea who the father was - it could have been anyone of a handful of guards, but it was obvious to the warden what had happened. Not wanting to cause a scandal, I was forced to have an abortion. But it was done off the record and in silence, so it was sloppy and damaged me so much that I will never be able to bear children. Not that I was planning to, considering I'm gonna be locked up for a long time. But I would have liked to have had the fucking choice.

And as for STDs - there's nothing I can do but hope for the best. So far, nothing has come up during my medical exams. Most of the guards put on condoms, claiming that I'm too filthy to stick it in me without some sort of barrier. Not too filthy to fuck, though.

I hurry my way back to the bathroom to wash myself off quickly before lights out.

"That was a long pee." I don't miss the mockery in her voice.

"Shut up, Neilson," I glare at her.

As soon as the officers have counted everyone, the cell doors close, and I immediately dive under the covers of my bunk. This is the only time I allow myself to - at least partly - let my guard down. No one can see or hear me here, so I can let my mind wander. I let it wander to a time before I came here, where - at least for a short time - I was happy.

I've developed a technique to keep the nightmares in check - at least sort of. I can't wake up screaming in the middle of the night. That would indicate vulnerability. I don't want Brad or anyone - or *anything* - else in here invading my dreams, so before I fall asleep, I force myself to think of something completely different, hoping that it will transfer into my dreams. It usually works, but sometimes I've woken up covered in a cold sweat from night terrors. Fortunately, no one has noticed - as far as I can tell.

It works this time. Instead of moldy bathrooms, flaking paint, and plastic trays, I dream of *him*.

I trace the edge of the swell of his left cheek, just below his eye.

"What was it?" I don't have to ask why or how it happened - I already know who to blame, and as for the reason, it's anyone's guess. When I reach a sensitive spot of his bruise, he flinches away in pain.

"A wooden spoon," he says, looking at the floor.

He thinks this is his fault. I guess you can only hear how worthless and unwanted you are so many times before you start to believe it.

"I must clean this. Otherwise, it'll get infected."

"Okay," he croaks. I put my hands on both sides of his face, careful not to hurt him, and push his hair back, drag-

ging my fingers through his soft, blond locks. He closes his eyes and seems to enjoy this moment. It feels surprisingly intimate.

I could tell him that none of this is his fault and that everything will be okay, but I know he won't believe me. Besides, I love him too much to offer him meaningless platitudes.

I swing my leg over his lap and straddle him, giving him a light kiss on the mouth. He slides his hands over the outsides of my thighs, letting them rest by my waist for a minute before gliding underneath my shirt. He groans when he palms my breasts, and I moan when he swipes his thumbs across my already-puckered nipples.

I reach down between us and start unbuckling his belt and unzipping his pants. He's already hard when I start stroking him through the fabric of his underwear. He keeps one of his hands on my breast while the other snakes under my skirt and starts rubbing me through my panties. For being so strong, his fingers can be surprisingly delicate. But I need more. So, I reach underneath the waistband of his boxers and bring his cock out of its confinement. At this, he pushes my underwear to the side, sliding his fingers through my folds.

"Oh, my..." I pant. He removes his hand and I instinctively scoot closer to him, dragging the tip of his erection from my entrance up to my clit, coating him in my juices.

"That's -" he gasps. "It feels incredible. You're incredible."

I put his cock at my entrance, and he pushes in without hesitation. It feels so good, the way he fills me up completely. It's the safest I've ever felt. He moves both of his hands, letting them linger by my waist, holding me in a firm grip.

He moans when I start moving my hips, but I let him set the pace with his hands. He needs this. He needs to be in control. He needs to know that somebody's always by his side, so I follow his motions, and it's not long before he starts thrusting into me, sending a wave of pleasure through me, and I know I'm close.

He's twitching inside me, and I know he's close too. I almost think he's gonna finish first, but when he moves his hand to where we're connected and start teasing my clit, it's my undoing. He keeps the same fast pace throughout my entire orgasm as he rubs me. A couple of more thrusts, and then he's coming too. His movements become wilder as he spills inside me.

After we've both come down from our highs, I move to stand up.

"Stay."

The look of pure innocence on his face melts my heart, and I know I can never deny him anything.

"Always."

I'm awakened by the horn, signaling it's 6:30 a.m. We

have fifteen minutes to come down to the dining hall, and then it's time for work. *Work.* They say it's a way of getting inmates assimilated into the real world when they get out. But really, it's just a way to get cheap labor. We're paid about a dollar an hour to use at the prison commissary.

My assignment is the laundry room, where we wash the bed sheets and the inmates' clothes. It's an easy job, and it's an upgrade compared to my first one, cleaning the toilets. I had to suck the warden's dick twice to get transferred. It was worth it.

You stand and fold the laundry as it comes out of the dryer. It's kind of therapeutic. I don't have to pretend in here. It probably sounds silly, but this is about the only secure place I've got. Sometimes you get new cellmates when old ones get released or transferred, changing the dynamic completely, and once in awhile you have to change cells. But this place is constant. It always smells the same, and you always do the same thing while you're here.

Whispers across the table break me from my thoughts. It's two of the girls with minor charges - I think it was drugs, but I'm not sure. I don't care, and I don't bother to learn their names.

"Hey." They snap their heads up, fear registering on their faces when they see it's me. *Good.* "Shut the fuck up."

"Sorry." They become silent and continue to work. But it only takes fifteen minutes before they resume their chatter. Are they *giggling*? I can't think of any reason to be giggling in this place, and their cackling brings to mind the sound of long nails scraping across a chalkboard. I slam the shirt I'm holding on the table, making as much of a noise as I can, and walk up to them.

"What could be so fucking funny that you're giggling?"

They somber quickly. "Sorry, but have you seen the new guard? He can cuff me anytime," one of them says, wiggling her eyebrows. They're crushing over a fucking *guard*? It's the pretty ones that are the most dangerous. They're used to getting what they want, and they will expect to get it here too. The ugly ones are usually happy with a handjob, or sometimes even just a kiss.

But a new guard poses a problem for me. I must get him on my side before bitches like Cash get their claws in him. We're in different parts of the prison and most of the inmates are either on my side or hers. She's been inside about two years longer than I have, and she gave me my welcome party when I arrived. After only a couple of days in here, she and her mercenaries beat me up and robbed me of the few personal belongings I had, only to assert her authority.

The bruises and cuts healed, and most of my stuff could be replaced - except for one thing. She took the only photo of *him* that I had. It's of both of us, me sitting in his lap, and we're laughing at something I can't recall. I tried to commit it to memory, but as the years went by it faded away. I never got the picture back, and I'm still biding my time to get revenge. But it's difficult considering we operate different parts and the few times I do see her; she's always surrounded by her "bodyguards."

"What's his name?"

"Radford. He'll probably grace us with his presence at lunch."

I spare a glance at the massive clock on the wall. 9:37 a.m. That won't do - I have to get to him as soon as possible. "Where did you see him?"

"In the hallway. I think he was going to Bowen's office."

"When?"

"About fifteen minutes ago."

That's good news. Hopefully, he hasn't met any of the other inmates yet. Maybe I can intercept him before he does. I haven't been to the toilet since I got here, which is a great opportunity. I walk up to the guard standing by the door.

"I need to go to the bathroom."

He checks the watch on his wrist. "You can wait till the break in twenty minutes," he responds dryly.

"I need to go now," I insist. "It's lady trouble," I say, trying to sound uncomfortable, squeezing my thighs together for effect.

He sighs. "Fine, but hurry back."

I scurry around him, making my way toward the bathroom. Before I enter, I look back at the guard, making sure he's not looking, and walk past the door instead.

As soon as he's out of eyesight, I pick up my speed to meet this new guard before anyone else does. Fortunately, the counselor's office isn't that far away from the bathroom, so I hope I can make this quick. It's usually enough to be the first to meet them and form some sort of bond. That way, when - or if - they chose their allegiance, you've already got them somewhat on your side.

But I'm out of luck. The office is locked, and I don't hear any voices inside. Bowen always has his door open - I think he has to, being a counselor and all. Here, they take the my-door-is-always-open-policy literally. So, if it's closed it must mean he's not there, and not that new guard either. Fuck. I can't go around looking for them, so I guess I have to wait until lunch.

"McKenzie!" a guard snarls behind me. Shit, the odds are not in my favor today. I turn around, flashing him an innocent smile. "What are you doing here?"

He's tall, with his dark brown hair in what looks like it's supposed to be a crew cut, but it's been a while since he's cut it. He has to shake his head to get rid of the hair from his gray eyes, almost the same shade as mine. He's holding a styrofoam mug, with what I presume is coffee, because based on how red he is around his pupils, he didn't get much sleep last night. It says 'Bailey' on his uniform. "I was looking for Mr. Bowen." Which is sort of true.

"Then you should come when he has visiting hours," he says, pointing at the sign next to the door. "Besides, aren't you supposed to be working? We don't pay you to wander around the hallway." His voice is stern. I stifle a snort. *Pay?*

I approach him. Hopefully, I can persuade him to not rat me out. "I'm sorry, Officer Bailey." They love when you address them as officers rather than guards. "I just needed to see him - it's really important. Please don't tell anyone. I'd owe you one," I say, sliding my fingers up his arm and hoping he'll respond like most men do. He doesn't seem to mind my touch, but he doesn't say anything for a while either.

He finally breaks the silence. "Just get back to work."

I scramble around him and half-run back to the laundry room. I spend almost two hours stealing subtle glances at the clock and only halfheartedly folding the sheets. Honestly, who's gonna tell the fucking difference? As soon as the sound blares, announcing lunchtime, I don't even finish the one I'm folding, just throwing it back in the dryer and hurrying to the dining hall.

As soon as I'm there, my jaw drops. I actually think it fucking drops. My eyes go directly to *him*. He still has the same effect on a room - it seems brighter and somehow more radiant. The lines on his face are more distinct, but it only makes him, oh-so-much sexier. His eyes are still the same, though, the same piercing blue gaze that could make any panties drop to the floor soaking wet with just one look. I can't reconcile this image with the battered, bleeding boy who used to haunt my dreams. He's put on some muscles, and he fills out his uniform perfectly - enough to get a hint of the chiseled pectoral and abdominal muscles he's sporting underneath. His hair is a little shorter than it used to be, but I think it's an improvement. He holds his hands behind his back with a straight posture. He doesn't need to assert his masculinity by gripping his belt or spreading his legs.

He's changed, but I can still see the innocence and purity as clearly as all those years ago. Instinctively, my hand covers my mouth, and for the first time in eight years, I let myself say his name. It comes out as a whisper, but inside I'm screaming.

Matthew.

Chapter Two

*N**o*. It's not him. It *can't* be him. During all this time I've been trying to keep him out of my head. Out of sight, out of mind. And he's been out of my mind for eight years. He will *not* make a reappearance now. I've worked too fucking hard for this. This will ruin everything.

"You're catching flies, McKenzie," an inmate announces.

"I didn't peg you for one of those who would fall for a cowboy," another one says.

They're right. I don't. I fell for him a long time ago. I think I'm still falling.

A push in my back jolts me back to reality. "Move along. You're holding up the line." If I weren't so confused, I'd probably send the bitch behind me a glare, promising that she'd pay for that comment later. But I don't. Instead, I catch up with the line, careful not to meet his eyes. He can't know I'm here. Besides, I think I'll crumble to pieces if I look at him one more time.

The food looks like it always does. It doesn't matter what they call it - I wouldn't be surprised if it's the same goo every day, but now I'm happy to have something to occupy my hands. I sit down at my usual spot. No one dares to take it. It happened once, and she ended up with a black eye.

"So, what do you want to do?" Cindy asks.

"What?" I look at her in confusion.

"That one that pushed you. We have to reciprocate." Cindy and Tanisha do my dirty work. In return for carrying out small favors for me, I give them security. I have a network full of inmates - and some guards - in different parts of the prison that do different types of work for me. It's everything from buying something in the commissary for me to taking care of troublesome inmates and smuggling drugs.

"What's she in for?"

"Possession, I think," Tanisha replies. "We should beat her up." She's resourceful and good at procuring weapons from what we have, but she's not that bright. There are better ways than always beating someone up to get your point across.

"Is she on the list?" I have a list of inmates who buy different types of drugs from me. It's good for moments like these to keep tabs on your customers and know their weaknesses.

"Yeah."

"Fine. Cut her off. She's not getting *anything* from *anyone* for two weeks. And let the others know that if they sell her anything, they'll end up in the infirmary."

A smile spreads on her face, but a whistle echoing across the hall catches everyone's attention. I turn to the source of the noise. *Of course.* It's Neilson.

"Finally. They realized we're women." Her gaze is set on Matthew. Yes, it's definitely him. "You can stay in the cell next to mine, cowboy!"

He doesn't flinch - doesn't even acknowledge her presence - and I'm filled with an odd sort of satisfaction.

"Neilson! Get back in line and shut the fuck up," another guard shouts at her. It's the one I met in the hallway earlier.

"You've got competition, Bailey." She looks back at him but follows his instructions. During the entire lunch, there are whispers and subtle glances Matthew's way. It's not until I'm about to leave when someone at the table next to us speaks up.

"Hey, Radford! I can give you a tour and show you the ropes around here. I'm sure we can think of a way for you to repay me," she smirks.

He strides up to her table, flashing her a gorgeous

smile. “Let’s get one thing straight.” His voice is still as soft as ever, albeit a little darker. It feels strange hearing it again after all these years. “I’ve been to three different maximum-security prisons. I know all the ropes. I know how you get stuff in and out, and I know where you hide it. Bother me again and I might do a spontaneous sweep of your cell. I know *exactly* where to look. Now shut up and finish your fucking meal.” His smile doesn’t falter once, and it’s eerie how he can deliver such a threat in that casual tone.

He walks back to where he stood and continues to observe the hall. I quickly finish my meal and try to leave as discreetly as possible. I walk past Brad, placing the tray where it belongs. He sneers at me like it’s some kind of victory for him. Any other day I would have done something to wipe that fucking grimace off his face, but not today.

I just walk past him and hope that Matthew doesn’t notice me.

When I get back to my cell, I throw myself under the covers, as if I could block him out with a piece of fabric. He invades my mind no matter what, and I curse myself for reacting this way to his presence. What fucking right does he have to waltz in here after all this time?

I hate him. I hate him. I hate him. No. I love him. Fuck, I still love him.

Neilson is still in the dining hall, and she’ll probably be

there for a while. I decide to take the risk and let my hand dip beneath the waistband of my pants. I need some release and I'm already wet. He's always had that effect on me - the sound of his voice, his breath on my skin, the touch of our tongues whirling in a dance we've perfected.

I think of his fingers skating across my breasts, hardening my nipples, and the way he would grab my ass and bury himself inside me a little deeper. My finger slides around my clit in tight, fast circles as I imagine the weight of his cock in my hand, feeling every ridge as I pump him before taking him in my mouth.

I think of the pants and moans he lets out when he fucks me, and it exhilarates me, knowing that I'm the only one who gets to hear those sounds. It fills me with a sense of pride. He fills me both mentally and physically. I'm completely at his mercy, and he knows it - just as he's at mine.

The thoughts of him bring me to the edge so fast, and I'm already frantically bucking my hips against the mattress, trying to stifle the moans that threaten to escape my mouth. When I picture his eyes locking on me as he's plunging into me with everything that he's got, it's my undoing. The pleasure explodes inside me in one of the most intense orgasms I've had in a very long time.

My heart is pounding in my ear, and I'm out of breath. Fuck. I hope I didn't make too much noise. It's not uncommon to hear inmates pleasuring themselves - and others. We all do it. You just don't want anyone to know exactly when or where. Because at that moment you are weak - you have no control, and you don't want anyone taking advantage of that.

When I've come back to my senses and caught my breath I turn to the side, facing the wall. What is he doing here? It can't be a coincidence. He must know that I'm here too, but if they knew about our connection, there's no way he would be allowed to work here. He must be fucking pissed at me. He must be here for revenge. He's here to kill me. That must be why he's here. It's the only explanation. Inmates, I can protect myself from, but COs are another matter. If they want to harm you, they will.

I don't know how long I've been lying here, but I'm too wrapped up in my thoughts to notice there's another person in the cell. I quickly snap my head around, and I'm met with Matthew's stare. He's standing casually, leaning against the door. My hand discreetly goes for the cavity in the wall next to the bed where I keep my knife.

"It's not there," he says, holding it up. My heart drops. He's unarmed me, and now there is nothing anyone can do to stop him from killing me. I've pictured this moment in a thousand ways, but neither of those has been by Matthew's hands. "It's the truth. I know exactly where to look."

"You saw me?"

"Of course, I did. You're the reason I'm here," he says calmly, which makes him even more intimidating.

"Just do it fast."

"What?" Confusion is written all over his face. "What are you talking about?"

"You're here to kill me," I say like I need to inform him.

"What? No. You couldn't be more wrong, Laura." He moves across the room, and I instinctively curl up against the wall. He halts, hurt registering on his face.

"Then why did you take my knife?"

"Precaution. You'll get it back, I promise. I didn't want to risk you throwing it at me." He doesn't move - only stands in the middle of the cell.

"So, you're not here to kill me?" He shakes his head. "Are you angry with me?"

"No," he replies sincerely, taking the knife and gently putting it by the edge of the bed. He doesn't have the same posture of confidence he had during lunch. There's a vulnerability in the way he looks at me. I grab the knife and rapidly put it back where it belongs.

He's still looking at me like he's expecting me to say something. I walk up to him so that our faces are only inches apart, and I can smell a familiar scent of mint. He still uses the same toothpaste, the one I said was my favorite. I raise my gaze, my eyes locking on his. "Then fuck you."

"Laura - " I know this voice. He's always used it to calm me down. But not this time. I won't allow it.

"Don't you fucking dare say my name again," I say

through gritted teeth. "You're a correctional officer, and I'm an inmate. We don't know each other." I can't stay here. I must leave.

The door is still open, so I bolt for the opening and hurry to the bathrooms. I lock myself into one of the stalls and sit on the toilet, my hands covering my ears. I can't hold it together.

Whatever reason he has for being here, I don't want to hear it. I *can't*. He left me in this fucking place. For the first time since the first night in here, I allow myself to cry. I cry for myself. I cry for him and us. It's gone. Whatever existed between us is gone.

A gentle knock on the door pulls me from my stupor.

"Occupied." I manage to keep a steady voice despite my sobbing. Another knock. I move to my feet, flinging the door open, and the girl on the other side instantly backs away. "Are you deaf or color blind?" I point to the lock. "See this thing here? When it's red, it means someone's in here."

"I know, I'm sorry. I just - " I sigh loudly, hoping it will get her to the point faster. "I need *something* ." She can't stand still, and she keeps rubbing her arms.

Something doesn't tell me anything - she must be more specific. Then I recognize her - it's the girl who shoved me in line at lunch. She must be desperate, coming to me so soon.

"No can do." I must keep up appearances, even though the only thing I want to do right now is curl up and die.

"I didn't even know it was you. Come on, cut me some slack," she pleads.

"How desperate are you?"

She licks her lips and puts her hand between my legs, rubbing me. "Very."

I swat her hand away. I'm no stranger to letting someone else finish me off once in awhile - you get tired of your fingers sometimes. But it's not the currency I use. I need a more long-lived commitment. "That's not how this works. If I let you have some, you are *mine*. You will do as *I* say, and if I catch you so much as looking Cash's way, I know many people in here who just can't wait to beat someone up."

She nods and rubs her nose. I go to the soap container and remove it - there's a loose tile, and behind it, I have a small bag with crystal meth. I take it and toss it to her.

"I move my shit every day, so don't you even think about going back here, thinking you can rip me off."

"I-I, won't," she stammers as I walk past her.

"You junkies are the easiest."

When I get back to my cell Matthew's gone, but Neilson is back.

"I saw you eyeing that new guard." Twice in two days. She must be in a chatty mood.

"Yeah, didn't everyone? He's the first one in here who

fills out his uniform." I pause. "In the right places. You announced it in front of everyone if I'm not mistaken."

"Just letting him know his options, is all. But you were eye-fucking him."

Shit, I didn't realize I was that obvious. "Hm? He would be a good distraction from Brad, I suppose."

She just snorts.

* * *

The next day he's back in the dining hall. I guess I shouldn't be surprised - he does work here, and I can't avoid him forever. I can't make him quit.

A hand waving in front of my face suddenly obscures my view. "Hey, wake up."

"What?"

"That meth head. She got her hands on a bindle," Cindy tells me.

"Yeah, I gave it to her."

"What? Are you going soft, McKenzie?" Tanisha asks in shock.

I point at her. "Listen. To get where I am today, you need brawns *and* brains." I tap my finger on my temple. "I could have denied her, but then she'd probably gone to Cash instead. Now, I've got another foot soldier. Besides, I didn't say she could have more than one."

"Ah, you're cruel." Tanisha nods her head, apparently liking my tactic.

"I am. And don't ever call me fucking soft again. I can cut *you* off too." Tanisha is also a drug addict. That's how I got her too. Her face falls, and she's quiet for the rest of the meal.

I try to steal subtle glances Matthew's way. I don't want to. I want to forget him, but I can't help myself from looking his way. He's shaved clean, with not even a trace of stubble, and his hair is perfect, just the right length and styled just the right amount. Why does he have to be so fucking gorgeous?

It's the same routine every day. I see him three times a day, trying not to get caught staring, and then I rub one off when I can. I can't help the way my body responds to him. It's the same as it was before - that hasn't changed.

One night I notice my knife's gone missing, and I know exactly who to blame. He's the only one who knows I have it. I go straight to the dining hall. Since he's always there, I guess he's also there between meals.

He's sitting by one of the tables, alone in the entire room. It feels weird, being here without a bunch of people eating. His shoulders are slumped, and he's leaning on one of his elbows, looking down at the table. In front of him is my knife. I take a quick look around to make sure the room is completely empty.

"This will get you sent to the max, you know that right?" he says, not taking his eyes off the table.

"Yeah. That's not the only thing I do in here that will," I say as I cautiously sit across from him. "Why haven't you turned it in?"

"I want you to hear me out," he says, pushing the knife in my direction. "But I won't force you. You can take it and leave. I won't turn you in, you have my word. But I will not disappear, and I won't give up," he says matter-of-factly.

I slam my hand on the table, grab the knife and quickly shove it into my pocket. "You've had eight fucking years," I seethe. "You left me in here to rot, and now you think you can come here and everything's gonna be alright?"

"I don't," he says solemnly.

"Good. Because it's not gonna happen, so save yourself the trouble. Turn me in. I don't care. That way I won't have to look at you every fucking day, reminding me that I'm here because of *you* !" I don't even mean the last part. I said it just to hurt him, and by the way, his eyes instantly tear up, I know I've succeeded. But I don't see it as a victory. It feels like we've both lost.

"I'm sorry that's the way you see it," he whispers.

Inside I'm screaming. I want to take him in my arms and comfort him. I see his pain, but I cannot give in to it. So, I leave before I do something stupid like cry.

It's a Thursday when it happens. I know because it says "soup" on the menu. Thursday is "soup day." Why they bother to call it a menu is beyond me - it's just a list of different names for the same thing.

I'm not listening to Tanisha's and Cindy's chatter. They're useful, but I don't particularly enjoy their company. As always, Matthew overlooks the dining hall. After he shut that girl up on his first day there have been no more catcalls. He has earned the inmates' respect.

I've managed to avoid any more encounters with him, but I don't miss his glances my way when no one else is looking. I can't say I hate it. I kind of like the feeling of him looking out for me. I know I shouldn't, but I do. Today, he's standing next to Brad. Their physical appearances are similar, blond with quite a muscular build, though Brad is one or two inches taller. But their personalities are opposites.

Brad says something to him that I don't quite catch - I usually don't, but his comment is funny because Matthew gives him a subtle laugh. How can he stand there and fucking laugh? With Brad, of all people? Is this place or this situation a joke to him? I don't know if it's the tension between us that has been building ever since he came here, or if it's something else, but my body moves of its own accord. It's like I'm on autopilot and I snap.

I leave my tray on the table and walk with determined steps to them. Both Brad and Matthew see me, but technically I haven't broken any rules, so they can't do anything. My hands automatically go for Matthew's chest, and I push him back. Hard. He manages to keep his balance, but the damage I caused isn't physical.

I instantly regret it. What in the world was I thinking? But before I can do anything to try to rectify the situation, an arm locks around my waist and someone harshly slams me to the ground. A hand holds my head down while my hands are cuffed behind my back.

"She's feisty, this one," I hear Brad musing as he holds me down. My face is pushed to the side, away from them, so I can't see Matthew. It's probably a good thing. "You know where you're going," he wheezes into my ear. I do, but I won't dignify him with an answer.

I'm brusquely hauled up to my feet by rough hands, and I'm sure it will bruise. Standing up, I catch a glimpse of Matthew. He's not embarrassed by being pushed by a female inmate, as most other guards in here would be.

"Hey, take it easy, man," he tells Brad calmly. "She's already cuffed." *Why does he care?* I just humiliated him in front of the entire dining hall, and he cares about how Brad's manhandling me?

"Why? These sluts can't go around here thinking that they set the rules. *We* fucking own this place."

Matthew flinches a little at his use of the word *slut,* but other than that, his expression is impassive. "Do it by the book. You don't want her getting off on a technicality." It doesn't matter if Brad does it by the book or not - they don't care about proper protocol here.

I've never heard him so calculating and cold before, and *that* scares me more than anything else.

Brad huffs, but his grip loosens a little, and he and another guard drag me away. Before we turn the corner, I manage to turn my head in Matthew's direction. He's not there, and a pang of regret hits me. I'm still angry, but I've gotten used to seeing him and being around him again.

But now it will be a long time before I see him again.

Chapter Three

Solitary confinement. That's what they call it. *The hole* is a more accurate description - that's basically what it is. I'd say it's a ten-by-five-foot room with a bed and a toilet. That's it. So far, I've managed to stay out of this place, so I have no idea what to expect.

The slam of the door behind me startles me, and I instinctively hurl myself at it, banging frantically.

"Hey! How long will I be in here?" No answer. I keep hitting the door until my hands are numb, and I slide down in defeat. I'd never would have thought that the reason I'd be down here would be for striking a guard, let alone Matthew. I've never used force against a CO before, and I've never planned on it, either. It's a foolish thing to do because I know they will retaliate - tenfold.

But that's not what's bothering me the most. It's the fact that I used violence against Matthew. *Matthew,* of all people. I've said some mean things to him, but I never thought I'd resort to using my fists. Our first physical contact in almost a decade - and I hit him. I'm no better than *her*. I deserve to be here.

After I've given up on anyone opening the door, I move to the bed. The mattress is thinner than I'm used to, so it's almost like sitting directly on the bed frame. There is no window or clock, so there's no way I will be able to keep track of time. It was lunch when I got here, so the next meal would be supper - if they planned on feeding me.

I guess they don't. I must have been here for twelve hours, pacing and counting the small cracks in the cement walls. Trying to sleep might help me forget about the hunger, so I lie on the bed, but the metal bars are poking through the bedding - it feels like they're poking my bones. The floor is at least flat, so I throw the mattress down there, alleviating some of the pain. It's hardly an improvement, but I'll take it, and at some point, sleep claims me.

I'm startled awake by the opening of a hatch on the door, and a tray slides into the room. Jumping up from the mattress, I bolt for the door, banging on it.

"Hey, how long have I been in here?" No answer. I give it a few more beats and kicks, but it's pointless. All I'm rewarded with is silence. A grumble in my stomach shifts my focus to the tray I've been given, but I lose my appetite as soon as I see its content. I didn't know it was possible to make food *less* appetizing than what I usually get, but it is. Refusing to eat it, I slide the tray across the floor.

I go back to my mattress, hoping to get some more sleep. That's probably the best way to pass the time, and I drift in and out of consciousness. There's no way of telling how long I've been out when I wake up, so I try to keep track of how many times I've been fed, but that is also a difficult task. They change the trays every meal, so I can't count them.

Every time the hatch opens, it's the same procedure - I slam my fist against the door, demanding to know how long I've been here and refusing to eat the food. There's never an answer, but if I'm going to die here, I will *not* go quietly.

Not eating is starting to take its toll on me, and the longer I spend here, the less powerful my cries are when they slide into the tray. But I still refuse it - I think I could die of hunger here out of spite. The lack of nutrients makes me hallucinate - at least, I think so. I'm sure that the blood covering the walls earlier wasn't real.

"It's Friday night." It's probably a figment of my imagination because the voice is oddly like Matthew's. "Please, Laura. Just eat the food." And then he's gone. I'm hurled back to another Friday night - back to when it all started.

I don't want to be here, but everyone is required to make an appearance.

"Just eat the food, and then you can go home," someone says behind my back, interrupting my staring competition

with the table full of side dishes. I turn around and meet a pair of stunningly blue eyes. They belong to the person whose fault we must be here - Matthew.

"I can't walk out of here without anyone noticing. They take note of attendance."

"So? You're already signed in, aren't you? I don't think they'll have a roll call. Besides, I feel bad enough already for dragging everyone here."

"It's not your fault."

"I think it is."

Last week the school's wrestling team - which Matthew is the captain of - won a statewide tournament. I know because I watched every one of his matches. Not because wrestling interests me - Matthew does. I wish I could say I don't care about boys. I have other issues that I should be more concerned about, like a dead father and an absent mother. But his ocean blue eyes, wavy blond hair, and warm-hearted personality are irresistible.

The board was so proud to have a winner representing the school that the principal organized a get-together - with mandatory attendance. I'm not enjoying spending time in a vast gymnasium full of people I don't know, but everyone's appearing to have a better time than I had expected.

"Okay, it is your fault," I smile, heat creeping up on my neck. "But it's a nice turn-out," I smirk, fidgeting with my braid.

Matthew chuckles. "Yeah, I think someone spiked the

punch, so..." he trails off, looking out over the crowd. Matthew? Breaking the rules? He's always struck me as a moral compass, which makes him even more interesting.

"Someone?" I question. Shit, did I flirt?

He looks down into his red solo cup. "Yeah, someone *." A smile creeps up on his face. Is he blushing? It's hard to tell with the lighting in here.*

"Congratulations on the win, by the way."

"Thanks. But I don't know if it was worth it, though. I've been paraded around on a victory tour like some trophy the entire week." He sighs. "Between this and school, *I haven't had time for anything else, you know? I haven't had any time alone whatsoever."*

People always surround Matthew - I thought he preferred it that way.

"Maybe it'll cool down next week."

"Hopefully."

It's a natural end to the conversation, so we fall silent after that. It's awkward - at least for me. I'm standing next to the guy I've been secretly pining after for the entire year, and now that we're alone, I don't know what to say. I don't even know why he's talking to me. We share some classes and greet each other in the hallway, but that's it. We're not friends.

"So, what do you do in your alone time?" I blurt out in a feeble attempt to end the silence.

He looks at me in surprise but answers without hesitation. "I draw."

"You draw?"

"Yeah, nothing much. Only sketches and doodles and stuff like that. But it's therapeutic." He seems lost in thought, a forlorn expression on his face. "Anyway." He turns back to me. "Can I offer you some punch?" he asks, gesturing for the bowl.

Ever since I first laid my eyes on him a year ago, I knew I could never deny him anything. "Yeah, sure."

The evening ends the best way possible - Matthew pressing my back into the brick wall behind the gymnasium and his tongue swirling around mine. I must be dreaming. No, not in my wildest dreams could I've imagined something like this happening. Or that it would feel this good.

His hands are on my hips, gripping me firmly, and his thumbs gently gracing the exposed skin above my waist will forever be etched to my body. I rest my hands on his solid chest, and when I lock them around his neck, pulling him closer, he moves my hips closer to his, and I let out a moan in his mouth.

At this, he skates his hands under my shirt and settles on my ribcage, right below my bra. There's an ache between my legs, and I'm suddenly aware of where this is going.

"Matthew," I sigh, breaking the kiss. His lips leave mine, and I instantly miss them. "I... I've never..." I don't finish the sentence, hoping he understands what I'm trying

to say. He's probably used to experienced girls, and here I am - a flat-chested virgin with no curves and no -

"Me neither."

"You mean, you haven't...?"

"No. Disappointed?" he asks dryly. He removes his hands from me, dragging one through his tousled hair and turning away. "I'm a fucking failure," he mutters under his breath.

"What? No, why would I be disappointed?" I question, putting my hand on his shoulders, beckoning him to return to me. "I'm surprised, is all." *I'm relieved.*

He puts his hand on mine, squeezing it gently. Taking a deep breath, like he's mentally preparing for something, he finally turns around. He smiles, but I can see something is bothering him right through it. "Let me walk you home," he offers.

"Okay."

We walk in silence, and when we're halfway to my house, Matthew envelops my hand in his, lacing our fingers together—a warm, fuzzy feeling from where we're touching spreads throughout my entire body.

Outside my front door, there's an awkward silence - neither of us knows how to say goodbye. But it's Matthew who speaks first.

"If you want to, I can... pick you up on Monday." He rubs the side of his neck. "So, you don't have to walk to school."

How does he know that I always walk to school? "Yeah, that would be great." I sound more casual than I thought, considering I'm bouncing up and down inside.

"Okay, see you then," he says, kissing me on the cheek.

He keeps his promise, picking me up Monday morning, and we walk into the school building hand-in-hand. Knowing what a statement that makes, I'm nervous as hell, but Matthew takes it in stride. I'm not famous. I'm a nobody, and our coming together raises quite a few eyebrows. But comments thrown our way roll off him like water off a duck's back, and I feel surprisingly at ease.

It takes about a week before I notice his first bruise.

It's a Wednesday, and I haven't seen him all day. He's had practice all morning, so when I spot him by his locker, I half-run to him, hugging him from behind.

"Ouch," he exclaims, instantly turning around. The look of pain on his face disappears and is replaced by a smile. "Oh, hey," he says, kissing me. I'm still not used to kissing in public, but I like the softness of Matthew's lips, and suddenly I don't give a rat's ass about who's looking.

"What's the matter?" I ask when we break apart.

"Nothing, just an occupational injury," he tries to joke it off, leaning in for another kiss.

"Let me see." I grasp for his shirt, but he stops me.

"It's nothing, really. Just drop it." He sounds annoyed.

I try to give him a stern look, and his expression softens. He sighs and lifts his shirt, revealing a bruise the size of a fist on his side, right above his waist. It's dark around the edges, but the center is turning yellow.

"Oh my god, Matthew. What happened?"

"I took a knee to the side during practice."

"This is not from today."

"So maybe it was last week?" he sighs. "Wrestling is a physical sport." He pulls his shirt down again, seemingly embarrassed. I do not know how common bruises like that are in wrestling, so I guess I have to take his word for it.

It takes a month before I meet his mother - she's a bitch.

Matthew and I are lying on his bed, tongues dancing around one another's and hands wandering. It started innocently - I came here to study. We have a calculus test next week, and Matthew was supposed to help me. We began by the fireplace in the downstairs living room, but he kept distracting me, drawing flowers in my notebook and trailing kisses down my neck.

His thumbs trace the outside of my bra, underneath my shirt, and my elbows rest on either side of his face as I thread my fingers through his hair. I rest my full body weight on him, but he doesn't seem bothered.

When he dips his thumb underneath my bra - skating it across my nipple - I don't know how to handle the sensation. Instinctively, I buck my hips against him, and I'm surprised by how good it feels. I want to feel more of him.

The sound from the front door startles us both, but Matthew looks downright scared. He bolts up, almost pushing me off the bed. Before I ask him about it, he quickly scrambles the papers and notes on the floor underneath the bed, along with his leather sketchbook. I adjust my shirt when the door opens, revealing a woman in her forties. Her blond hair is pulled back in a tight bun, and her icy blue eyes give me the chills.

"Hey, Mom," Matthew says carefully.

She doesn't say anything, her eyes not meeting either of ours. Matthew seems paralyzed in her presence. Without warning, she walks into the room, picking up his sketchbook from under the bed. She inspects its content with suspicion and shoots a glare Matthew's way.

"Downstairs." Then she leaves.

We sit still for a couple of seconds before Matthew moves to leave. "I'll be right back," he whispers, standing up and dragging a hand through his hair. Is he going to listen to her? Granted, I don't know their kind of relationship, but that was weird - disrespecting our privacy and snatching his personal belongings right before our eyes.

"Matthew?"

He turns around. "Just wait here," he croaks, carefully closing the door and leaving.

As soon as I hear him walking downstairs, I dart for the door, pressing my ear against it. After a few seconds, I hear hushed voices, but I can't determine what they're saying. Curiosity gets the better of me, and I sneak out in the hallway, allowing myself to hear the conversation.

"Is this what you're wasting your time on?" she questions. "Scribblings and girls?"

Silence.

"Let me tell you one thing, Matthew. This - it stops now."

"Please, Mom. Don't." His voice has never sounded weaker.

"Drawing is for sissies." There's a thud, but I can't determine what caused it. "Are you a sissy, Matthew?" she taunts. I can't believe what I hear - she's bullying her son.

"No."

"Then you better wipe those tears away. Boys, don't cry," she hisses.

I can't stay up here - not when she's talking to him like that. Even if we've only been together for a month, I feel like I've known him forever. He always stands up for what he believes is right. That's why I don't recognize this, Matthew. Why doesn't he stand his ground? He's never at a loss for words.

I make a point of walking down the stairs loudly,

announcing my arrival. Both Matthew and his mom jerk their heads my way. His eyes are red, and he looks a little surprised. Something smells off, but I can't put my finger on it.

"Do you think you can take me home, Matthew?" I want to take him out of this toxic environment.

"Yeah, sure."

He puts his arm around my shoulder, and we leave. But I don't miss the addition to the fireplace - the remnants of a book with leather casing.

It took a year to realize his cuts and bruises were not from wrestling.

Today is Matthew's eighteenth birthday, and I'm about to surprise him at home. We're going out tonight, but I want to see him every hour of the day. I'm about to ring the doorbell when I hear loud voices from the open kitchen window. I peek through the window next to the door, where I can see part of the kitchen through the foyer. Matthew's sitting by the table, his shoulders slumped, and he's lazily spinning a spoon on the table. Their voices are loud enough for me to hear.

"Do you want to drink your life away? Fine, be my guest."

"It's one night, Mom. And it's my birthday."

"Don't remind me. Eighteen years ago, since the worst day of my life." Matthew doesn't even react to her hurtful words - as if he's heard them before.

"Then you don't mind me spending the night elsewhere," he says calmly. Like they're having a casual conversation.

"As long as you live under my roof, you live by my rules. And you will not spend the night with that harlot."

"Her name is Laura. And she's not - "

"I don't fucking care! Do you want to become a teen dad, Matthew?" Silence. "Because that's what you'll become if you spend all your time with trash like that. Lord, I hope you use protection before sticking it in her."

I balk at her words, and Matthew raises his voice, pointing a finger at her.

"Don't." He pauses. "Just don't," he says with remarkable steadiness.

"You will come home right after school," she responds, changing the subject. "Understood?"

"Why? It's not like we're going to celebrate."

"Are you giving me attitude?"

Then she slaps him. Hard. I stumble back in surprise and disgust, almost tripping on the stairs. After I've regained my bearing, I gather enough strength to look through the window again. This time I only see his mother hunching over something and swinging her arms. Back and forth. It takes me a few seconds to realize it's Matthew she's hitting.

I know that Matthew and his mother have a strained relationship - to put it mildly. I've heard what she says to him in person and by Matthew's account. But it never occurred to me that she was violent. I hate her, but now I wish there was a stronger word. Hate isn't enough.

Instinctively I start banging on the door, hoping it will stop her.

It feels like hours, but I think it's seconds before Matthew opens the door. His cheek is red, and he's upset. He tries to put on a neutral face for me, but I see right through it.

"Laura, hey. What are you doing here?"

I don't answer him. Instead, I take his hand, yanking him outside and closing the door shut. I put my hand on his face, and he's doing his best not to flinch at the touch. It all makes sense to me now. The cuts, the bruises. They're not from wrestling - he's used it to keep his mother's abuse from the public eye. But I should've seen it. I should've understood.

"How long?"

There's confusion in his eyes at first. Then he realizes, sighing before answering.

"All my life."

It takes two years before the last time she lays a hand on Matthew.

I get a call from his father.

"It's Matthew," he says. "There's been an accident."

I don't know what to say. I only hear that Matthew's in the hospital before hanging up and rushing to get to him. When I get there, I search for the room number his father gave me, ignoring the nurses saying that only immediate family is allowed - I'm the closest thing to family he's got.

Walking into the room, I notice his father in a chair by the window, but I don't acknowledge him. I've barely seen him for the two years Matthew and I've been together. Matthew's unconscious, the white sheets a chilly contrast to his bloodstained and bruised face. His hair usually shines a golden blonde, but now it's covered in a white bandage, and the few visible locks have dried in red and brown lumps. If this is how he looks, I can only imagine what shape his car is in.

"Matthew," I whisper, approaching the hospital bed and taking his hand in mine. He's always warm, but now I'm caressing cold, lifeless fingers. Blood has settled and dried in his cuticles, and I'm instantly annoyed that someone hasn't cleaned him up. He deserves more dignity than to be lying here in his blood.

There's a small adjoining bathroom, and I take a couple of paper tissues, soak them and walk back to Matthew. I start with his hands, wiping the blood away. It dissolves readily in the water and drips steadily down his fingers, forming a red pool on the floor. Moving to his arms, I notice several old cuts and scars. Some have been there for as long as I've known him, but a few have occurred over the last few years.

I take another wet paper tissue and swipe it across his forehead, but his face is so bruised that it barely makes a difference. Instead, I clean the few free locks, dissolving the blood and running my hands through it, massaging his scalp, careful not to touch the bandage covering most of his head. I clean his entire body, and only when I've wiped his upper body and my hands start to move downward does his father excuse himself, claiming he will get some coffee.

"What happened to you?" I whisper as soon as we're alone, but I'm not expecting an answer. I've heard that familiar voices can be calming even if you're not conscious.

Not long after his father returns, the doctor also decides to make an appearance. I don't understand what she's saying - blunt force trauma, medically induced coma - everything jumbles around in my mind.

"The worst part was the hit to his head," she says, pointing at the bandage, and I can't help but feel that she's treating him like a mannequin instead of a human being.

"Will he be alright?" I interrupt her volley of medical terms that no one understands.

"We can't know the extent of his injury until he wakes up." She takes a breath. "But there is something else I want

to discuss with you. There are some older injuries that concern me."

"Matthew's a wrestler," his father says immediately.

The doctor scrunches her nose, eyeing him. "Well, these injuries aren't consistent with wrestling," she says slowly.

"What are you trying to say, doctor?"

"Don't play dumb," I snap. "You know she's been hitting him his entire life. How you can stay married to that fucking shrew is beyond me."

The doctor touches my shoulder, urging me to calm down. "Do you want to press charges?"

"Can you do that? For old injuries? I ask.

She looks confused. "No, I mean this incident. We've documented the injuries."

I whip my head around to look at his father. His eyes are downcast. When he said there had been an accident, I assumed it was a car crash. His mother hitting him is not an "accident" - it's assault. She's caused all types of injuries, but I never thought she would - or could - go to this extreme.

" She *did this?" I croak.*

"Normally, I'd wait until the patient is awake, but with injuries like this, the assailant is considered a flight risk. So, if you want to contact the police, now is the time."

"No. Thank you, doctor."

"What?! She deserves to rot in hell for everything she's put Matthew through." I can't believe what I'm hearing. He has neglected his wife's abuse of Matthew's entire life.

Now he has the opportunity to redeem himself and, for once, make a statement. And he decides not to stand up for Matthew when he has the chance - it's the ultimate betrayal.

"Since he is over eighteen, I won't be contacting child protective services." She throws Matthew's dad a stern look. "But know this, if this would have happened before he turned eighteen, I would be required to, and would gladly, call CPS. By the number of scars of varying ages, he was physically abused long before he turned eighteen." She pauses. "But since Matthew is of age when he regains consciousness, he is within his rights to contact the police himself."

He won't. I know he won't. Then he would have done it a long time ago, and I think the doctor realizes it, too, because she gives me a sympathetic look before leaving the room.

"That evil bitch almost beat your son to death, and you're letting her off the hook?" I hiss, my hands grabbing the armrests on his chair.

"It's a little more complicated than that, Laura." His voice is pained, like he doesn't even care.

"No, it's not complicated at all. She did this to him," I say, gesturing to Matthew. "Everything else is irrelevant. There are no mitigating factors."

"Contacting the police won't help. She will retaliate, and it won't be directed toward me - it will be toward

Matthew," he tries to defend his decision, but I'm put off by how he uses his wife to escape his responsibility.

"You've been watching him getting beaten day after day and turned a blind eye. It doesn't work. It would be best if you did something. For Matthew," I try to reason with him, feeling tears prickling my eyes.

"This will not happen again. I promise."

He's avoiding the issue, and I know in my heart that if no one does anything, everything will go back to how it was before - or worse.

"No. It won't."

Dad taught me to shoot once. I often joined him when he went hunting before he died. I only used the rifle once, shooting at inanimate objects. I am - by no means - an expert, but I'm a fast learner. There's also a pistol inside the gun locker - I've never fired it, but I've seen Dad use it. It's heavier than I'd imagined, and the cool metal against my fingers sends chills down my spine.

I don't remember much of the drive over here. The door is unlocked, and I'm surprised she's still here. I'd figured she would have left town by now. I'm partially correct because, by the looks of it, she's planning to go soon, packing her bags.

"Why?"

She whips her head around, her eyes widening when she sees me.

"Why do you hate him so much? What has he ever done to you?" I say, pointing the gun at her face. My hand is surprisingly steady.

"It was self-defense," she tries to argue, holding up both hands.

"Don't lie."

"I'm not," she pleads. "He hit me."

Her words send my anger spiraling. All his life, she's been abusing him - physically and mentally. Not once has he reciprocated out of fear of turning into her. Now, he finally did it, and it earned him a bed in the hospital. And somehow, she still manages to pin this on him.

This must stop now. It's been going on way too long. I cock the gun, holding it with both hands now. She looks at me, but she doesn't seem afraid.

"You won't do it. You're a pussy, just like him."

I'm thrown back to the hospital, seeing Matthew's lifeless form, covered in bruises, cuts, and a bandage around his head. This cannot happen again - I won't allow it.

I close my eyes and squeeze the trigger. Again. Again. Again. For every shot, I remind myself why I'm doing this. For Matthew. For Matthew. For Matthew.

She will never hurt him again.

The sounds from the gun blend with the noise outside, and I'm thrown back to reality. The noise sounds oddly close to knocking. Why would anyone knock on this door?

The hatch they use to slide in the food trays is open, and I approach it carefully, peeking out. I must still be hallucinating because Matthew is standing there. And instead of the usual stale brown mess on the tray, there's a loaf of bread.

"Walnut and raisins," he says. My favorite. *He remembers.* I wish I had the willpower to refuse it, but at this point, I'm so hungry I can't leave it. I take a large chunk - it tastes heavenly.

I don't speak until I've devoured almost the entire loaf. "Why are you here?" I ask, my voice breaking.

"You want to know?"

We haven't talked since before the "accident." At least I can let him explain why he left me here in this hellhole. If out of nothing other than curiosity.

"Yes."

Chapter Four

"You have one more day in here. I'll come find you after that," he says quietly, almost in a whisper. "I have to get back before they notice I'm gone."

He's about to close the hatch when I call out to him.

"Matthew?"

He stops his movement, holding the window half-open.

"I shouldn't have pushed you," I whisper.

"Don't worry about it." He stands still for a couple of seconds, like he's contemplating saying something else, but eventually closes it.

And once again, I'm left alone with nothing else to occupy me besides my thoughts. But the knowledge of having only one more day in here puts me at ease. I'll take Neilson's company any day over this.

If I'm not mistaken, they slide in a new tray three more times. But I don't bang on the door after Matthew's visit anymore. I still refuse the food, though - the loaf of bread Matthew brought is enough for the remainder of my stay here.

The fourth time someone approaches my cell, the door opens, revealing one of the few decent guards in this prison. I'm sitting on the floor, and Thresh looks down at me from the door opening.

"Come on, McKenzie."

I consider not moving, anything to make my stay here harder for everyone. That way, maybe they think twice before sending me down here again. But that would only force Thresh to carry me out of here, and I have no quarrel with him. So, I walk up to him, letting him cuff me and lead me back to my cell.

"You're usually smart, McKenzie. Why did you have to go against a CO? You know how some of the guards react to shit like that."

His concern is genuine, and I know what he means. I WAS SAFE when I was in the hole - no one could touch me there. Now that I'm back, there is no stopping some of the guards from getting back at me for hitting Matthew. It doesn't matter to them if he wants revenge. Most see the guards as a brotherhood - mess with one, and you mess with all.

Our first stop is Bowen's office. I feel like a kid who's

come back from detention and now must face the principal to talk about the consequences of their behavior.

Thresh closes the door, and I slump on the chair across the desk.

"Well, I never thought I'd live to see the day."

There's no question, so I don't feel the need to answer him. Instead, I lock my eyes on one of his pens on the desk, trying to look indifferent.

"Yeah, I know you're not a talker," he says, refilling his cup with something stronger than coffee. "What did the Radford boy do to you?" He pauses, the cup inches from his mouth. "Did he introduce you to little Radford? He doesn't strike me as the type, but you never know."

I huff, annoyed that he even considered Matthew forcing himself on someone. "No."

"So?" He gestures for me to explain. I could lie, but Bowen would see right through it, so I stay silent.

He sighs. "You're not going to tell me, are you?" I glare at him. "Fine, I'll just make something up for the report. You can leave."

As I stand up, he puts his feet on the table, pinching his eyes with his thumb and forefinger. "Hey, McKenzie," he barks when I'm at the door. "I'm not the enemy."

As soon as I'm out of his office, I head for the bathroom - I need a shower. The only way of cleaning myself the last two days has been the small sink in my cell, but that doesn't cut it. This is not the time I usually shower - there's a schedule. But the guard outside is one of mine. I've blown him so many times I've lost count, so he lets me pass anyway. The door to the stall closes behind me, and I swiftly slip out of my clothes and let the water rinse me of everything from that place. There's typically a line to the showers, so I usually make it quick. But today, the place is empty, so I decided to take advantage and stay a few minutes extra under the cascading water.

I'm back just in time for supper. Tanisha and Cindy chatter my ears off, but I try to concentrate on the food. It's pretty good - considering. I quickly finish my meal and return to my cell - I've missed my bed. The corridor is seemingly empty. Most people are probably still in the hall.

A hand covers my mouth and yanks me backward, and an arm wraps around my waist to keep me from falling. It's one of the guards coming to retaliate - probably Brad. I'm forced into a narrow corridor I haven't seen before and then into an ever smaller one. You'd probably never find it if you don't know it's here. The grip on me loosens, and I'm taken aback when I see Matthew bringing me here.

"I'm sorry. I didn't mean to be so rough," he says, releasing me completely. He switches places with me, putting me between him and the only opening out of here.

"I've had rougher."

He doesn't speak for a couple of seconds, letting the impact of my statement settle in.

"So..." He rubs the back of his neck. "What do you want to know?"

I have so many questions I don't know where to start. So, I start with the most important one, the one burning a hole in my soul. I did what I did for Matthew. I know that. But if he can't see it, everything's been in vain.

"When did you find out that...? That I was the one who...?" For some reason, I can't bring myself to say the word, murdered your mother. It sounds so cold. But then again, that's probably what I have become.

"As soon as I heard the news, I knew," he says quietly.

"And how did you feel about that?" I ask carefully, afraid that he hates me for it.

"Relieved. Is that weird?"

Nothing about his family situation was normal, so there is no right way to react to something like that. "No."

"I wanted to go to your trial, but I couldn't. I couldn't even leave the hospital. Hell, I could barely walk. My leg was pretty fucked up, so I had a lot of physical therapy. I still have a limp."

I remember searching for Matthew in the courtroom, but I never saw him - I assumed it was because he hated me. I chose not to testify - I didn't want to talk about Matthew's and my relationship or the one he had with his mother. It was too personal. Besides, if I did, Matthew would be forced to testify, and I couldn't put him through that too.

My lawyer wanted to argue temporary insanity, that seeing Matthew caused me to snap, and that I didn't know what I was doing. But I was completely sane at the time and knew full well the consequences of my actions. I didn't regret it - I still don't.

"I've been wanting to see you ever since I woke up."

There is a visiting room and telephones, both of which he could have used. "So, you waited eight years?" I ask dryly, the bitterness evident.

"I know how it looks. You think I abandoned you, but that's not it. At all. I - " A beep from his radio interrupts him.

"Yeah?" he says into the comm without removing it from his shoulder.

"You're needed in cellblock C," the voice on the radio says.

"Okay, I'll be right there," Matthew answers. He looks back at me. "I have to go." As he walks past me, he raises his hand as if to put it on my shoulder, but it lingers in the air. He must change his mind because he retracts it again. "I... I've missed you," he whispers. Then he's gone.

That was the longest conversation we've had since before I was incarcerated, but it doesn't feel like I got that much information out of it. If anything, it raised even more questions. Why hasn't he come to see me if he didn't abandon me? And even if his reason is legitimate, will I be able to let it go? I've been angry for so long that I'm unsure I can feel anything else.

When I return to the hallway, it's bustling with inmates returning from supper. Tanisha grabs me by the arm and drags me toward another corridor.

"Come on, you've got to see this," she says without looking at me. I don't like how hard her grip is on my arm, and after this, I will let her know that. But for the time being, I relent and follow her.

"What is it?"

"You've got to see it for yourself."

I'm not going just blindly to follow her wherever she leads me, so I pull to a halt, forcing her to do the same. "That's not how this works." She seems to have forgotten that we are not equals. "Tell me what it is, and then I'll decide if it's worth my attention."

She glances over my shoulder, and I follow the direction of her gaze - big mistake. When I turn my head, I'm shoved into the closet outside, and I fall over, fortunately managing to let my hands break the fall. Someone is blocking the door - Bailey.

"If I'm not mistaken, you owe me something," he taunts, closing the door. That's what this whole charade was for?

"You didn't have to go through someone else for that," I say, trying not to let my fear show. The look he's giving me is terrifying, but I don't want him to know that.

He approaches me, and I decide to stand where I am - I will not back away from him. He grabs my chin, bringing my face closer to his. "I think I did." Without warning, my feet are swept from under me, bringing me to my knees. I'm at eye level with his crotch - he wants a blowjob.

I start unbuckling his belt. The sooner this is over, the better, but his dick is only half-hard. I throw him a glance as I start stroking him. He takes out a knife from his pocket, putting it on my throat - he must've talked to Brad. "Don't you give me that look, inmate. It's in your best interest that you do a good job."

Trying not to acknowledge his threat, I take him into my mouth. He removes the knife and puts it back in his pocket, getting lost in the moment.

I don't know his preference, so I do the shit that most men like - sucking the head, fondling his balls. I have a feeling I'll soon know exactly what he likes. I don't know how long I've been sucking his dick, but it doesn't seem to work. So, I put my hands on his hips, taking in as much of him as possible. I try not to gag as I look up at him, locking my eyes on his, and finally, he starts bucking his hips.

"Yes. Take my cock, you little cunt," he pants, fucking my mouth. "You've been missing a real man's touch." I have missed a real man's touch, but it's not his. Instead, I hum, creating vibrations that I'm sure will bring him even closer.

He grabs my hair, pushing my head faster and harder toward him. I close my eyes shut, trying to stop the tears that are threatening to spill over the brim of my eyes. I hate this. I fucking hate it.

The only thing that keeps me going is that I can feel how close he is. Only a few more seconds, and then we're done. He's about to finish when he pulls out, frantically stroking himself.

"Oh, fuck yes," he gasps. A few more pumps, and then he spurts his cum on me, mostly my face. "Take it," he exclaims, stroking himself through his orgasm. It's not the first time someone has come to my face - they do it all the time. I don't say anything, letting him have his seconds of bliss.

He doesn't do anything for a few seconds, coming down from his high. When the waves of his release subside, he tucks himself back into his pants.

"Clean your face, inmate. You look disgusting." He's no different from the others. My touch is wanted until they come, and then I'm garbage again. I wipe his cum off my face and stand up to leave.

"Where do you think you're going, inmate?" he snarls. I don't know if his always addressing me as an inmate is a powerful thing. Maybe it turns him on. Probably both.

"I'm going to my bunk. I owed you. Now I don't," I state. And I owe Tanisha a fucking beating.

"We're not finished." He needs time to recover, so I doubt he wants to fuck me too. But right when I'm about to ask what he's talking about, the door opens, revealing Brad and two other guards.

Fuck.

"Well, hello there," Brad mocks, one of his characteristic smug smiles. He swipes his thumb across my cheek. "Bailey, have you already had your fun?"

"What was I supposed to do?" he smirks. "Besides, she owed me. And from what I've heard, McKenzie always pays her debts."

"She does," Brad sneers, licking my face. "She does."

Four guards against me. I stand no fucking chance whatsoever. Brad and his companions walk into the room, closing the door. I can't do anything but hope they go easy on me - I doubt it. The COs are here for the inmates' protection, but who will guard the guards themselves?

Brad closes the distance between us, his face only an inch from mine. "You assaulted an officer. Now you will pay the price," he seethes. He doesn't care about Matthew - oh Matthew - he's just using this as an excuse to fuck me, but it doesn't make it less real. It doesn't matter the reason - it hurts just as much.

The guards behind Brad grab me by the arms and push me onto a table, face down. I don't have time to react before my hands are cuffed to the legs on either side. I'm utterly defenseless in this position, and when they pull my pants off, there's nothing I can do. I could try to resist, but I know it's pointless, so I just let them. I will not give them the satisfaction of winning over me.

Brad pushes his groin against me, his erection pressing against my bare ass. He leans over me, his chest flush against my back. His breath against my skin and the reek of his cologne disgust me, but I try not to show it.

"Have you ever taken it in the ass, inmate?" I don't answer him. "It doesn't matter. Soon you will," he hisses in my ear. There is no mistaking the sound of pants unzipping, and then he drags his dick along my ass.

I try to prepare myself for the pain. I will not scream. I will not. He will not have the satisfaction of knowing that he's hurting me.

But before he pushes himself in, the door opens, and for some stupid reason, I let myself hope that it's someone who's come to rescue me. My heart drops when I hear Bailey's words.

"Well, here's the man of the hour."

There's a short intake of breath and a couple of seconds of silence.

"What the fuck is this?" Matthew's voice is strained, and I don't know what's worse - being in this position or Matthew seeing me like this. So vulnerable.

"She needs a lesson in hierarchy. And I think you'd be

the perfect teacher. Or at least you can have the first round," Brad explains calmly and slaps my ass - that's going to leave a mark.

No one says anything. Now I know what the worst part is. Matthew will have to rape me right here on the table while these guards watch. There's no way he can talk his way out of this. What little relationship we'd managed to rebuild will be destroyed today. Pain I can live with, but Matthew will never recover from doing something like this. And it's my fault. I caused this.

Brad walks around the table so that he's standing in front of me, his dick hanging out for all of us to see. I still can't see Matthew.

"How many inmates have you fucked, Brad?" Matthew asks behind me. He sounds surprisingly calm.

"Too many to count," he answers, a smug look on his face.

"And how many of them follow your rules?" His smile drops, and Matthew walks around the table, his eyes locking on Brad's. Their faces are so close I'm sure they can smell each other's breath. But despite Matthew being shorter, it's Brad who wavers. "Didn't think so," Matthew continues. "You can't fuck them into submission."

"It's the only language they understand."

"No, it's the only language you understand." He pauses. "You've only worked in this prison, right?"

"So?" Brad's confidence falters, and I feel slightly satisfied at his discomfort.

"How do you think we do it in max - where it's not this easy to sneak off for a quick fuck? Making sure they drop the soap?"

Brad doesn't say anything. But I don't think he's angry at Matthew for shutting him up. I've seen his angry face, and that's not it. That's when I notice that Matthew has an emblem on his shirt sleeve that Brad doesn't. Matthew outranks him.

"Try to make sure some of your blood rushes to your brain instead of your dick, and I might just tell you," Matthew says calmly, glancing down.

"That still doesn't mean you can't have a little fun," Brad tries to reason, tucking himself back in.

"Oh, I'm planning to. But I won't be getting it up with your ugly faces here. No offense, but I think I prefer this pretty little one here," he says, patting my head. "Now get the fuck out."

The guards behind me huff but don't say anything. Brad walks toward the door and, when he passes me, puts his hand on my ass, squeezing it just enough to hurt. "We'll take a rain check, sweetheart."

This is the first time I see Matthew flinch today, but he manages to regain his composure. When the guards close the door, he rushes over to it, locking it and putting a chair against it so that no one outside can open it, even with keys.

Without another word, he hurries back to my side, unlocking the handcuffs. "I'm sorry," he whispers.

I know that this was all Brad's doing. Matthew could've taken advantage and fucked me and gotten away with it, but he chose not to. He also saved me from a painful and humiliating experience. "This wasn't your fault," I tell him as soon as I pull up my pants.

"I mean about everything. For making you think that I didn't care. I should've tried harder to...." He pauses. "I should have reached out to you, but I didn't know how."

"There is a visiting area."

"You must sign in for that. Besides, there are cameras everywhere." He takes a seat on the floor, leaning against the wall.

"So?" I sound impatient, but I've waited too long for these answers. I take a seat next to him, but we don't touch. Only an inch separates us, but it feels like a mile.

"What kind of relationship would that have been, Laura? A meeting once a week is the only touches allowed at the beginning and end of every visit, every phone call and conversation monitored." He exhales. "I'm sorry, but that's not good enough for me."

He's right. That wouldn't be much of a relationship. But what were we supposed to do? And is this good enough for him? We won't be able to have a real relationship in here either if that's his reason for coming here.

"When did you start working as a CO?"

"As soon as I could. I started basic training right after my leg healed. They normally let new recruits start in minimum security prisons, but they were so understaffed that my first job was at a max." That explains why he's already worked at three of them.

"How did you end up here?"

"I've only worked in all-male maximum security. I said I wanted to 'broaden my horizon.' I always intended on ending up here. With you."

Even if that's true, why didn't he let me in on it? "You could've told me."

"How? If I'd come here, people would have known. The wrestling wimp visiting the psychopathic killer. That would make a great headline," he says dryly.

He's never been one to care what other people think, so I don't understand why that would've stopped him. But how did the media find out about the truth?

Matthew senses my question. "After your trial, the teachers and coaches started talking. How they'd suspected but didn't do anything, like they couldn't have. They were crying their eyes out in the newspaper like some fucking martyrs." Matthew clenches his hands into fists in frustration. I instinctively want to cover his hand with mine but refrain.

"They called you a wimp?" I don't know why I ask that - it's not the most pressing issue.

"Yeah." He lets out a humorless chuckle. "I was too much of a wuss to handle Mother myself, so I sent my girlfriend to do my dirty work."

I don't know what to say. I had no idea how the outside reacted to what happened - I had assumed that no one knew the truth, but apparently, everyone did. After the trial, my mother severed what little bond we still had. She hasn't visited me once, and I don't expect her to. I don't have any other contacts - except Matthew.

"I thought no one knew," I say quietly.

He looks at me, blue eyes locking on gray, and for the first time since he came back, my first emotion isn't anger or betrayal; it's compassion. He's suffered as much as I have.

He's the first one to break eye contact. "Anyway." He drags a hand through his hair. "I focused all my energy on training as soon as I was discharged. I didn't talk to the media. I never confirmed or denied any of the rumors. I just wanted everyone and everything to disappear."

I can understand that. He never wanted the abuse to be public knowledge, and suddenly it was plastered all over the news.

"That's why you changed your last name?"

"Partly, yes."

"Then why couldn't you come here?" I ask in frustration. "People wouldn't know it was you."

"They run background checks on all the guards. If anyone ever found out about my past, or if there were records of me being here before, visiting one of the inmates, I would never have been able to start working here. It had to look like we didn't have any connection. I couldn't risk it."

I don't say anything, stunned to silence. Since leaving the hospital, he's been putting all his effort into seeing me again. I thought he'd abandoned me, but it was the opposite.

"I know you think I gave up on you. On us. But everything I've ever done has been to end up here," he says quietly.

"I didn't know."

"Now you do. If you never want to see me again, I'll respect that." He pauses, closing his eyes. "I've never stopped loving you. If you don't believe anything else, believe that."

I felt sorry for myself, convincing myself that he had deserted me here and hated me. I hated him too. It made it easier to cope, blame someone else and be angry. But he never stopped caring about me. And instead of accepting the situation, he's been doing everything in his power to see me again - for real.

He stands up, straightening his shirt, and heads to the

door. He won't press me for answers - he's changed, but some things remain the same. But he can't leave this room thinking that I hate him.

"Matthew?" My voice is weak, but I don't care. No one else can hear me right now. He turns his head when he's about to open the door. "Don't leave."

He looks up at me, a silent question in his eyes. Tears prickle my own. It's been so many years, but it still comes as natural as ever. Loving him. I've never stopped. Closing the distance between us, I let him embrace me. I've spent so much time building walls that now crumble to the ground at his touch. In his arms, I am free. He breaks the chains.

It's a simple request, but it weighs a million tons, constricting my throat and clouding my mind. "Stay."

His grip tightens. His one-word answer is just as simple, but the impact is unfathomable. "Always."

Chapter Five

His words will probably echo in my mind forever. Matthew's the only one I've ever been able to trust - even when I thought I couldn't. I thought he abandoned me, but it was the opposite. My abandonment was emotional - I gave up on him, and that's worse than what I thought he did to me. I should have known better. I should have known that, if anything, Matthew sticks to his words.

How many times did he tell me that he'd never leave me? That he'd always love me. That he wanted us to be together forever. I heard it, but apparently, I wasn't listening.

I don't know how long he holds me. It could be seconds or hours - I can't tell the difference. Only when he finally releases me, his warmth leaving, I don't ever want to get used to a life without him ever again.

We stay in the room a little while longer, long enough for Brad and the other guards not to get suspicious that we'd done anything other than what they thought we were doing. I even make point of limping a little, in case anyone is watching.

"No guard will ever lay a hand on you again. I'll make sure of that," Matthew promises before we part ways. The corridor is almost empty, so I guess it's almost lights out. I wish I'd had the time to pay Tanisha a visit. She sold me out, and she knows it. I wonder if she knows what that will cost her.

The horn signaling 6.30 cannot be more welcoming. For the first time in a very long time, I allow myself to feel hopeful again. I look forward to seeing Matthew again. Knowing that I have him as an ally makes me less dependent on other guards and inmates. Like Tanisha. But I don't see her at breakfast - she's probably too afraid to show her face. I hope she spent the night fearing today - fearing me.

I don't see Matthew either. He usually overlooks the meals, but I guess he has other duties too.

"Where is Tanisha?" I ask Cindy during breakfast.

"I don't know."

"You're in the same cell block. How can you *not* know?"

"We're not that close."

Hm? They always come in a pair, so I assumed they were close. But I don't pay that much attention to them because I don't care. They're assets, and that's it.

I don't see Matthew until lunch when he's back in the mess hall. Every other inmate in here throws him appreciative glances, so I don't see why I can't too. When his shift ends and he leaves, I quickly get up to leave too, making sure to put the tray where it belongs not to attract any extra attention.

I catch up with him outside the bathrooms. I walk beside him, but I don't look at him.

"Have you seen Tanisha?"

"Who?" he asks in a hushed tone.

Fuck, what's her real name? "Allison..."

"Marcus?"

"Yeah."

"I oversaw her release this morning," he says casually. "Why?"

No, no, no. "Son of a... That motherfucking... "

Matthew stops, looking around before opening a door to an empty office. "What's the matter?" he asks as soon as we're inside and the door is locked.

"She's the one who lured me into that room yesterday."

He drags his hand through his hair. "Fuck, I didn't know, Laura. I'm sorry." He turns away, not looking me in the eye. I know exactly what he's thinking. I can see it in his slumped posture and hanging head. He thinks he's a failure. His mother's abuse cut deep, and he still hasn't fully healed.

"It's not your fault."

"Yes, it is. You said it yourself. You're here because of me." He sounds defeated, and he still has his back to me.

Fuck, I knew that comment would come back to bite me in the ass. I only said it because I wanted to hurt him - I didn't mean it.

"No. I didn't mean it, Matthew. It was in the heat of the argument." I put my hand on his shoulder, a wave of fire spreading through my arm. We've barely touched since he came here, and I'm not used to it.

He turns around, locking his eyes on the floor. "You wouldn't have said it if the thought never crossed your mind." He's right. I *did* blame him. I'm about to argue, but he beats me to it. "It's okay, Laura. I don't blame you."

I can't lie to him, so I leave the past be. "I don't think that *now* ."

"What *do* you think now?" He still doesn't look at me.

"I think that... That I never stopped loving you either."

Finally, he lifts his gaze. We don't need any more words. His lips crash against mine - they're as soft as I remember. His tongue brushes the seam of my mouth, asking for entrance. I eagerly let him in and put both of my hands on his face.

"You have no idea how much I've thought about you," he whispers between kisses. My hands travel down his shoulders and toned arms, unbuckling his belt. He suddenly puts his hand over mine, stopping my movements. "Wait. I want to savor this moment. Let me taste you again."

The way he says it. *Again.* Like this - *me* - is what he's been living for since we've been separated. All I can do is nod. His mouth is on my neck in no time, kissing the sensitive spot right below my ear. The flick of his tongue on my earlobe sends a jolt right through me, settling between my legs.

"Fuck," is all that escapes my mouth before his lips find mine again. He sucks my bottom lip and presses me gently against the wall, silently asking for permission to give in to his urges. We haven't done this in ages, but it's like it was yesterday. We're in sync, always knowing what the other wants. "Yes."

He moves his hands down to the hem of my sweater. Not wasting any time, he cups my breasts underneath my shirt. He can probably feel my already puckered nipples through the fabric of my sports bra because he hisses at the touch - I do too. He drops down to his knees, lowering his hands to the waistband of my pants. He looks up at me, again asking for permission to proceed. I know he will never do anything that I don't want him to, but he seems more cautious than I remember. So, I take his hands in mine, guiding them to my waist, and pull down my pants.

He plants kisses along my legs, his hands roaming the outside of my thighs.

"Matthew," I pant. "Touch me," I plead. I need to feel the touch of a man who truly cares about me. I need to feel Matthew.

When his fingers find their way between my legs, slowly stroking me through my soaked panties I know that Matthew is what I've always craved. Even when I thought I hated him, he's always been what I wanted.

"I've dreamed of this for so long," he whispers, kissing my stomach. He probably doesn't know that I will never be able to bear his children. I've never been mother material, but if anyone deserves to be a parent, it's Matthew. I wonder if he'll resent me for it. But I'm too selfish to tell him now, allowing myself to get lost in this moment.

He keeps moving his fingers back and forth, but he doesn't slip his fingers inside. He needs me to say it.

"Matthew, I want to feel you. Only you."

He seems to understand what I'm trying to tell him because he pulls down my cotton underwear. I haven't had the time nor the tools to properly shave, so when he doesn't do or say anything I'm afraid he's repulsed by the fact that I'm not completely bare for him. But when I look down at him, he just stares at me in awe.

"You're so beautiful. You're more perfect than in my wildest dreams," he says, his voice hoarse. Without another word, he licks me along my slit, and my eyes flutter shut. The touch of his soft tongue on me is like a completely new sensation. He doesn't only do it because he's trying to make me come - he does it because he wants it. And that makes all the difference in the world. Without hesitation, he takes my right leg and hoists it up on his shoulder, opening me up for him. He puts his hands on my hips and starts working me with his mouth.

"You taste so good," he says between licks. He alternates between sucking my clit and flicking it with his tongue. If he keeps doing this, I won't last long - I already feel that familiar sensation starting to build. But Matthew doesn't want me to finish fast. He stops working my clit and plunges his tongue into me.

"Oh my god," I cry out. At this, he puts his hand on my mouth, stopping his ministrations.

"You can't be too loud. Bite my hand if you have to."

He starts fucking me with his tongue again, sending another rush of pleasure through me, and I have to bite down on his hand not to cry out again. The way he's working me is bringing me so close to release, but he slows down again, licking me with a featherlight touch. It's enough to keep me close to the edge but not completely push me over.

"Matthew," I gasp.

"I'm gonna make this last as long as possible," he growls, sliding his tongue gently around my clit before sucking on it. I must bite his hand so hard I think I'm drawing blood, but he doesn't seem to mind. His other hand grabs my hip, keeping me from meeting his movements and holding off my orgasm even longer. I'm so sensitive right now I think the slightest touch will probably send me spiraling.

Matthew seems to understand this because he pulls his head back, staring at my center.

"You're so wet, Laura."

Instead of putting his hands where I want them the most, he skates one of them up my waist, underneath my shirt and bra, carefully rolling my nipples between his fingers. I push my head back against the wall at the sensation. He keeps working my breasts, squeezing and kneading.

"Harder, please." I need to feel him. Completely. I don't care if it hurts - I need to know that this is real. He pinches my nipple harder this time, making me ache for more. Instinctively, I want to cry out his name, but I try to suppress it, biting down on his hand once again.

My clit is throbbing, desperately needing his touch.

He gives me a tentative lick like it's the first time, and once again I have to suppress my moans, but I can't stop the labored breaths from escaping my mouth. He keeps stroking me with his tongue, and when I instinctively buck my hips, he slows down.

I can't take it anymore. "Matthew, make me come."

At this, he starts sucking my clit with such determination that I almost come immediately. But it's only seconds before I'll snap. He doesn't stop, fervently sucking and flicking his tongue. It doesn't take long before it happens, and as I feel the first wave of my orgasm, he pushes two of his fingers inside me, deepening and prolonging the feeling.

The intensity is too much to handle. I slam my hands against the wall behind me to have something to hold onto, but there's nothing. Instead, I desperately tug at Matthew's hair as I come around his fingers.

"Ah, fuck!" I don't fucking care if anyone can hear me. It feels too good. Too good to keep quiet. Too good to not let him know what he does to me. Matthew keeps sucking and thrusting his fingers into me until my shaking stops.

He kisses my inner thighs before standing up, his lips and chin glistening from my arousal. I notice the bite marks on his hand and immediately grab it, tracing the wound.

"I'm sorry," I whisper.

"I've had worse," he shrugs.

I pull my pants back up and sit down on the floor.

"Can I ask you a question?" I ask when my breathing has returned to normal.

"Yeah." He sits down next to me, resting his arms on his knees. "I have to get back soon, though, before anyone misses me."

"What did you mean by what you said to Brad about keeping inmates in check? How do you do it?"

"I wish I could say something like 'treat them like people' or something noble like that." He sounds distant, and he doesn't want to look at me. "I tried that."

"Did you try... fucking them?" I ask carefully.

Finally, he turns his head to me. "No."

It's a relief. I wouldn't blame him if he did if that was what he had to do. But there's a pang of hurt when picturing him being that intimate with someone else - even if it doesn't mean anything. But I have no claim to him. Not anymore. "Did you... fuck anyone else?"

"Are you seriously asking me that question?" he snaps. "You thought I was lying when I told you how I got myself here?"

"No."

Matthew stands up, distancing himself from me. "Then why do you feel the need to ask me that?"

He's avoiding the question. "Why can't *you* answer the question?"

He holds out both of his arms. "No. I haven't fucked anyone. Happy?"

I *am* happy about that, but I don't tell him. Instead, I

let my old hurt and anger take over and I snap too, taking it out on him.

I push myself up to my feet. "What? You want a medal?" I can't stop the vile words from escaping me. I can't say I'm sorry. "I wasn't expecting you to live in celibacy, so don't act like you're some sort of saint. You don't know what it's like to be in here. Being at the mercy of assholes like Brad, thinking that they own you. You don't know what it's like to have to regularly fuck these pieces of shit. Your presence here can't change that - *you* can't change that. I'm not as good as you. I never will be. So, fuck you."

I'm doing it again - the only thing I can do is hurt Matthew. I couldn't stop it before, and I can't stop it now.

"You think I'm good? I'm the opposite of good, Laura! I said I didn't fuck anyone else. I never said I always did the right thing."

I close the distance between us. I want to hold him again and say I'm sorry for what I said, but I don't. I don't even reach out to touch him - I don't why. Maybe I'm a heartless monster. "What do you mean?"

He takes a breath as if preparing himself for what he's about to tell me. "Most of the time it's all about illusion, making the inmates think that you have more power than you do. I can't authorize a search of an inmate's cell, but now everyone here thinks I can. And that's usually enough."

"So, you lied," I state. "Everybody lies, Matthew."

He lets out a humorless laugh. "I wish that's the worst thing I have done. For most prisoners, it's enough to think you have more power, but sometimes you must prove it."

"How?"

He sighs, crossing his arms over his chest. "There were beatings that I was made aware of. And I didn't do anything to stop them. Just made sure that they saw me watching. If they thought I ordered it, even better. I'm not a saint. I'm a fucking monster." He's quiet for a couple of seconds before adding, "Like mother, like son, right?" He's sacrificed so much to be here. He even thinks he's turned into his mother and lost his sense of self in the process.

"No," I say sternly. "You are *not* like her." I take his hand in mine. He can't think like that - I won't allow it. He might be a lot of things, but he's *not* his mother's son.

"What's the difference, Laura?" he asks in defeat. "I might as well have beaten them up myself, using my position to hurt others." He looks down again. "You know what the worst part is? I don't even regret it. *I'm* the one who should be locked up. I destroy everything I touch."

"No. You can't think like that," I plead. My desperation probably shines through, but I don't care. I loop my arms around his waist, trying to convey whatever strength I have left to him. "You must stay strong. Don't you see it, Matthew? When you are strong, I am strong."

He sighs into my hair, returning my embrace.

"I'm sorry I snapped."

"No, you were right. It's none of my business." He's put everything on the line for this - for *me* - and I shouldn't have questioned his commitment.

"There's never been anyone else. Only you," he reassures me.

We stand like that for a couple of seconds. I haven't asked him about what happened when he ended up in the hospital, what caused his mother to lose it like that. Might as well get it over with.

"How much do you remember of that day?" I don't have to specify. He knows.

"Nothing."

Nothing. He remembers *nothing.*

"So, you don't know what made her hurt you like that?"

"No. But with her, it could've been anything. Sometimes my presence in the house was enough to set her off."

I'm not surprised, and that makes it even more horrifying. I can't imagine growing up with a parent who hates you with everything that she's got.

He doesn't know that he hit her back. To be honest, I don't know if his mother told me the truth, but it sounds reasonable that something like that could've sent her rage completely out of control. And Matthew would be too ashamed to fight back again. Should I tell him? He's always been afraid of turning into her. Afraid that he might carry that gene. Will he completely break if he ever finds out?

Thankfully, I don't have to make that decision now because Matthew speaks next.

"I must go. And you have to go to the laundry room." He's right - my shift starts soon.

He leaves first, and then I wait a couple of minutes before exiting the room. I see him during lunch and supper, but we don't talk. There is no need to raise unwanted suspicion about our relationship.

When I arrive back to my cell before lights out someone is sitting in my bed. Neilson is nowhere to be seen, and I know there's only one person within these walls who'd have the guts to violate my personal space like that. There is not much privacy in this place, but your bed is yours and no one else's. You don't touch my bed unless you're looking for trouble. But she's the only one who doesn't fear retribution from me. Cash. Her long blond hair is in a ponytail, reaching the middle of her back, she probably heard me coming but keeps her back to me. Instinctively, I look around to make sure none of her "friends" are here.

"Move." She doesn't flinch.

I enter the cell, somehow feeling like a stranger even though I've spent most of the last eight years in this small space.

"If your ears don't work, I might as well cut them off," I

say, approaching her. Since she's sitting down, I've got height on my side, so I stand right behind her, towering over her.

At this, she stands up, taking back the leverage. Standing up, she's got several inches over me. She's taller, but I'm faster, and I quickly take out my knife, holding it close enough to her to intimidate her, but not to be too obvious of a threat. That's what we've always done. Both of us always skirting that fine line.

"Heard Radford fucked you," she sneers.

I don't know how that rumor started circulating. I'd heard some whispers during the day, but that's normal. Besides, it's good if they think he fucked me in that room. It wouldn't look good for Matthew if he passed up a chance of getting back at me for what I did. And the more people who think we hate each other, the better.

"I didn't know you were into girl talk." I tap on the bed. "Let's braid each other's hair and have pillow fights," I say sarcastically.

"So did he?" Why does she care so much? She knows I've been with more guards than she can count, so why is Matthew so important?

"He's no different from the rest of them," I lie.

"So that little thing in the mess hall is history?"

And the true nature of her visit reveals itself. She wants to know if he's up for grabs. She must know about Matthew having more authority than the others, otherwise, she wouldn't pay me a personal visit - without company.

"You can have him if you want." I do my best to sound disgusted when talking about Matthew, not wanting to let her in on our real relationship.

She huffs at my offer - expected. She's too proud to accept that she has something because I let her. So, fucking predictable. She won't approach him now - she's not interested in my sloppy seconds.

Slowly, she walks around me, our eyes locked on each other, making sure the other doesn't try anything. I guess we're too focused on each other to notice the footsteps outside because we're both startled by the voice from the door opening.

"Collins." I recognize his voice anywhere - it's Matthew. What is he doing here? He doesn't think I can handle Cash on my own? "What the fuck are doing you here?" He points at her with his baton, eyes fiery with rage. "You're one small misstep from ending up in the hole. Leave now and maybe I didn't see you."

I send him a glare - I don't need saving.

Cash walks over to Matthew, stopping only a couple of inches from him and eyeing him up and down. "I don't do leftovers, but for you, I might make an exception." I don't like the way she looks at him like he's a piece of meat. If this wasn't a prison, she'd probably be dry-humping him right about now.

But Matthew pretends he doesn't see her advances. "One misstep," he repeats, holding up his index finger for good measure. "I can be very thorough when I search your cellblock," he says slowly.

This seems to get her moving, and she leaves without further ado.

"I could have handled her by myself," I tell him after I make sure no one can hear us.

"I know that. That's not why I'm here." He straightens his shirt. "I'm here to take you to the warden's office."

Oh no.

He removes the handcuffs from his belt. "Turn around," he says sternly, but his eyes are full of regret. I do as he says, crossing my hands behind my back. The cold metal of the cuffs feels like ice when he locks them around my wrists.

"You do know why he called me to his office, right?" I whisper. His hand on both of mine tells me that he knows exactly what the warden wants.

"I'm sorry."

I don't know how many times I've been called to his office, but this is different. I've accepted my role here, but with Matthew escorting me there it feels like I'm ruining him in the process.

The walk is relatively short, but it feels longer now. I concentrate on moving one foot in front of the other while

Matthew gently holds the cuffs behind my back, helping me keep my balance.

When we're outside his office Matthew raps his knuckles on the door. "It's Radford," he announces. "And guest."

"Enter," the familiar voice of warden Thorn booms from inside the room. Matthew opens the door, gently nudging me to step inside and he's right behind me. I don't know if I want him here for this, though. The office is cluttered with diplomas randomly strewn across the walls like someone put them up only to show them off and for no other reason.

He's sitting by his desk, pretending to write something. Like he's so fucking important.

"Sit down," he commands without looking up. Matthew uncuffs me and directs me to the chair but remains standing by the door. "I looked through Bowen's report." He lifts his gaze. "Slipped and fell?" he questions, lifting his eyebrows.

If that's what he wrote, I'm sticking with that. "It *is* a slippery floor."

"Hm. It is, isn't it?" There's a sense of satisfaction about him - I don't like it. "And we wouldn't want me to slip and accidentally drop your file into the maximum-security folder now, would we?" he sneers.

I don't say anything.

"Would we, *inmate* ?" he repeats, apparently irritated.

"No," I croak.

"I didn't hear you."

I clear my throat. "No."

"Glad that we're on the same page." He moves the papers on his desk, putting them in a stack to his right. "You can wait outside, Radford."

"I need to escort her back before lights out."

Thorn only waves him off. "Don't worry about that. You can take her back after we're finished here."

"Sir? I thought it was the same routine for *all* inmates, no exceptions."

"I'm the warden of this fucking prison!" Thorn erupts, standing up and pushing his chair against the wall behind him. "What are you? A simple guard. Don't question my authority, boy."

I turn my head around, facing Matthew, and give him a subtle nod, silently telling him that it's okay.

He tries to put up a professional facade, doing his best not to crack at the knowledge of what the warden intends to do. At what has already happened so many times. His eyes quickly avert to mine, begging for forgiveness. Forgiveness that he shouldn't feel the need to ask for. This is not on him. This is on me. I chose this. This is what I have become.

My discreet nod to him convinces him to accept that it's okay for him to leave. I *want* him to leave. Seeing my pain reflected in his eyes would be too much for me to handle. I'd rather suffer alone. He sends me a glance before leaving the room.

As soon as the door closes, I stand up and walk over to the other side of the desk, doing my best not to meet Thorn's gaze. I'm about to bend over the table, but he pushes me over before I get a chance. Without hesitation, he pulls my pants down.

"You've been a bad girl," he growls, dragging a whip against my ass. Fortunately, Thorn is one of those who always use a condom. He doesn't want a repeat of what happened seven years ago.

Thankfully, he finishes fast. But my main concern isn't the time or my well-being. It's the fact that Matthew probably heard the whole thing. Thorn is fast but vocal, and his thrusts caused the desk to scrape against the wooden floor, creating loud noises.

He barely has the time to pull out before he tells me to leave. I'm trash again, easily disposed of. I open the door, and as expected, Matthew's there. His hands are balled into fists, and his jaw is clenched. He knows exactly what happened in there. I put my hands behind my back, and he cuffs me again. His hands barely touch mine, but it's enough to make me feel safe again, knowing that he's here.

"I'll kill him," he mutters while he guides me back to my cell. "I'll fucking kill him myself."

"Matthew." I want to throw my arms around him, letting him know that I'll be okay. But the chains around my wrists and the fact that we're in this fucking place make that impossible.

"What?" he snaps, but it's not because of me. He's angry about the situation.

"What did you expect?"

He lets out a long sigh but doesn't answer. He *did* expect this. He knows exactly how it goes. Since it's already past lights out the corridors are empty, enabling us to speak more freely. "This is how it works. You can't protect me, no matter how hard you try." With so much experience in max, this can't come as a surprise to him.

"I know."

"If it's too much for you, maybe it's better for you to leave." It pains me to say the words, but he can't change the way things are in here, and I hate to see him ruined because of it. There's no way we'll be able to have any sort of relationship anyway. We'll get caught eventually.

When we get to a crossing hallway where we usually turn right, he directs me to the left. Away from the surveillance cameras, he puts his hands on my arms, turning me around. "I *am* leaving."

Horror and relief wash through me. He won't be spending more time in this hellhole, but I'm selfish enough to want to have him near me, if only for the subtle glances and the delicate touch of his fingers.

He swallows hard, his eyes piercing through mine. "And I'm taking you with me."

Chapter Six

I don't register his words immediately, and I don't know how to respond.

"Matthew, we're in prison. I can't just walk out the door." I feel dumb for pointing out the obvious, but I want to make sure he's talking about what I think he's talking about.

"Listen," he says, putting his hand on the wall behind me, his face inches from mine. "Do you think I'm happy with this?" He makes a motion with his hands, gesturing to the surroundings.

I know he isn't - I'm not either. But what did he expect? Maybe he didn't think that I could do the things I have had to do in here, half of which I don't even think he knows about.

"No."

"I don't want it to be like this. In here. I want

you. *All* of you. I meant what I said earlier. This is not good enough."

This is not good enough for me either. But is breaking out the answer? Besides, what would we do if we somehow managed to escape? People would be looking for us. Do I want to live like that, always looking over my shoulder? Does Matthew?

But I don't want to voice those thoughts to him right now because I'm afraid he'll take them the wrong way - that I don't want him. I *do* want him, but I've built a life for myself here.

I don't know what to say to him. I'm at a loss for words, as I always seem to be around him. "It's impossible," I manage to get out. "You're talking about breaking out." I only mouth the last words, afraid that someone or something will pick them up.

"Laura. You don't deserve to be here. It kills me knowing that you wouldn't have been here if you hadn't met me." He blames himself for this. *Of course, he does.* He grazes the skin underneath my eye with his thumb, cupping my cheek. "Tell me. What do you miss the most?"

I answer without hesitation. "The stars." We're only allowed outside during the day and there's no window in my cell. I miss being able to stargaze in the woods where there's barely any artificial light. The minuscule living quarters, the food, and the company I can live with, but I miss nature, being outside without restrictions or fences.

"Then will you let me bring you to them again? Please." His voice is so tender, so soft, that it fills me with a sense of security - and I want more of it.

Are we actually considering escaping?

Matthew's hand is still on my cheek, and I lean into it. A warm sensation spreads throughout my body at his gentle touch. But I can't allow myself to dream. I'll only be disappointed when I wake up to the real world. "Matthew. Even if I agree to this, this is prison. There are alarms, guards, fences..."

A subtle smirk mixed with pride spreads on his lips. "What do you think I've been doing for the past eight years?"

I can't sleep. When Matthew dropped me off in my cell, Neilson was already asleep. Or she pretended to be - I can't tell the difference, and I don't care.

Of course, I want to leave, but I'm not sure life as a fugitive is what I want. That's what I will be, and Matthew will be a wanted man. I don't want him to suffer anymore - especially not because of me. The alternative is to wait until my sentence ends, but that won't be anytime soon. I've probably got another ten years in here - at least. And, in a way, having Matthew right under my nose without being able to touch him whenever I want is more torturous than constantly being physically and mentally abused. That's its form of torment.

Matthew's put a great deal of effort into this, and I don't want to let him down. But I can't make this decision lightly - he can't expect me to.

Sleep never comes, but when we get up at 6:30 I'm surprisingly alert. When I get to the mess hall, though, there's an atmosphere that I'm not comfortable with. Eyes linger on me longer than they should if they know what's best for them. More heads than usual pop up when I enter, and it feels strange. I'm used to getting people's attention, but this is different. It's not fear on their faces - it's curiosity. Were they somehow privy to my conversation with Matthew? No, no one could hear us.

That's when I see her. *Cash.* The meals are scheduled, and her times normally don't coincide with mine. It's not uncommon for us to be in here at the same time, but it's not the fact that she's here that causes me to waver. Cindy is sitting next to her. *Fucking traitor.* That's why these bitches are staring at me. They want to know how I will react to this.

She must have known about Tanisha's deception, otherwise, this is a huge fucking coincidence. The smug smirk on her face when she meets my eyes leaves a bad taste in my mouth, but I try not to show my disgust. How much has she told Cash about me? How much *does* Cindy know? I try to wrack my brain and sort through if I've ever said anything personal to her. I don't think so - I've never confided in anyone, not even Bowen, who's bound by law to keep his mouth shut.

Leaving the line, I walk up to their table. She will know that this will cost her, one way or another. "I thought you said you didn't do leftovers," I say to Cash. I don't acknowledge Cindy, knowing that she craves attention.

Cash puts her hand on Cindy's cheek, locking her eyes on me. "Cindy here isn't leftover." Cindy stretches her back - she's so desperately in need of validation that it's almost painful to watch. Almost. "One of your own made a fool of you. You are *weak*, and people don't want to associate themselves with weaklings."

I want to punch her face if only to wipe that fucking smile off it. But I can't. This is not the time nor the place. It would only get me sent back to the hole.

Instead, I shift my focus to Cindy, temporarily giving her some much-needed attention. "You will regret this," I say matter-of-factly, turning around to leave.

On my way back to the line something hits my back. "Your threats are empty," Cash yells after me. Now we've got everyone's attention, including the guards. It takes everything in me to not throw myself at her and shut her up the way I want to, and I say a silent prayer that Matthew doesn't intervene now. That would only give Cash's words merit, weakening my position further. Subtly, I try to send him a glance, hoping that he'll understand. He's still standing by his post, his hand on his baton, ready to engage if he must. But he seems to understand what I'm trying to say. Or he's figured it out on his own.

There's nothing much I can do right now. She wants me to lash out, but that will only give her what she wants. But if I don't do anything it'll look like she's won. Neither of those options are good. By the looks of it, the entire mess hall knows how I got played. I must somehow stand my ground and show them that I'm no pussy. I do the only thing I can think of. It's suicide maybe. I give her the middle finger - it's very common. But then I curl it around my index finger - not so common. It means 'I hate you.' It means 'I loathe you.' It means that we will meet again and then we will settle our differences. And there will only be one victor - one way or the other.

The sign is a well-kept secret from the guards, so they'll only see one inmate flipping the other off, missing the secondary meaning.

Of course, she takes the bait. She can't resist the challenge or the possibility to get rid of me. I don't blame her - I feel the same way. Her smile is wicked as she gives me a subtle nod, accepting the invitation.

"McKenzie," Matthew barks from the cell door. "You're wanted in the warden's office."

"Ooh, someone's in trouble," Neilson quips.

"Shut the fuck up," Matthew cuts her off immediately. He's pissed.

When I walk toward him, he doesn't look me in the eye before I turn around for him to lock my hands together. His touch is almost rough, and he's breathing heavily. *What's happened?*

When he closes the door to the cellblock we're alone in the hallway between the actual prison and the offices. There are cameras, but they don't pick up sound. But this is not the shortest way to the warden's office. "What's going on?"

"Not here," is the only response I get, his tone terse. Neither of us speaks again until he opens the door to an empty office and uncuffs me.

"What the fuck are you doing?" he growls as soon as I turn around to face him.

"What do you mean?" Those beautiful blue eyes pierce a hole through my brain.

"Don't patronize me, Laura. Why are you challenging Cash to a fight?" *Oh.* I should have known.

"What was I supposed to do, Matthew?" I throw out my arms, his anger rubbing off on me.

"You could have walked away."

"I couldn't do that. You know how it works. If I had left, I'd have no power whatsoever in here. No one would respect me, and that would be the end. Now, I at least have a chance."

"And the price, if you lose, could very well be your life. It'll be on my watch. What do you expect me to do, just stand there and look?" His jaw clenches, and his hands ball into fists.

"Why not? You've done it before," I snap.

Silence.

I crossed the line. I know I did. He doesn't answer, only locks his eyes on me. His stare is intense, and I almost buckle under it. I must stop taking everything out on him. "I didn't mean it like that." I reach out to him, but he backs away. It hurts more than I want to admit.

"Of course, you meant it," he spits.

"Fine, I did. But what's the difference, Matthew?" I try to reason with him. He's acting like he came here thinking he didn't need to get his hands dirty. "This is prison. You of all people know how it works."

"It doesn't mean I enjoy it." He's calmed down a little, but he's still angry. "And you don't get to decide what I do, or how I do it."

I put my hands on his cheek, but he doesn't acknowledge my touch. He's still upset. "I know. But I need your help with this."

"How?" He moves my hand from his face, not meeting my eyes. "What do you want from me, Laura?"

"I don't know."

* * *

The next couple of days I barely speak to Matthew - he seems busy, always on his way to something, and he never seeks me out. But I don't miss how Cash always linger on him. Did she change her mind about 'leftovers?' I don't have to worry about that. I trust Matthew. I *have* to.

He's not meeting my gaze anymore; not like he did when he first arrived here when I could feel his eyes on me every time we were in the same room. Now he seems more set on doing his actual job than I would want him to. I've spent such a long time in here without him, but now I miss him more than I ever have. He was right - the only way for us to truly be together is to somehow leave this place. And now he acts like he doesn't even want that. It hurts like hell.

Since Tanisha's gone and Cindy's with Cash, I eat by myself. I'm fine with that. I don't want, or need, anyone's company. It's an odd sort of relief not to hear them cackling all the time.

"Hey," a tender voice says from the opposite side of the table.

"Leave," I say, not raising my gaze from the food. I don't want to chit-chat, but she sits down anyway. I lift my head, exhaling loudly. "You deaf?"

"No," she says carefully. "I have information."

"Yeah, everyone does," I try to blow her off. Bitches

often come up to me with "information." It's usually vague or something I already know.

"It's about Collins. I think she's trying to rig the fight."

"Of course, she does. It's her M.O." I look up at her. She's the one I gave the meth to a couple of weeks ago. "That's it?"

"I've just noticed that she's been talking a lot to Radford this past week. With him being the superior guard and all, I just thought - "

"Yeah, you *thought*. Your theories don't interest me." For all, I know it's Cash who sent her here. I have no way of knowing if she's telling the truth or feeding me Cash's lies. She doesn't take the hint, so I slam my fist on the table, catching the attention of some inmates around us. "So split."

When she goes back to her place, I catch Matthew out of the corner of my eye. He's leaving, and only seconds after Cash leaves too. That can't be a coincidence.

If they need privacy I know exactly where they are. I find them in the small hidden corridor where Matthew took me. Their voices are hushed, and I can't see them, but I can make out what they are saying.

"You want to get rid of her, don't you? She humiliated you in front of everyone. I'd never do that," Cash says.

"I know."

"Then help me with this. Don't back down now." I can

practically see her fingers sliding up his arm, and I hate her for it.

There's a couple of seconds of silence before Matthew answers quietly. "Okay."

During dinner, I manage to sneak away a plastic knife from the mess hall. It's not that difficult, and I at least have some of the guards still on my side. As it is now the knife can't do much harm, but I can carve it, making it pretty lethal if it hits the right place. Since I was the one to challenge Cash, she chooses the weapons - there are plenty within these walls and they're not that difficult to steal. She chose no weapons.

"You think you're gonna win?" Neilson asks. Of course, she knows about the fight. She has ears fucking everywhere. Most inmates don't know when or where the fight will take place - the more that know, the bigger the risk of the guards finding out and stopping it.

I don't answer her because I don't think I'll win. Going head-to-head with Cash is terrifying - she's taller and more muscular. And during my 'inauguration,' she threw the hardest punches. Maybe my plastic knife will make us even.

No, it won't.

After dinner, but before lights out, is the best time.

Many of the guards' shifts end soon, and they're tired after the day, making them less likely to intervene even if they suspect something is up. *Lazy fucks.* I tuck the makeshift knife inside my braid, trying to conceal it with my hair the best I can.

When I meet Cash in the hallway between the cells, she's not alone - Cindy and two of her other lackeys flank her.

"Really? You don't fight your own battles?" I taunt, trying to get a rise out of her.

"You wouldn't either if you had anyone left," she responds quickly, not missing a beat.

"Bathrooms," I say. Since Cash chose the weapon, I decide on the place. The bathrooms have more furniture that you can accidentally hit your head on. I won't be winning this fight by raw force, so I have to rely on some luck.

When we get there, Cash takes a look around. "I don't like this. There's too much preventing a fair fight." *Like she knows anything or cares about what's fair.*

"It's not your choice to make," I say, trying to stand my ground, but I'm outnumbered.

"It's supposed to be fair," she points out.

"I don't care what you think is fucking fair. You choose the weapon; I choose the place."

A satisfied smirk spreads on her lips like she's been

waiting for something. "So, you didn't bring anything with you?"

I don't know what she's playing at. "No."

"Prove it."

I unbutton my shirt and slide it off my arms, tossing it on the floor. Loosening the drawstring of my pants I peel them off my legs and pile them on top of the shirt. She gives me a look, clearly not satisfied. I remove my top and cotton underwear too, leaving me completely naked in front of her. I have no problem with nudity, but I feel exposed here like this.

"Your turn."

She does the same and we search each other's clothes. She doesn't have any weapons, and they don't find anything either. When we put our clothes back on, I don't miss her toned arms and well-defined abs. *This is going to hurt.*

"Let's stop messing around and just do it here," I say, my voice raised. "Let there be some fucking pretense of honor."

"You seem very eager," Cash sneers, looking pleased with herself. Like she knows something I don't.

"Just as eager as you are to make sure I'm clean. Are you sure you don't want to look up my pussy too?"

"Pass." She gives Cindy a nod and walks up to me, a devilish grin on her lips. Then she yanks my braid. I try to swat her hand away but I'm too slow.

"Well, what do we have here?" she snickers, unweaving my braid and taking the plastic knife. She walks back to Cash and gives it to her.

"Radford saw you take this before leaving dinner," she says, sliding it between her fingers.

I jerk my head up in surprise, a look of betrayal and hurt probably evident on my face. There's a lump in my throat at the mere thought of him ratting me out. To *her* of all people.

Cash continues. "Just because he fucked you doesn't mean he's forgotten what you did. He's not as simple-minded as Brad or Bailey."

"Piece of shit," I curse under my breath.

"Okay, now that that's settled, let's move on, shall we?" She's very chipper about all of this.

I have no choice but to follow. Now she's chosen both place and weapon, giving her an even bigger advantage than before. We end up in the TV room, and I can understand why. It's easy to clear - we only have to move the chairs and tables, leaving a large, empty area.

The rules are simple. We'll continue until either one of us yields or dies. But knowing how stubborn Cash is, she will not yield. Neither will I.

I take the table closest to the door, move it to the side, and turn it around. When I'm done, the others have already cleared the rest of the room.

I'm not prepared when the first hit comes. Cash's fist

connects with my nose, and I stumble backward, almost falling, but I manage to stand my ground. I dry my nose on my sleeve, soaking it in blood.

I swing my arm against her, trying to get a hit, but she evades me every time. I get in a few punches, but nothing severe, only hitting soft tissue. Instead, she lands another hit right on my mouth and I can taste the blood now. *It hurts like a motherfucker*.

I don't have time to recover because she takes the collar of my shirt, dragging me toward the middle of the room and hauling me into the brick wall. I try to brace the impact with my hands, hearing what I think are bones breaking when my arm gets squashed between the wall and the rest of my body, and I collapse on the floor. But I'm so hyped on adrenaline now that I barely feel it.

Before she attacks me again, I steal a glance at the clock. *Wear her out.* When Cash comes at me again, I throw up my foot, hoping that it'll hit her stomach. It does, and she loses her breath temporarily. I take the opportunity to hit her right on the nose, and I feel it breaking under my knuckles.

"Not so pretty anymore," I taunt. This causes her to let out an animalistic scream, and she charges at me with all the force she's got. But I'm quick and throw out my leg, tripping her, and she crashes into the wall face-first. With our ragged hair, blood-covered faces, and feral eyes we probably look like Carrie's deranged sisters.

I might be quicker, but her stamina is better. I can't keep at this for much longer - my heaving chest makes that pretty obvious. And now I've pissed her off even more. I have to win this - now.

But Cash grabs me by the sleeve and tries to throw me against the wall again. I manage to put my foot down and steer us in another direction, and I land on a table next to the door. *That's gonna leave bruises.* Cash's on top of me, turning me over so that she's straddling me, effectively pinning me down. She takes hold of my injured arm. Hard. I scream out, and I think I'm going to pass out from the pain.

"Give up, bitch," she snarls, the blood from her nose dripping down on me.

"No," I growl.

In the corner of my eye, I see the door open, and it takes everything in me to wrench my right arm free from under Cash. I throw it backward, feeling the underside of the table until I find it. It only takes a second, but that's all I need. I yank the knife free, pull it over my head and stab her in the gut. Warm blood covers my hand as I press the knife in as far as I can.

There is pain, but mostly shock in her eyes when she realizes what's happening. A silent moan leaves her lips as I release the knife and push her off me. Matthew catches her, putting her on the floor, and her eyes widen when she recognizes him. There's a pool of blood growing underneath her, and even if she survives this, she'll spend weeks in the infirmary. Cindy and her friends have already left - they probably fled as soon as they saw Matthew. *So that's how far their loyalty goes.*

"M... Matt..." Cash stutters.

Matthew sits next to her, grabbing the knife still in her stomach. He looks her right in the eye, twisting it, and a groan of pain leaves Cash's mouth. He twists the knife again before pulling it out, a subtle smile on his lips. He slowly wipes the sides of the blood-covered knife on her cheeks before handing it to me, not breaking eye contact with her. "So, you gained a few friends. I've got friends too." His voice is so dark. Cold. Sinister. It stirs something inside me that I can't quite describe.

"Pl... please..." she coughs.

"I heard about how you welcome people in here. Consider this your going away party," he says. She knows exactly what he's talking about. When I told Matthew what happened when I first arrived here, he got furious, and he hates her as much as I do. Probably more.

Being here was *our* plan. It was *Matthew* who suggested it to her because of the lack of cameras, and *he* left the knife here for me. I knew they would find the plastic knife on me - she's not stupid - and by getting us here she thought she had the upper hand. And that was her downfall.

I pull my blood-soaked shirt over my head and dry my

face with it. I can't stay here - Matthew must call for backup. Seeing him like this, doing all this for me, makes me love him more than I think I ever have.

"You have to go," he whispers.

"I know." I put my hand on the side of his face, and he leans into my touch. My fingers leave a streak of blood on his cheek, and I kiss him there, licking it off.

I don't care that Cash sees. No one is going to believe her anyway. When Matthew says that *she* attacked *him* with a knife, it's only going to seem like a desperate attempt from her to get off the hook. Especially considering that I hit him openly not so long ago.

I quickly leave the room and find the nearest bathroom to wash off. I don't care if any of the inmates see me like this, but I don't want the guards to have any suspicion I was in a fight, possibly undermining Matthew's story. I manage to avoid any COs on my way to the bathrooms, and when I'm back in my cell I change into a clean set of clothes that I stole from the laundry room.

"Where's Cash?" Neilson asks.

"I don't know. She was a no-show," I lie. I don't care if she believes it or not. She's not a snitch anyway.

I don't see Matthew for several days. He's probably being questioned about what happened with Cash, and during the investigation, he won't be working here. I hear rumors about what happened, though. The consensus of it seems to be that Cash attacked Matthew for an unknown reason and now she's in the infirmary, recovering, before being sent off to max. *Good.*

There are also some less frequent rumors among the inmates that it was a result of the fight with me. I don't mind.

When I finally do see Matthew, I want to run into his arms like some cheesy romance novel, but I refrain myself. He's back in the mess hall, which must mean that they believed his story.

It takes another day before we have a chance to be alone. During a break in one of my shifts at the laundry room, we manage to sneak off to one of the closets. He doesn't waste any time. As soon as the door is closed, his hands frame my face, and he kisses me. Hard. I open my mouth, his tongue slipping in, and we feed off each other's hunger.

"Tell me what happened," I say after we break apart, trying to catch my breath.

"They swallowed it. Hook, line, and sinker."

"Really?" I can't believe everything went off without a hitch.

"Yeah, they really didn't investigate it that deep. They just seemed relieved that someone provided them with a plausible explanation for what happened and went with it." *Finally, the lack of regard for inmates works to my advantage.*

"And Cash?"

"Infirmary. She lost a lot of blood and will stay there for about a week. And then she's off to max."

This wouldn't be possible without Matthew. If it weren't for him, I'd probably be back at the bottom of the food chain, cleaning toilets and getting regularly beaten. He's devoted his life to this. To *me*.

"How much time do we have?"

He looks at his wristwatch. "I've got fifteen minutes, but you need to be back in five."

"Good." I crush my lips against his. "Fuck me."

"Now?"

"Yes, I've waited long enough. I'm tired of the other shitheads. I want you."

He returns my kiss with eagerness and takes hold of my legs as I lock them around his waist. He pushes his hand under my shirt, kneading my breast, and I groan into his mouth. At this, he thrusts his hips into me, allowing me to feel his cock pushing against my pussy. I'm already wet, and he hits just right.

Knowing that we don't have much time, he releases my breast and shoves his hands down my pants, rubbing me a few times before I lower my legs and he pulls down my pants and underwear.

"You have a condom?"

"Yeah." I unbuckle his utility belt as he reaches into his back pocket. My fingers work fast, and I release him from his boxers before he tears the wrapper to the condom. We don't have much time, but I *need* to taste him. I drop to my knees and instantly start sucking the head. He tastes so good, a bit salty mixed with something that is so Matthew. Just like I remember it. "Oh my god," he growls at my initiative.

I let him go and he swiftly rolls the condom on, grabbing my legs so that I lock them around him again. Without hesitation, he pushes himself inside. I have missed this. I have missed *him.* For the first time in almost a decade, this doesn't hurt. I kiss his lips to prevent the sob that threatens to escape my mouth, but I can't stop a tear from rolling down my cheek. Matthew's eyes are closed so he doesn't see it. I'm glad he doesn't.

He still hasn't moved, like he's relishing this moment as much as I do. "Do you have any fucking idea how many times I've dreamt about this?" he groans, showering my neck in open-mouthed kisses. I lock my arms around his neck to spur him on, and when his tongue reaches that spot below my ear, I instinctively buck my hips. He meets it with a thrust of his own, and it's not long before he drives himself into me with more force and speed.

I thrive on his lustful grunts, and there's a burning sensation in me that starts to build. "Matthew..." is all that escapes me when I feel how close I am. He moves his hand

and starts rubbing my clit, and I know that's it for me. With one more snap of his hips, the fire I've been containing for so long finally spreads throughout my entire body, out to the tips of my fingers. When I come, my walls contract around him, pushing him further to his release, and it's only seconds before he comes too. His movements become more erratic as he spills into the condom.

He puts his forehead on my shoulder after we've come back to our senses, his warm breath on my skin. He stays inside me for a little while before pulling out, and I miss him already. I make my decision, but I somehow know that this would have happened anyway.

It only takes a minute before we're both fully dressed, but his cheeks are still flushed. "Matthew." I wrap my arms around him, and he returns my embrace. "I don't want this either." He stiffens at my words, maybe misunderstanding what I'm trying to say. "I mean... This is not good enough for me either. I want to be with you. Fully."

"What are you saying?" he asks carefully.

"I want to leave."

Chapter Seven

Matthew silently looks at me in disbelief. His jaw is slack, and there's a question in his squinting eyes. Is he wavering in his decision? He must have realized what a monster I've become - retaliating against Cash without a second thought or any regard for her. We could probably have gotten rid of her without using violence, but I'd wanted her to suffer, to feel the pain that I felt. I'm sure he's finally figured out how many guards I'd have had to fuck and suck off, and it's too much for him.

He opens his mouth as if to say something but changes his mind. I want to say something, reassuring him that whatever I've done in here has been out of necessity, not desire. But he doesn't give me a chance to react. His mouth is on mine again, sucking my bottom lip, and I eagerly meet his tongue as it probes for entrance. The heat from where we are connected spreads through me, and I feel myself getting wet for him again. But I can't let myself get carried away.

I break the kiss. "I have to get back."

"Yeah," he croaks, sliding his thumb across my bottom lip, getting rid of the evidence of our kiss. "Laura," he speaks, before I open the door. "Are you sure?" He's not unsure about his own decision - he's making sure I want this too.

"Yes." I had made peace with myself about being here for a long time. But Matthew's opened the door for me, showing me that I can have more. More than this.

I must get back to the laundry room. I can't risk anyone missing me and finding me here with Matthew. I press my lips against his in what I hope is a reassuring kiss. "I promise. I want this. I want *you*," I tell him before leaving the room.

"Fuck, yes! More!"

He's kept me on the edge for too long. I need to come *now*. I desperately grasp his hair, trying to make him do something. *Anything*. He knows how close I am, but seems unfazed by it, not changing the speed or the pressure of his tongue. Matthew's on his knees, with my right leg resting on his shoulder. I frantically buck my hips against his face, trying to get some pressure to push me over the edge.

Then he stops, and I can't hold back the groan of disappointment leaving my mouth. He raises his head, looking up at me. His lips and nose glisten from my arousal, making him so sexy that I would kiss him on the spot if I wasn't so close. He replaces his tongue with his thumb, making an agonizingly slow circular motion around my clit without touching it. "How badly do you want this, Laura?" he purrs. My name rolling off his tongue like that is the sexiest thing I know.

"Please, Matthew." I don't care that I sound desperate and pathetic. I'd do anything for this man.

"Say it," he whispers, licking the inside of my thigh. His tongue is warm and wet, leaving a trail of goosebumps in its wake.

"I'm yours, Matthew. Only yours," I pant, knowing that this is what he wants to hear and hoping it will make him continue what he was doing.

At my words, he returns to his task, fervently sucking my clit, and my head falls back, hitting the wall behind me. It's like I'm on autopilot, grabbing the metal shelves above me as I start to rock my hips again. Matthew snakes one of his hands up under my shirt, stroking my nipples through the fabric of my bra.

"Fuck, I'm gonna..." After that, everything is pure bliss. My orgasm washes over me as Matthew continues to work both my clit and nipples. Exactly the way I want, licking and sucking until I've stopped shuddering. He wastes no time and stands up, pushing his tongue into my mouth, and I taste myself on his tongue and lips. It only turns me on even more. I want more.

"Do you know how many times I've jerked off imagining you saying that?" He presses his hips against mine as if to prove his point, letting me feel how hard he is. "Exactly like that."

His admission only adds to my arousal, even if I just came. That he thought of *me* while bringing himself to completion. I can't help picturing him stroking himself, making those beautiful sounds of lust and pleasure when he comes.

I'm filled with an eagerness to please him, so I drop to my knees, unbuckling his belt and unzipping his pants. I lick him through his underwear, and he groans at the contact. I impatiently push his pants and boxers down his hips and immediately take him in my mouth without breaking eye contact.

"Tell me," I say as I release him.

"The thought of your sounds, your smell, your taste... It always does it for me," he says, his voice hoarse, panting. I lick the underside of his cock and suck the head when I reach it. "Oh fuck, that feels so good."

His sounds. *His* smell. *His* taste. Everything about him is perfection. I grab him at the base and suck him off with more determination. When he gets closer to his release, I let him go and fish out a condom from the pocket of his pants that are now pooled around his ankles. Tearing the wrapper, I put it on him and give him a few extra strokes before rising again.

Before I get the chance to kiss him, he turns me around and starts sucking the side of my neck while squeezing my nipples. Hard. "Bend over," he growls in my ear.

The way he says it, demands it, makes me weak in the knees, and I have no choice but to obey him. I'm on my hands and knees on a wooden bench and Matthew wastes no time plunging into me. His hands are on my hips, pulling me against him. It doesn't take long for us to find a fast pace. His powerful thrusts cause my knees to scratch against the boards underneath me, but I don't care. This feels so fucking good, and I already feel myself closing in on another orgasm.

He's close too. "Matthew, I want to see you." He stills his movements, and I take the opportunity to quickly turn around. His cheeks are flustered and he's out of breath. I'm still on all fours when I roll the condom off him and start sucking him off again.

"Fuck, Laura." His head falls back, and his hands find my hair, guiding me. He's rock hard, but the skin is smooth, allowing me to feel every ridge with my tongue. I grab his hips, pushing him in a little more, and I can feel how close he is. It's only a couple of seconds before he comes. The warm liquid fills my mouth as my name falls from his lips. He tastes exactly like I remember. I love it.

After I've made sure to swallow everything, I rise and kiss him full on the mouth. I'm sure he can taste himself, but he doesn't seem bothered by it.

"You didn't finish," he says as we break apart.

"It doesn't matter," I say, trying to shrug it off.

Instead of answering, he moves his hand to the juncture of my thighs, threading his fingers through my folds. "It matters," he whispers in my ear as he strokes my clit before slipping two of his fingers inside. He extracts them before pushing them back in. He has such an effect on me - everything he does to me feels so good, and I can't help but cry out as he pushes me closer again.

My legs give out, and Matthew supports my weight with one of his arms. His ministrations soon send me spiraling to the point of no return, and he covers my lips in his as I come around his fingers. I've missed this.

Matthew knows the blueprints of this compound, allowing him to find a spot where we can go unnoticed and not have to worry about the sounds we make, and he knows how to sneak off unnoticed.

"Listen," he says, securing his utility belt around his waist. He hesitates before continuing. "Despite this place being the worst run-prison, I've ever seen, it's well-monitored. And the guards outside carry some heavy rifles."

"What are you saying?"

Where is he going with this?

He doesn't meet my eyes. "I think our best chance is from the administrative building. The security there is not as heavy, and no one would suspect it." His voice is clinical like he's reciting a recipe.

I've only been in that building for one reason. "So how do we get there?"

Finally, he lifts his gaze, looking me in the eye. He doesn't answer, confirming my suspicions. I can't believe it. The only way to get out of here is through the warden. Not only have I been forced to sleep, suck, and lick my way to the top here - now I must fuck my way out of here too?

"You want me to fuck Thorn?!"

"You know I don't," he answers immediately. "And if everything works out, you won't have to."

Of course, he doesn't *want* me anywhere near Thorn. I saw how angry and hurt he got when I was there last time. "I didn't mean to - "

"Don't worry about it," he reassures me, opening his arms for me. His hands travel up and down my back, and I revel in the little time we can spend like this. Alone.

"It's just... I hate him so much. When Cash beat the hell out of me, he let it slide and..." I bury my face in his shirt, so I don't have to face him.

"And what?" he asks carefully.

I haven't told Matthew about the abortion. It's still

difficult to talk about, especially with him. He puts his finger underneath my chin, nudging me to raise my head.

"Laura. Tell me what he did." He's so sincere that I can't brush it off.

"I got pregnant," I croak, but he probably can't hear it.

"What?"

I clear my throat. "I got pregnant," I repeat. Matthew's eyes widen in shock, but I continue before he says anything. "I don't know whose it was. It could've been Brad's or anyone else's." I pause. "I guess it didn't look good, so he decided to get rid of it."

He hugs me tight, pressing my head against his chest. "I'm sorry. I'm so sorry," he whispers, rocking me back and forth. "I should have been here. I should have..." he trails off, sobbing.

He thinks this is on him - that he somehow could have stopped it. There's nothing he could've done, but he still blames himself. The next part will probably shake him to his core, but he needs to know. "There's more."

He doesn't say anything, only keeps hugging me.

"I can't..." *How do I break his heart?* "I can't get pregnant again," I whisper. He releases me from his embrace, putting his hands on my cheeks and searching my eyes. I can't quite read his. Is he angry? Hurt? Sad?

I don't know how long we stand there, looking at each other before Matthew drops to his knees, pressing his face to my stomach. "I'm so sorry, Laura. Please forgive me," he pleads. "It's my fault. I should have stood up for myself, so you didn't have to. She was right. I'm a pussy."

I can't stand him begging for forgiveness for things he couldn't do anything about. I drop to my knees too so that I'm at eye level with him, but he won't look at me. "Matthew." His eyes are still locked on the floor. I cradle his head in my hands. "Matthew," I repeat. "Don't apologize for things you can't control. I knew what I was doing. *I* chose this."

"Laura, you shouldn't sacrifice yourself for me. You won't be doing me any favors." He blinks away some of his tears. "I would gladly take a beating every day if it meant keeping you out of here." He pauses, taking a breath. "But I get it. I understand why you did it."

I believe him. He understands why I couldn't do it. Because he'd rather get physically assaulted than for me to be here. Because we're the same. Just like he'd sacrifice himself for me, I'd do the same for him.

"Did you mean what you said before? About Thorn. Could you, do it?"

He looks at me in confusion. "What do you mean?"

"Kill him."

He hesitates, but only for a moment. "Yes."

"Then help me balance the scale."

He swallows. "Okay."

I don't want to admit it, but getting my revenge on Cash was so liberating, I can only imagine how it would feel to let Thorn gets what he deserves, and maybe Matthew will feel the same, getting some peace of mind.

I kiss his lips. "Then let's do it." *Let justice be done.*

* * *

The meth head who told me about Cash rigging the fight is probably our best bet. A junkie's loyalty is better than the ones who stayed with you for years. When many of them betrayed me, she tried to do me a favor. It was probably because she was looking to score some drugs, but still. I'm sure she'd let me beat her up for the rest of my stash. That'll send me back to Thorn's office.

"Krista? No, not her," Matthew says without looking at me. "It's too risky. You'll only end up in the hole again."

We're in a corner in the laundry room. It's semi-secluded, allowing us to talk almost freely. Matthew overlooks the room while I empty and refill the washing machines.

"I can live with that. Besides, she can have all the drugs I have left. I won't be needing them."

"I know you can, but then there will be reports to fill out, and Bowen will get involved. Too much can go wrong."

I don't say anything for a couple of minutes, contemplating his words. "What did you mean by 'not *her* ?'"

He exhales. "Do you remember Justin Denver?"

Justin Denver. A CO that worked here a couple of years ago. He was gorgeous but untouchable. Every inmate tried to get him on their side, but no one succeeded. I never bothered to try - he seemed too easy to lose that I didn't think it was worth the effort.

"Yeah."

"He transferred to the same prison I worked at two years ago. He's a great CO - stern, but fair. He stopped a fight once when she was getting beat up, and she took a liking to him. She started imagining that they were in a relationship and followed him around all the time. To be honest, I don't know why she's here. She should be in psych."

"Why isn't she?"

"She *would* have been if it weren't for Denver. I guess he felt sorry for her, so instead of turning her in, he transferred to another prison. I said I'd look out for her. I can't break that promise." He pauses. "I take it she turned to drugs after he left because he didn't mention her being an addict."

He crosses his arms over his chest. "Besides, if Thorn gets another guard to take you to his office..." he doesn't finish the sentence. I guess he doesn't want to think about that. Neither do I.

"Hadn't you been planning this for eight years?"

He throws me a look. "You can't plan everything. It's difficult to find out the routines in each prison without being there. I got some inside information from Denver, but I couldn't ask him too much without raising suspicion."

Matthew runs his hand through his hair, apparently not knowing what to do with it. "It's been a while since they searched your cells, right?"

"I guess. They don't seem to have a schedule."

A subtle smile settles on his lips, apparently amused by it. "Of course, they don't."

Ever since Cash disappeared, the inmates have been pretty calm. The mess hall's been remarkably quiet, and I've gotten a few meals in peace, without anyone approaching me trying to 'make friends.' Not even Brad has been as big of an asshole as he usually is. I've barely spoken to Matthew either. Even if he knows his way around, we can't risk being seen too much together, so we have to choose our moments carefully.

It's Thursday because it's 'soup' again. When I finish my bowl I leave the tray on the table, making sure Brad notices. It's only seconds before he's yelling at me.

"McKenzie!" I halt. It's not Brad - it's Matthew. I turn around slowly, meeting his eyes for the first time in several days. "That's the *third* time this week." It's not - it's the first. His gaze is stern like he's trying to tell me something. I understand. I love how fast we got back to how we were before any of this ever happened. How can we communicate without words as if these years apart never happened? "Pick up your tray and put it where it belongs, or I'll drag your ass down to the hole myself."

Not wanting to call his bluff, I pick it up and put it with the others. Brad smirks behind Matthew, snickering something about me being 'dick whipped.' I don't care. He can have this one, and I'll have *his* dick on a platter later.

Three days. Three days before I'll be leaving this place. Either with Matthew or in a body bag.

I realize I might not be able to speak to Matthew before everything goes down, but I must see him. I must talk to him. I can't let him go through with this without him knowing everything. He'll resent me for it if I don't tell him. If we are going to do this there needs to be complete honesty between us.

The meth addict - was it Krista? - gets a few bindles to help me out. I know Matthew's routine, and when he walks around the corner, she shoves me into a closet where there aren't any cameras.

"Guard!" I yell, and it's only seconds before he appears at the door opening. I immediately push her out and lock the door, leaving me alone with Matthew.

"What the fuck are you doing, Laura? This is way too risky."

"She won't tell anyone. She's afraid she'll end up like Cash. Besides, this is important."

He puts a chair against the door, making sure no one can get in.

"I have to tell you something."

He freezes, seemingly terrified of what I have to say. He doesn't say anything, silently urging me to continue.

"It's about that day." It's still too difficult to say it - *the day I killed your mother* - but he knows what I mean. "I should have told you sooner, but I didn't know how and - "

"Laura," he interrupts, approaching me and putting his hands on my shoulders. "What is it?"

"She told me something, right before..."

It's a couple of seconds before he speaks. "What?"

"She said that you... That you hit her." He relaxes his shoulders, but I can't quite read his facial expression.

"I know," he murmurs. *How could he possibly know?* He was unconscious. As if sensing my question, he continues. "I mean I don't know what she said to you. But I've somehow always known what I did."

"How?"

"I've dreamt about it several times. But it's always felt so real, so I thought there was more to it." He pauses. "Like a memory. It's only fractions, so I don't know the details.

Just that feeling. I was so angry that there was only one thing I could think of to relieve it."

There seems to be more to this, but he bites his tongue. "Tell me everything, Matthew," I urge him. "If you remember anything else, now is the time to tell me."

He envelops me in a tight hug, holding me like it's the last time. "It felt good. It felt *so good,* Laura. I *should* regret it, but I don't," he sighs into my hair. "She deserved to suffer for what she did and to die for it. I fucking hate her, and I only wish she'd be alive so that I could kill her myself. I wish I was ashamed for feeling that way, but I'm not."

It feels like a balloon deflating like he's been holding it in for too long and now finally letting all his guard down.

I don't argue with him, because he's right. We *should* be ashamed of what we did. It *shouldn't* feel good, but it does. We did what was right. Why should we have to apologize for righting a wrong?

I loop my arms around him, gripping his back and burying my face in his chest. "Then don't. Embrace it."

This is the day. The day I'll finally be out of this place. I had resigned myself to spending the rest of my life in here. Now, I can't imagine being another day in here. Matthew has shown me that there is more to this life, and he wants to share it with me. We'll be branded fugitives. Criminals, menaces, and a danger to society. *What else is new?*

I couldn't care less about those things - I've been called worse. The only thing that concerns me is that whatever happens, we will do it together. If something happens to him, I will not continue my life here. There *is* no life here. I know it now - even before he came here, I lived for him. Knowing that he could live his life made my incarceration bearable. If he dies, and I live, there is no life at all for me. In one last act of rebellion against this fucking place I'll kill one of the rapists posing as noble officers, and then I'll die for my troubles.

I think I'm imagining the sound of their shoes meeting the concrete floor because I hear it for hours before they arrive. When the key slides into the lock I bolt up from the bed, but Neilson is still sleeping. Should I have warned her? We're not friends, not even allies, but I have no beef with her. Hell, I think I even respect her in some weird sort of way. No, I can't focus or worry about her right now.

When the door opens the guard looks surprised that I'm not lying down, but he says nothing. Neilson starts to stir when Matthew's voice echoes through the cellblock. "Inmates, line up outside your cells." That's all the instructions we get. Clear and simple.

There are two inmates in each cell, making it twenty-four people in the hallway, excluding the COs. I catch a glance at Matthew before someone cuffs my hands behind my back. The reek of cologne alerts me to who it is before I see him - Brad.

"You better pray that I don't find anything, or we'll have field day later," he wheezes in my ear. His breath causes me to shudder, and he seems satisfied by my reaction.

"Alright, ladies," Matthew starts, getting everyone's attention. "This is an unscheduled inspection of your cells. I'm assuming you have nothing to hide, so this will probably be quick. Nonetheless, you will wait in the hallway during the inspection." His voice is almost robotic, and I wonder how he does it. I'd be a shivering mess if I were in his shoes.

We wait while they search through the small spaces, turning the mattresses, and looking for cavities in the wall. I know the second he finds it - Brad's snickering turns my stomach, and I try not to throw up in his face when he approaches me.

"Taken up carving as an extracurricular activity?" he taunts, holding up my knife only inches from my nose. I don't dignify him with an answer. He just sneers. "Radford!" he calls over my shoulder. "I think McKenzie needs a lesson in what objects are allowed in the cells."

Matthew walks over - I sense him even though I can't see him.

"Hm?" Brad grabs my arms, forcing me to turn around, and I settle my eyes on Matthew. He's holding my knife, inspecting it. "I thought we settled this a couple of weeks ago, McKenzie. Didn't we?" Damn, he's a good actor.

"I guess not," I mutter.

"Brad, can I trust you to finish this?" I can only imagine Brad's look of pride when he realizes he'll be in charge.

"Of course."

"Good. I think medium security is too lenient for you," Matthew says, making sure the other guards hear him. He turns me around and lowers his face, so his mouth is close to my ear. "You're going to the warden's office."

Chapter Eight

He holds my hands behind my back, but his touch is soft. Since most of the guards are working with the inspections the corridor is pretty much empty - except for Bailey. I can tell the exact moment Matthew sees him, his grip on my wrists tightening.

"Making new friends?" Bailey quips, looking at me.

I want to spit in his face. That motherfucker and I have unfinished business. But I can't do it now - it would only cause a scene, and attention is the last thing we need right now.

"Found a knife in her cell," Matthew responds immediately. If he thinks Matthew's taking me somewhere to fuck, maybe he'll mind his own business. Matthew carefully yanks me backward, his mouth by my ear. "There's only one hard object you're allowed in your hand."

His meaning is not lost on Bailey, and he smirks at Matthew's comment. He looks at Matthew. "Thorn will send her to max."

"Probably."

"Does he know?"

"Not yet."

Bailey approaches us - I have to suppress the gag reflex, but I try not to show it. He grabs my chin, turning my face left and right as if inspecting it. "It's a shame. She gives a decent blowjob." Then he addresses me. "What do you say, sweetheart? One last time? As a parting gift," he mocks.

"I told you, Bailey. Don't touch my things," Matthew says in his most authoritative voice.

"What makes you judge of that?" He looks and sounds annoyed. He's probably still pissed because he couldn't have his turn. He seems like someone who can hold a grudge.

"Hierarchy. Would you like a lesson?" Bailey's got a couple of inches on Matthew, but Matthew makes up for it in confidence.

He squints his eyes at Matthew, then surrenders, only now seeming to realize that Matthew outranks him. He looks down at his feet. "No." I can't suppress the smirk on my face.

"Good. If you don't have anything better to do, then

you can help Brad with the inspections. They're a man short."

Bailey drags his feet as he passes us, and I'm sure that if we didn't want the extra attention Matthew would reprimand him for it. He's been a pain in the ass to the guards who were involved in the incident in that room. And I love him for it.

The rest of the walk is quiet. Fortunately, we don't meet anyone else, and I appreciate these few minutes of silence, his hand on my wrists, his soft breaths - this closeness.

Before Matthew knocks on the door, he unlocks my cuffs. "I need a couple of minutes. You sure you can stall him?"

I turn around so we're face to face. Since he came back, he's never faltered, but now there's a vulnerability in his eyes - he's nervous too. "Yeah."

He looks around, making sure no one can see us, and puts his hands on my arms. "You can still change your mind about this."

"I know, but I won't," I tell him with the firmest voice I can muster. I'm sure of my words and I'm determined to leave, but I'd lie if I said I wasn't nervous.

He slides his hands up to my cheeks, grabbing my face and pulling me in for a kiss. I part my lips, and our tongues meet as I skate my hands up his arms, grabbing him as if my life depended on it. *It does.* We don't know how everything will play out after I enter that office, so I pour every emotion I can into this kiss, and he does too. The insane roller coaster we've both been on is about to come to an end, and the weight of it hits me. He suckles on my bottom lip before pulling away, and I instantly miss his touch. We *will* leave this place. Or die trying.

We don't have to say anything else. His fingers linger on my arm a little longer before he knocks on the door.

"What?" Thorn shouts from inside.

Matthew opens the door, and we both walk in. Thorn doesn't even look up from his papers, and Matthew clears his throat to get his attention.

"We found a knife in her cell." Matthew pushes me forward. "I figured you'd want to speak to her about that."

A smile of satisfaction spreads on his face. "You figured right," he says, licking his lips. *Motherfucker*.

Matthew subtly caresses my wrist behind my back before letting me go. "I'll wait outside."

"This might take a while, Radford. You can continue with the inspection. I'll make sure McKenzie is well taken care of," he says, a smug look on his ugly face.

I don't have to see Matthew to know that he's shooting daggers at Thorn. But his voice is still steady. "Alright, sir."

As much as I want to look at him one more time before he leaves, I restrain myself from turning around. When the door closes, I take my seat across from Thorn. He stands up right away, walks to the door, and locks it.

In an instant, he's behind me. I don't like it.

"Whatever are we going to do about you, little missy?" He puts his hands on my shoulder and lets one of them shamelessly slide down my shirt to my breast. He grabs it with such force that I have to suppress a cry of pain.

"A knife, huh? Unless you want to be shipped off to max, you have some serious groveling to do."

"What's your price?" I ask, trying not to let the pain he's causing seep into my voice.

"You're not in a position to negotiate. We'll see how well you do today, and then I'll decide if it's good enough. You're a pain in my ass, McKenzie, but you do have a decent cunt."

He unbuckles his belt, turns my chair around, and stands with my legs between his. His dick is right in front of me, and I try not to let the disgust show on my face.

"You want to stay here, don't you?" he murmurs, sliding his dick along my left cheek.

"Yes," I whisper.

"Good," he says, backing away from me a couple of inches. "On your knees."

I hesitate a second too long, and he slaps me. Hard. It takes me by surprise because even if he uses his whip from time to time, he's never used his fists.

"Do I need to repeat myself?"

Instead of answering I get off the chair and do as he

says. He immediately takes my seat. "Take your shirt off," he commands as he strokes himself.

I obey, not wanting to aggravate him. He needs to have a false sense of security.

"You'll probably won't need your pants either."

He barely has time to finish his sentence before there are four rapid knocks on the door. This catches Thorn's attention, and I act as if on autopilot. I pull out a knife Matthew slipped in my pocket earlier and put it at his dick. No, this is not a knife - it looks like a scalpel.

"Don't say a fucking word, or I swear to god, I'll cut it off."

The door is locked, but Matthew has a spare key, and when Thorn sees him there's a Tanisha of hope on his face. But instead of rushing to his aid, Matthew slowly closes the door and locks it again.

"Radford?"

"Shut up, you fucking piece of shit," he spits. Matthew puts down the bag he was carrying when he came in and pulls out a roll of tape to strap Thorn's wrists and ankles to the chair. "They'll be needing dental records when we're done with you," he says in Thorn's face after being silent during the entire process. Matthew's words have the desired effect - Thorn's scared shitless. I've never seen him so weak. It's a wonderful sight.

"What are you - "

"Didn't you hear the officer?" I move the scalpel to his throat. "You will speak only when addressed," I seethe.

Matthew looks at me, seeing my state of undress. "What did he do?" His voice is completely different from when he talks to Thorn.

I stand up, putting my shirt back on. "He complimented my pussy." I direct my gaze to Thorn. "Or how did you put it? My *decent cunt* ."

Matthew takes out a gun, pressing the muzzle against Thorn's jaw, only inches separating them. "It's fucking better than decent."

As Matthew moves away from Thorn I stand on my toes and give him a quick kiss on the cheek.

His hand snakes around my waist and he puts his mouth by my ear, making sure Thorn can't hear him. "You alright?" His genuine concern for me makes me want to shut everything and everyone out. This moment is about him and me, and us alone.

"Yes," I whisper, pressing my cheek against his and feeling his warmth. I guess it'll have to do for now - we're not out of here yet.

Matthew shifts his focus back to Thorn as I stand behind him. He tries to follow my movement as if he's afraid I might do something he won't see coming. *Good.* But Matthew brings his attention back to him.

"Do you know why McKenzie is here?"

"You found... You found a knife in her cell." It looks like he's trying to reposition himself in the chair, but the tape prevents him from doing so.

"No," Matthew says impatiently, exhaling. "In prison."

"I... I don't know," he says carefully, apparently afraid of saying something wrong.

"Sure, you do. You must have looked at her file dozens of times, every time you threatened to send her to max."

Thorn hesitates, his eyes flickering. *Matthew* doesn't hesitate. He punches him right on the nose, causing it to start bleeding. "Don't go forgetful on me now, warden. You had no problem remembering every single one of her missteps during my installation."

Thorn's hand jerks, probably instinctively wanting to wipe his nose. "She... She killed someone."

"That's right. Do you know who?"

"I don't remember the name. What does it have to do with - "

Matthew pulls out a card from his pocket, throwing it on Thorn's lap.

"Ring a bell?"

It's his old driver's license. The one he had before changing his last name. Thorn stares at it for a couple of seconds, putting the pieces together.

"You," he says, looking up at Matthew again. "You're the wimp who - "

He doesn't see my fist coming, and I punch him square

in the jaw. "He's not a fucking wimp!" *Fuck, that hurts a lot more than I thought it would.*

It takes a little longer for him to recover this time, but when he does there's a sneer on his face. "Always hide behind a woman when things get rough?" he taunts. He's very cocky for being in this position, and I want to slap the grin off his face. But that would only be grist to his mill.

Matthew seems unaffected by Thorn's mocking. "I can understand why a strong woman might make someone like you feel emasculated. But I really don't like your attitude," he says calmly, before turning the gun around in his hand and hitting Thorn with it, exactly in the same spot he hit him before. Matthew backs away, giving me the space. "All yours."

I move so I'm only inches away from his face. Blood runs freely from his nose, dripping down on his shirt. I want to yell. Yell at him for forcing the abortion, raping me, letting almost every guard rape me, ignoring the beatings, and for all the other shit that's going on in here. But it won't change anything - *he* won't change.

I let out a huff. "You're not worth my time or my energy."

My words seem to make him think I'm having second thoughts, a Tanisha of hope glistens in his eyes.

At first, I think I miss. I don't feel the knife slicing through his skin. It appears Thorn doesn't realize what I did either. It takes a couple of seconds before his hands instinctively try to move to cover the open wound where I slit his throat, but they're strapped down. The blood squirts from his artery with such force it soaks me. The red liquid is warm, the feeling liberating.

Matthew grabs my arm. "We've gotta go."

I don't know if Thorn's dead or alive when we leave his office. It doesn't matter. If he's still breathing, he won't be for long.

"Come on, this way." Matthew pulls me through a door leading to a tiny room. It reminds me of the hole, but this one has another door on the opposite side. It looks like it's a way out. "This is an emergency exit for the administrative staff."

"Won't the alarm go off if we open it?"

"No. It's been broken for years. I checked." He takes out a long cylinder from his bag, threading it on his gun - a silencer - and hands an identical one to me. It feels cold and heavy in my hand. The last time I held one was when I killed his mom. You'd think that it would stir up a string of emotions, but it doesn't. "Listen, when we get out there, you run. Okay? I don't know if we're gonna get fired at. It depends if the guards on watch see us. You remember how to use one of these, right?"

I stare at the gun in my hands. "Yes."

"It's the white Ford. It's open, and the keys are under the driver's seat."

Why is he telling me this?

"Don't you have the keys?"

"Yeah, but..." He swallows. "Whatever you do, keep running, okay?"

I put my hand on his chest, and he grabs my fingers, closing his eyes briefly. "Matthew..."

"Please, Laura. Whatever happens, get to that car."

"Matthew." I wrap my arms around his neck, pulling him to me. "Don't expect me to just leave you." After everything we've been through, how does he think I'll be able to keep on living if something happens to him?

He puts his hands on my hips and kisses my hair. "I hope it won't come to that, but - "

The door we just came through bursts open. Neither of us has time to react before the intruder spots us - it's a guard. He must've seen us. Fuck.

We all stare at each other for a while - I have no idea how long - no one seems to want to make any sudden movements. Only when the guard slowly moves his hand to the radio on his shoulder does Matthew break this weird stalemate, and swiftly point his gun at the guard. "Don't."

He seems at a loss, not knowing what to do, and frankly neither do I. But Matthew slowly approaches him, pulling the cuffs in the back of his utility belt off with one hand, leaving only one of the guns. The guard sees this as an opportunity and tries to knock it out of Matthew's grip. It doesn't work, but it's enough to shift Matthew's focus for a split second and my heart sinks when I see him getting tripped and falling to the ground.

On instinct, I drop the gun I'm holding and throw myself at the guard, who's now on top of Matthew, desperately trying to pull him off. His ugly hands are locked around Matthew's throat, and the sight makes me lose all control. "Let go of him!" I scream as I try to claw at his arms, neck, and face. Whatever I can think of to get him off.

It's enough to get his attention, turning around to throw me off him. With a grunt, he manages to land a fist on the side of my stomach. The force knocks the wind out of me. My vision gets blurry and the sounds of the scuffle next to me drown in silence.

The next thing I see is Matthew's face above me. It's pale. Why does he look so scared? He looks down between us. His hands are covered in blood. *Oh no.* He can't leave me now. Everything spins. White lights dance around Matthew's head.

He's my angel.

"Laura? Stay with me. Please. Stay with me."

Why am I lying down? Matthew's terrified. I lift my hand to his face, caressing it. There's something red on my finger. I paint a flower on his cheek. *I'm here. I'll always be here. With you.*

"Laura?" He pats the side of my face with his hands. "You need to stay with me." *Why does he think I'm leaving?*

He opens the bag, pulls out something white, and pushes it to my stomach.

Then pain. *Oh, the fucking pain.* The lights disappear when the intense burn from my stomach flashes through my entire body, out to the tips of my fingers.

"Matthew!?" I cough.

"Hey, you're going to be alright, okay." I don't know if he's asking or telling me, but I believe him. He never lies. Not to me. You have to try to stay awake, okay? Can you do that?" The blood on his hands isn't his - it's mine.

The realization throws me back to the present, my brain letting me feel the full extent of my injury. It hurts like hell.

"Yes." I don't know if I can, but I will give it my all.

"Listen, there's a lot of bleeding. You need stitches. The fucker had a knife." Matthew's voice is calm - he's switched to survival mode, methodically working on my wound. He wipes his forehead with the back of his hand, his jaw clenching. But we're sitting ducks here. Someone is going to find Thorn, and then we'll be stuck here, our only chance of leaving slipping through our fingers.

"We must go, Matthew. We can't stay here." They will find us here if we don't leave.

"Laura, if we don't do anything about this, you're gonna bleed out." That's when I see it. He's not calm. He's terrified. I've always thought that if something happened to me, he'd survive it. He's strong. But now I see in his eyes that he won't. We're the same, dependent on each other and unable to survive without the other.

"We *have* to go."

"I know. I'll get you out of here. I promise." He takes my hand. "Do you trust me?"

He doesn't even have to ask. "Yes."

"Good. I managed to put on a bandage, but that's not gonna last. The infirmary is not too far away. I'll carry you."

No, that won't work. Both of his hands will be tied. "No, I can walk." *I think.*

Matthew helps me up to my feet, but he might as well have carried me - I'm putting pretty much all my weight on him.

"The guard didn't have time to call it in, so no one suspects anything yet, at least," Matthew assures me. I look down at the body. One shot. In the head.

We don't take the shortest way to the infirmary, trying to avoid most of the cameras. We can't evade all of them, but Matthew says they're not monitored all the time, so hopefully, no one in surveillance sees us.

I lean on Matthew the entire way, doing my best not to put all my weight on him. I wish I could stand and walk on my own, but it hurts too much. Thanks to me, we're forced to go back, leaving us extremely vulnerable. "Matthew, I'm so sorry."

We stop after we round a corner. "Hey, listen. Do you remember what you used to tell me after Mother hit me?"

I do - I told him the truth.

"That it wasn't your fault."

"And this isn't yours."

"But you didn't believe me."

"No, but I'm a lot more persuasive than you." Even now, when we're facing the hardest challenge we'll probably ever meet, he manages to put a small smile on my face. And I know he's right. He doesn't say it to placate me. He says it because he believes it. And I believe *him.* "Come on, we're almost there."

The infirmary is a large room with beds along the walls. When Matthew opens the door it's eerily empty. What if they already know? But it doesn't take long before a middle-aged man enters the room from a door opposite the one, we came through. Doctor Aurelius. He's done some of my medical exams. He freezes when he sees us.

Before he gets a chance to do anything Matthew points his gun at him.

"Radford? What - "

"She needs stitches, and you're gonna do it."

"Are you asking me to - "

"This isn't a fucking discussion, Aurelius. You either do it, or I'll shoot you and do it myself. I prefer option number one, and I think you do too."

Aurelius looks at me and Matthew for a couple of

seconds before making his decision. "Put her here," he says, motioning to one of the beds. Matthew carries me to it and gently puts me down. As soon as he lets me go, I grab his hand, holding on to it as hard as I can, searching his eyes to have something to hold on to.

The doctor carefully lifts my shirt and removes Matthew's temporary bandage, which is now completely soaked. Some of it has even smeared onto Matthew's shirt, leaving a red stain. "What happened?"

"A knife," Matthew says, without breaking eye contact with me.

"I have to clean this," he says robotically. Matthew holds my hand the entire time, his eyes going between me and the doctor. "Are you feeling nauseated?"

"No."

The doctor takes my blood pressure and measures my pulse, everything under Matthew's watchful eyes.

"There doesn't seem to be any internal bleeding, and from what I can see the knife missed any vital organs."

Matthew sighs in relief. "Good. Then finish up and we'll be on our way."

Aurelius hesitates again, and I can see Matthew's losing his patience, exhaling loudly.

"It would go a lot smoother if I didn't have a loaded gun pointed at me at all times," Aurelius mutters.

"Well, doctor, it just so happens that I don't trust you.

So why don't you focus on what you're doing, and I'll make sure this doesn't *accidentally* go off?"

I don't feel anything when the doctor stitches me back together. Did he give me something? I feel myself drifting off, Matthew's face turning blurry. But he keeps talking to me, whispering assuring words in my ear that keeps me in the present.

"Look at me. Just a little while longer. We'll be out of here in no time." I try to focus on his eyes to keep myself from losing consciousness.

"Matthew?" I whisper. "Tell me a story."

He brushes a tear from my cheek and gives me the subtlest of smiles. "Did I tell you about the final game in the state wrestling competition?"

"No."

"I was nervous as hell. The guy I was up against was bigger than me. Not much, but sometimes that's all you need. I wanted to win so badly - not for the school or myself, but for Mom."

I furrow my brows. "Why?"

He closes his eyes as if to gather strength before continuing.

"Because maybe then she wouldn't see me as a constant failure and disappointment anymore. Or at least for the day." His confession breaks my heart. He did everything he could to get her to care about him, even though all she ever did was break him down. She didn't deserve him.

"Anyway, I'd seen you in the crowd during some of the games, and my foolish, lovestruck teenage mind had somehow convinced me that you were there to watch *me*," he says, shrugging his head as if chastising his younger self.

"The minutes before the game I tried to find you in the sea of people. And then my opponent came out, looking down on me. He wasn't *that* much taller, but it's a lot of psychology, and he was already winning. It wasn't until we stepped onto the mat that I saw you. It was like the entire room fell silent. And just like that, I knew that I could beat him."

He saw me. He saw me in the audience, and it gave him strength. I've relied on him for so many things, but he depends on me just as much. Lying here, hand in hand, I don't want to be anywhere else. Wherever he is, I want to be there.

"Okay, you're done," Aurelius says, breaking us from our moment. Matthew helps me up to a sitting position. The pain radiates from the right side of my stomach through my entire body. "She can't walk, or the wound will reopen."

"Give me your phone," Matthew says to Aurelius. He pulls it out from his pocket and gives it to Matthew, who hurls it across the room, breaking it against a wall. "Where's the bathroom?"

The doctor points to a door close to the one we came from. "Get in there." Aurelius looks at Matthew in horror.

"They'll find you eventually. You won't like the alternative."

As soon as Aurelius opens the door, Matthew closes it and props a chair up against it, making it impossible to open from the inside. He smashes some of the cupboards, takes most of the stuff, and puts it in his bag before swinging it over his shoulder.

"Put your hands around my neck," he instructs when he's back by my side. "There's been a slight change of plans. We'll go through here. We have to get outside before the alarms go off. Many of the doors lock automatically."

"How far are we from the parking lot?"

"Too far. I have to get the car first and come and pick you up."

He scoops me up in his arms. I know he's doing his best not to make my pain worse, but it hurts like hell. "Fuck," I exclaim. I'm afraid I'll pass out.

"I know. Just hold on a little longer." He carries me through the same door Aurelius came through and then a short, narrow corridor. At the end of it is another door that looks like it leads outside. When we get to it, Matthew uses one of his knees to prop me up, freeing one of his arms so that he can use his keycard.

The light almost blinds me. The sun shines right in my face. It's warming. Comforting. Matthew carefully puts me down on the ground. I'm an easy target, waiting here for Matthew to come back, but it's our only chance. I'll only slow him down if he takes me with him, leaving us too exposed to the guards.

"I'll be back as soon as I can," he promises and hands me a gun. I know he will. He'll put his own life at risk to save me. And that scares me more than anything.

I think I drift in and out of consciousness because I have no idea how long it takes before I hear the car. That's when the alarm goes off. There's a click from the door we just came through. If I'd slowed us down any longer, we'd be stuck in there. I've never heard this alarm before. It's different from the 6.30 wake-up call - louder and more high-pitched. I wait for the shooting to begin. But it doesn't.

Matthew parks the car right in front of me, shielding me from the watchtowers. He opens the passenger door from the inside. Stepping out, he helps me get in the car. I do my best to help him, but the wound hurts so fucking much that Matthew ends up doing all the work. He even makes sure to buckle my seatbelt before we take off.

That's when the shooting starts. This car isn't bullet-proof - one shot in the right place and we'll never get out of here.

"They're shooting at the tires," Matthew says as if that will calm me down. If they hit one of them, everything is over. We can't get away if they blow a tire.

But Matthew manages to get away from the bullets,

skillfully turning left and right before we're out of their sight.

We come to a wider road, and we're both silent for a couple of minutes before he takes my hand.

"How are you feeling?"

It hurts like hell, but I want to sleep. "I'm tired."

He grazes his thumb over my knuckles. "It's okay. Go to sleep."

I close my eyes and see seventeen-year-old Matthew right before the last game in the wrestling tournament. That moment when his eyes locked on mine. I'd written it off as a coincidence, a figment of my imagination, that he was looking at me.

"Matthew."

"Hm?" He squeezes my fingers.

"I *was* there to watch you."

I don't have to open my eyes to know that he's smiling.

Chapter Nine

The sound of sand crushing beneath the tires wakes me. Where am I? I open my eyes slowly, trying to adjust to the light.

I'm leaning with my side to the back of the seat, my face to the driver's seat, so the first thing I see is Matthew. He hasn't noticed I'm awake yet, and I take the opportunity to simply look at him, taking him in. He's here. He's *real*.

"Hey."

He quickly turns to me, giving me a subtle smile and taking my hand. "Hey. How are you feeling?"

"Like someone stabbed me."

"That's a good sign," he says before concentrating on the road again.

That's when I notice that we were in a pickup truck. "What happened to the other car?"

"I ditched it in the woods a couple of miles after you fell asleep." I didn't even think about that. Of course, they'll be looking for that car - everyone saw it, and it's probably all over the surveillance footage.

"How long was I asleep?"

"A couple of hours. Aurelius gave you some sedative."

"Where are we going?" We're not on the same road anymore. Trees tower over us on both sides of the dirt road, which is just wide enough for one car.

"There's a cabin about half an hour's drive from here."

"Matthew?" I say, putting my hand on his arm. "Thank you."

He doesn't say anything. He doesn't need to. Instead, he squeezes my fingers again. The rest of the car ride is silent. I can't stop looking at the woods. I'm finally here. I try to take in as much as I can, afraid of waking up in a hard cell bunk.

"Where are we?" I ask when Matthew stops the car in front of a small wooden cabin close to a lake.

"I bought it from a local farmer. The property line stretches about half a mile in either direction from here. There's a fence, and the only road here is private. The nearest town is twenty miles that way, and the prison is seventy-five miles that way."

"Isn't that a little close?"

"This is the farthest place I could find that's still inside the state line. We can't risk crossing it yet."

"They won't be able to track this place through you?"

"Probably not. I paid cash and didn't use my real name. And it was a couple of years ago. If they run a search for newly bought properties in the area, this won't come up."

"Well, haven't you figured everything out?" I manage a smile.

"See, there's more to me than a pretty face," he says, exiting the car.

It's not until I reach to unbuckle my seatbelt that I remember my injury. If Aurelius gave me painkillers, they're wearing off now. Matthew opens the passenger door and helps me with the seatbelt. Scooping me up in his arms, he carries me inside the cabin.

"I guess now I'll have to marry you," I say when we cross the threshold.

He snorts. "Right, because we are so traditional."

I smile at his words, but it fades the instant he puts me down on the bed and I see myself in the full-length mirror. I'm still covered in blood. Thorn's blood. It's dry and brown now. My face is almost clean, but my neck is still covered, and I can only imagine what the rest of my body looks like.

"I need a shower," I say when Matthew comes back from the car.

He takes a seat next to me. "You can't take a shower yet. The stitches are too new."

I must get this blood off me. I can't stand another second of it. "Matthew, I can't - "

"Okay. Let me help you."

He lifts me in his arms again, and I rest my hand on his chest, letting the closeness to him soothe me. I miss him the moment he puts me down on the toilet and leaves to get something. When he comes back, he's carrying a simple chair of some sort and puts it in the shower stall.

Matthew offers me his hand and I take it, letting him help me to the chair. Slowly and carefully, we work together to get rid of my clothes. I take one of my arms out of the sweater, and he gently takes it off. He helps me with my bra, tentatively pulling it over my head. I manage to stand up for a little while to shed my pants, leaving me only in my panties.

He sits on his knees in front of me. He's still wearing the same clothes, the blood stain on his shirt only serving as a reminder of what we did. With my left hand, I tug the hem of it. "This needs to go to."

Matthew swiftly unbuttons it and shucks it off, throwing it on the bathroom floor. The blood leaked through his shirt, staining the t-shirt beneath it. Without prompting, he takes it off too.

Taking the shower head, he turns the water on and soaks the cloth in his hand. The moment he puts it on my body I feel free - like he's cleansing me of my sins. *Our* sins. But they're not sins. The blood dissolves in the water, pooling around the drain before disappearing. The water is cold, but I don't care.

He wets the cloth again, repeating the motion. I close my eyes, letting him wash me.

"You did this for me once. That's real, right?"

"Yes, but you were unconscious."

"I know. The doctor told me someone cleaned me up. I ruled out my dad quickly."

He takes his time, making sure I'm clean from all the blood, dragging the cloth along my arms, throat, chest, and fingers. I close my eyes, reveling in this. His touch. I've missed this. I don't think I realize it until now. How much I've missed being free. If they catch us tomorrow, I can live with that, knowing that we have tonight.

I don't think I told him in there. I was afraid that someone might hear it, tainting the words that are so special. Because they are for us, and us alone. I couldn't risk it. But now we're away from all of that. No one can hear us here. We're alone. Safe.

"I love you." I don't think I've ever told anyone else. And I never will.

"I love you, too." He doesn't question why I didn't say it before.

He turns the water off, and I put my hand on his shoulder. If I could I'd use both my arms to pull him to me, but I can't. It hurts too much.

I let my fingers slide along his arm, goosebumps

breaking out on his skin. His pants are soaked from washing me, but he doesn't seem bothered by it.

He turns the water off and gets out of the shower. Once again, he picks me up and carries me back to the bedroom. When he puts me on the bed a wave of exhaustion hits me. "I'm so tired, Matthew."

"I know." He strokes my back. "Let me just get the rest of the stuff from the car, and we'll go to bed."

He moves to get up, but I grab his arm. "Stay. Please."

"Okay."

He quickly takes off his wet pants and pulls the cover up over us. I turn over to my good side, tugging at the waistband of his boxers. I need to feel all of him, without the restriction of clothes. He readily complies and helps me with my underwear too. He lets me rest my head on his arm, our noses almost bumping into each other.

He strokes my cheek. "Whatever happens, I don't regret anything."

"Me neither."

He pulls me closer, his hand on my back. It won't be long before I fall asleep - my eyelids are like lead. Pushing my forehead to his, I sigh, letting every worry leave me. Tonight, it's just us. Together.

Because of my injury, I'm pretty much incapacitated for the next three weeks. The intense pain from the wound subsides to a dull ache, and I must refrain from any physical activity - if Matthew had his way, I'd be in bed the entire time, but I can't lie idle for so long. I need to do *something*.

Matthew's stocked up on cans and other non-perishables, making it possible to stay here for weeks without having to leave the premises. We have fresh water, and electricity from time to time. It's unreliable, but fixing it isn't worth the risk, or the trouble.

I'm pouring pasta sauce from a can into a pot when Matthew enters the kitchen after chopping wood. He wipes his forehead with his discarded t-shirt. Our only reliable heat source is a fireplace and since I'm barely allowed to move Matthew's been forced to do all that work since we got here. He tends to the physical labor, and I cook. I think this is the most traditional we've ever been or ever will be. It's boring.

Unfortunately, having to stay away from physical activity means *all* physical activity. And when he walks in like that, sweat outlining his perfectly sculpted chest, it's torture. I may be physically injured, but my libido is not. And the way my body reacts to his hasn't changed. I feel fine, but Matthew's cautious, afraid that we'll do something to cause an infection or rip the stitches.

"Matthew, put your shirt on," I say, annoyed that he's

teasing me this way. He's probably not even aware of it, and that makes it even more infuriating. Becoming a correctional officer did well for him. He was in good shape in his teens too, but this is sick. Up until now, I haven't been able to fully appreciate his body. Our few moments have been brief, and at least one of us has had some piece of clothing left on. Out of all the feelings, I thought I'd have now; sexual frustration wasn't one of them.

"I have to wash off first," he responds casually, giving me a quick kiss on the cheek before leaving.

He returns only minutes later, thankfully with some clothing on his upper body. Putting his hands on my waist but avoiding the Band-Aid on the right side, he rests his chin on my shoulder. "I think we can take out the stitches tonight."

"Really?"

"Yeah, it looked okay last time I reapplied the Band-Aid, but I wanted to wait a few extra days." Since Matthew's had medical training, he's been taking care of my wound, making sure it heals properly and without any complications.

I turn around in his arms, locking them around his neck. "Good." I pull his face to mine, pressing our mouths together in a kiss. His tongue traces my lips, and I part them for him. We both explore each other's mouths as he cups my face with his hands. I love the way he takes control of the kiss, pulling my face toward his and plunging his tongue greedily into my mouth. I'm weak in the knees before he releases me.

"As much as I appreciate all of this, we have stuff to do. If you take the stitches out tonight, how long before we can get to it?"

He sighs, putting his forehead against mine. "A couple of days, depending on how it looks tonight."

"Okay."

* * *

I lie down on my side as Matthew sits in front of me. The adhesive sticks to my skin as he carefully pulls the Band-Aid off.

"Looks good. No infections," he assures me after cleaning it up. Using tweezers and a small pair of scissors he starts removing the stitches. His gaze is intense and focused. I thought it might hurt, but when he pulls the thin thread from my skin there was only a dull, tingling feeling. "Are you feeling alright?"

"Yeah."

Now and then, his fingertips graze a part of my side that's not affected by the wound, causing goosebumps to break out on my upper body and down my arms. If he notices he doesn't comment on it.

Cleaning it one more time, he puts on another Band-Aid, and we're done. When he returns from the bathroom after getting rid of the old Band-Aid, he's only wearing his sweatpants, ready to tuck in for the night.

When he was gone, I shed everything but my panties and found one of his shirts in the closet. It's long enough to cover my ass, and I've only closed one button. If this doesn't work, nothing will.

"Laura..."

I don't want to talk. I want to fuck. So, I get up from the bed, keeping him from saying anything else with a kiss. His lips easily part for me, and his hands settle on the sides of my ribs, right next to my breasts. He sighs, breaking the kiss.

"We shouldn't - "

"Matthew doesn't treat me like I'm a porcelain doll. I won't break. You know I won't."

"I know. It's just... Having you here with me. I've dreamed about this moment for so long, Laura. Now that it's here, I don't want to ruin it."

"How could you ruin it?"

He cradles my face in his hands, pulling me in for another kiss. He gently sucks on my bottom lip before pulling back again.

"I'm scared," he whispers.

I've seen many emotions from Matthew - love, anger, hurt, pain, hate - but I think I can count on one hand the number of times he's been scared. He was cautious around his mother, but not scared. "Why?"

"Are you sure that this is what you want, Laura? For real."

What kind of question is that? Of course, I want this. Why would I go with him if I - *oh.*

"Because if you don't, tell me now. If you want to leave, I'll respect that. Hell, I deserve it. You don't need me anymore."

Why can't he see that I've always needed him? I always will. "I need you."

Before he can say another word, I press my mouth against his, trying to convey that his fears are unfounded. This time he responds with eagerness, sliding his hands around my head and threading his fingers through my hair. His tongue on mine is like a completely new sensation, sending jolts of fire through every nerve in my body. Before, there's always been a subdued worry in the back of my head, afraid of someone walking in and not letting me enjoy his touch to the fullest. Now, we can take our time.

Stepping closer to him I let my hands roam all over his back, sliding them over his shoulders and exploring his chest and taut abdominals. He takes my hand in his, effectively stopping my movements, and breaks the kiss. His eyes bore into mine, full of love and desire. For a moment I think he'll stop where this is going, but when he opens the button on the shirt I'm wearing and gently nudges me back, I know we're on the same page.

When the back of my legs hit the foot of the bed I sit

down, my hands skating down his sides and settling on his hips. My fingers dig into the fabric of his pants, trying to tug them down. But he stops me once again, taking my hands and kissing the knuckles.

"Matthew," I sigh, falling back on the bed.

Before I get a chance to say anything more, he's on top of me, showering my face and neck with open-mouthed kisses. The tip of his tongue connects with my skin in all the right places. When his knee presses in between my thighs I scoot back. I want him to rest more of his weight on me, to crush his body to mine, but he won't until I've healed properly.

When his knee presses against me again all those thoughts go out the fucking window. He's doing everything right, and I wouldn't change a thing even if I could. This little motion of his spurs me into action, pulling his face to mine for a proper kiss and plunging my tongue into his mouth. He rewards me with a groan from the back of his throat and the sound is music to my ears.

Matthew's strong and could resist my every attempt, but instead, he follows my every direction. So, when I gently press my hands against his chest, urging him to the side he complies. Instantly, I climb over him - if he can't press his body against mine, we'll have to do it the other way around. This position allows me to move more freely, and I can adjust so that my wound doesn't hurt without

Matthew having to worry about it. I throw off the shirt, leaving me only in my panties.

His hands find my outer thighs, moving me on top of him. When he does, I cry out in pleasure - and he's still in his pants. Fuck. Me.

At my cry of approval, he sits up, supporting me with his hands on my back. His mouth finds my breast, and if I wasn't already so turned on, the feeling of his tongue swiping across my nipple would certainly do it. Locking my legs around his waist, the heels of my feet dig into his back, urging him closer. He kisses his way to my other breast, and when he envelops it with his mouth my hips roll against his, sending the next wave of pleasure through me.

My hands find their way to his hair, my fingers digging into his scalp as I push my hips against his again.

"Fuck, Laura," he pants when he needs to come up for air.

"I know." Because I *do*. We've both been craving this moment, being together like this. For real. Completely alone. And now that we're here we want to make as much of it as possible, not letting it go to waste.

Without warning he pulls his head back, looking up at me. The look on his face is filled with adoration. Love. Lust. He scoots back, pulling me with him. My hands on both sides of his head support me as I lower myself down to his face, locking our lips together. Purposefully, I roll my hips again, and his fingers dig into my skin, his body responding exactly like I want to. He sucks on my bottom lip, his hands roaming all over my upper body.

When he cups my face, pulling me closer to him, the hunger I feel for him is too much for me to handle, so I climb off him and peel off his pants. Now he's only wearing a pair of boxers, and they do very little to hide his erection. There is little I can do to mask my disappointment when he stops my hands from removing his last piece of clothing.

"Matthew..." I sigh.

"Laura," he murmurs. "We don't have to rush this."

"I know."

"Prove it." He's using his authoritative, stern voice. How can his voice alone turn me into a pathetic pile of mush? "Climb up on top of me."

Oh. He's never done *that* before. He's made me come with his tongue countless times, but never with me practically sitting on his face. I make quick work of my panties, straddle his waist, and slide up his torso using my knees. I lift myself over his shoulders, so my crotch is right in his face. He loops his arms around my thighs, pulling me closer to him, and when his tongue connects with my clit, I automatically grab the headboard, so I don't fall over at the sensation.

But he doesn't continue, and when I look down on him, he only smiles. "Good?"

I would comment on the smug grin on his face, but I want this too much to answer with anything other than the absolute truth. "Yes."

Pulling me closer to him again he continues to work me with his tongue. Every flick leaves me wanting more. More of everything. More of *him.* It doesn't take long before my hips uncontrollably start rocking against his mouth.

"Jesus, fuck!" It feels so good. In this position, I'm so open to him as he sucks and teases my clit. I'm afraid he won't be able to breathe, but his hands and arms hold me firmly, just allowing me to move my hips. When I feel the telltale tingling letting me know that I'm close to cumming, he stops. "No," I pant, but I'm too worked up to form any coherent sentence.

"There's no rush, Laura," he purrs, pleased with himself.

"I know. I just... I want to come." I *need* to come.

"Why didn't you say so?" he smirks and plunges his tongue inside. I love having him inside me, connecting us on a whole new level. I can barely support my weight anymore - Matthew holds me up and I do my best, holding onto the headboard.

There it is again. That sensation. But he doesn't stop. I'm close. So, fucking close. I need to be closer to him. I need. I want. I want more. More. More. I search for something to hold on to. There's nothing. I fumble for something, finding only his legs. When something swipes over my nipple it's the only thing, I need to completely lose myself. Surrender to this intense pleasure. Surrender to him. This feels so good. *He* feels so good. Let me freeze this moment and stay in it forever.

His name falls from my lips as I come down from the most intense high of my life. My muscles give out and I fall back, his torso against my back. "Oh, my fucking god."

He sits up, his hands on my back, pulling me to him. I'm glad he's so strong because I can't trust my muscles for shit right now. His lips find mine, and I taste myself on his tongue as I suck it into my mouth.

"Can we fuck *now*?"

He turns me over so we're in the same position as before, with him above me. "Yes," he says before kissing me thoroughly. I hook my fingers in his underwear's waistband, tugging them down, and he helps me get them completely off.

Naked, he settles his hips between my thighs, his cock pressed against my slit. I'm still a little sensitive, but it feels incredible, to be like this with him again.

"Fuck," he growls in my ear as he rocks his hips against mine. This man. I don't deserve him, but I'm too selfish to do anything about it. Whatever he gives me, I'll gladly take it.

"Did you bring - "

"Yeah," he interrupts, fumbling with his hand in the drawer next to the bed. He works fast, and before I know it, he's got the condom on and is back on top of me. Grabbing himself, he pushes inside.

This feels like the first time all over again. In a way, it kind of is. Not being afraid that someone might come barging in is a feeling I've almost forgotten and am now rediscovering.

He stretches me just the right amount, filling me without hurting me.

"You feel so good," he whispers before taking my lip between his teeth, tugging gently, and pushing into me once more. A moan escapes my lips, and he moves his hips again, this time with more determination. He must be as impatient as I am because it doesn't take long for him to pick up his speed. My legs wrap around his waist, meeting his every thrust and urging him to keep going. There's pain on my side, but I don't fucking care. What Matthew's doing to me right now overshadows everything else.

Locking my arms around his neck, I pull him to me, capturing his lips in a wet, sloppy kiss. The tip of his hair swipes over my forehead back and forth as he drives into me. He keeps our lips connected as he increases his pace, neither of us barely hanging on to control. He knows exactly what I want - how I want it. He hits every spot, exactly right. This is perfect. He's perfect. *We're* perfect.

The familiar feeling rises again, and I let out a moan at the sensation.

"More," is the only word that escapes me.

At this, he stops his movements, pulling me up so we're both sitting up with me straddling his thighs. He swiftly enters me again, and in this position, I get more control of the pace. Instantly, I buck my hips, trying to find release. With every thrust, I get a little closer, but when his tongue lavishes my nipple, it drives me so much closer.

"Don't stop," I pant, trying desperately to keep this pace, my nails digging into his back.

"You're so fucking perfect, Laura. Come for me."

And I do. I come for him so fucking hard. I clench around him, and he lets out a string of expletives I don't catch. I frantically rock my hips against his, trying my best to prolong this indescribable feeling of completeness.

I'd thought that contracting around him would make him come too, but when I come back to my senses, he was still hard inside me, and his eyes are filled with pure hunger.

He puts his hands on my hips, lifting me off him. I know what he wants - he doesn't have to say it. Turning around, I kneel on all four.

He slides his fingers along my slit, checking if I'm ready - as if this fucking session didn't make me dripping wet for him already. Immediately after retracting his hand, he slams into me, filling me up once again. I won't come again like this, but that's irrelevant. This is about Matthew. I'll give him whatever he wants.

But this is still so good. Hearing how much he loves

this. How close he is. I meet his every movement by pushing my ass against him. His hands find my hips again, guiding me and pulling me to him.

"Fuck, Laura. I'm gonna - " And then he comes. With a grunt, he fucks me through his release. With every thrust of his, I meet with a groan because I can't hold it back. Why should I? He pulses inside me as he fills the condom. We stay like this for a couple of seconds, catching our breaths, before he pulls out.

He quickly comes back, and I snuggle against his chest. "That was unbelievable." It's an understatement, but it's the only word I can think of in this post-fuck haze.

"Yeah." I draw patterns on his upper body as we fall into a comfortable silence. When he turns around to his side, resting his head on the back of his hand, he turns somber. "Listen. I didn't mean to doubt you. It's just... If you'd used me to get out of there, I wouldn't blame you."

I don't know how to respond to that, so I kiss him, hoping that'll convince him that I want to be here - with him - and that *this* was my goal, *not* getting out of prison. When we break apart and he opens his eyes I know that he believes me.

The bedroom has two closets - one of them contains our clothes, and in the other are items I'd never in my life thought I'd need. Wigs, glasses, guns, pharmaceuticals, passports, and money. *A lot* of money.

"Matthew, where the fuck did you get all of these things?"

"Collected a few favors," he shrugs.

"What kind of favors?"

"Laura..."

"I'm not judging you." I don't. I'm smart enough to know when I'm standing in the proverbial glass house. "I just want to know. Why do they owe you?"

"For looking the other way, mostly."

He comes up to me, close enough for me to feel the coffee on his breath, and I notice he hasn't shaved in at least a day. His hands slide up my sides, lingering on the Band-Aid.

"How does it feel?" He's not asking because he feels like he has to - he asks because he's genuinely concerned.

That's why I can't blow off his constant worrying. "Good. I think the sex helped."

The grin on his face reminds me of when we were younger before any of this ever happened. Innocent. At least more innocent than we're now. "Let me know when I can be of service."

"You're my go-to guy."

"I better be." He gives me a brief smile before pulling out the map. "I don't think they've found the other car yet.

They haven't alluded to anything like that on the news anyway."

We don't have TV or internet out here, but the radio in the car works. The news reported the breakout and two deaths, but they haven't released details about them. Our names are repeated frequently, and I can only assume that our faces are all over the news. They don't seem to have found the connection between us yet, or they're consciously not disclosing that information.

To be honest, I don't care if they find out about our past. It doesn't matter anymore now that we're out. If anything, it would be sticking it to the system for missing it and letting Matthew work at the prison where I was serving time.

Since we're all people seem to talk about - the talk show hosts keep discussing theories on what happened and why - both Matthew and I are hesitant to return to the city. But we can't stay out here forever. Eventually, they will find us - we haven't even left the state - and we still have work to do.

"Are you ready?"

I press my lips against his again. We're ready for anything. "Always."

Chapter Ten

Matthew's marked all the places of interest on the map. We'll have to be careful with it, though, because a paper map is hard to come by these days, and we don't want to make more trips to town than necessary.

I'm sitting on one of the chairs and he's leaning over the table, his arms stretching the fabric of his shirt perfectly. After that wonderful round of sex last night, I want him again. And again. And again.

He points to the prison that served as my home for eight years and follows the marked path to the outskirts of town. "He lives here. There's a supermarket a mile in this direction where he makes almost daily trips."

I give Matthew a look. *He goes grocery shopping every day?*

"See here?" He moves his finger to a spot not far from

the supermarket. "The hob. The worst-kept secret in town."

"Hookers?"

"Yeah. And drugs. Whatever you want, you can find it there."

"Why am I not surprised?" *And why does Matthew know so much about this?* Was he a visitor there? No, he told me that he'd never done anything like that, and I believe him.

"He's a piece of shit. Did you think he'd stop once he's outside the prison walls?"

"Guess not."

"I pulled his schedule from the database, but that might've changed now after..." He drifts off. "Anyway, he alternates between the day and night shift. It's the day shift this week, so he's usually home by six."

Matthew points to another marked route on the map. "Every other day he takes a detour here. Except for weeks, he works night."

"What's there?"

He hesitates. "You know I'll support you no matter what you decide, right?"

"Matthew." I put my hand over his. He's scaring me. "What is it?"

He looks down, refusing to meet my eyes. "A daycare. He has a son."

I stare at Matthew. I did not see this coming. He's the

last person I expected to have kids. He shouldn't even be allowed to.

Does it make a difference? *Should* it? No. He made this life for himself - now he'll pay the price.

"The mother?"

"They're not together. She seems decent - works at the DMV, goes to yoga on Tuesdays and Saturdays, and does laundry on every other Sunday. No criminal record."

I bet this kid is in better hands with her than he'll ever be with Brad.

"You grew up without a father," Matthew says. "Do you want the same for this kid?"

"Matthew. The worst thing about not having a father was how my mother shut me out. We'll be doing this kid a favor, ridding the world of his father. And if he's lucky, his mother is better than mine. Maybe he doesn't see it now, maybe he never will, but Brad deserves to die for everything that he's done."

"Okay. Like I said, I'm with you one hundred percent if this is what you want to do."

"It's not like people haven't grown up without a parent before! Look at you. Your mom beat you half to death and your dad didn't care. And you turned out fine."

"I don't think everyone agrees with you on that one."

"Does it matter, Matthew? To me, you're perfect. Don't sell yourself short. Anyone else would have crept into a shell, not caring about anyone but themselves. But you didn't. You made something of yourself and that's the biggest 'fuck you' to you mother if I ever saw one."

Tipping my chin up with his fingers, he captures my lips in a kiss. "I love you."

"I love you, too."

"If he decided to put a kid on this earth, maybe it's our job to keep him from tainting it."

"You're right."

Through the scope of the rifle, we get a good view of his apartment. He's sitting on his couch, seemingly enjoying a TV show. He got home about an hour ago, and after warming something up in the microwave he's been parked on the sofa. We must wait until dusk - we can't risk getting recognized.

Matthew's lying next to me, his arm brushing mine. The warmth he radiates calms me, anchoring me in the belief that we're doing the right thing. "You sure you don't want to just do it now?" he asks from the left of me. "It would be an easy kill."

"That would be a clean, humane death. He wouldn't know what hit him. What good would that do?"

He doesn't answer.

"Matthew? You're with me on this, right?"

"Of course, I'm with you. Say the word, and I'll strangle him myself for what he did to you."

"I want him to know why he's dying. Otherwise, it's pointless."

"Okay."

He's quick to open the door when we finally knock. He's wearing a T-shirt that says, *Correctional officer. Because badass isn't a job title.*

Please.

He looks at both of us in confusion before he recognizes us. There's a moment of silence before he speaks.

"You - "

Matthew punches him in the mouth before his next word. "You fucking piece of shit."

Brad stumbles back, almost tumbling over, and covers his blood-soaked mouth and nose. One of his hands goes to his pocket, but I put my gun in his direction. "I wouldn't do that if I were you. I'll blow your fucking head off before you get your hands on that cell."

He holds up his hands in surrender. "All right, I won't." His voice is weak, insecure, a complete one-eighty from when he used to rape me.

"Brad, Brad, Brad," I taunt him because it's my turn. "You're a much bigger pussy than I gave you credit for. A gun to your face, and you're the biggest fucking pussy I ever saw."

"Two."

"What?"

"There are *two* guns pointed at my face."

"Well, you've got a lot of fucking nerve. Back up," I say, pointing my gun to his groin to make a point. The thought of getting his dick blown off must terrify him because he staggers back. He thinks he's getting out of this alive. He's scared shitless, and I enjoy every second of his misery.

Matthew walks ahead of us, pulling a chair from the kitchen.

"Sit," he commands, but Brad seems unsure. "Sit the fuck down, or I'll cut your fucking balls off." The way he says it, without hesitation, lets Brad know he's telling the truth. He *will* follow through, and Brad understands it, sitting down on the chair. Instead of saying anything, Matthew straps Brad down, his legs and arms taped to the chair just like Thorn was.

"You're a fucking - "

He doesn't get to finish his sentence before Matthew punches him in the face again.

"Watch your mouth, or I swear to everything holy, I'll shoot you right now."

He seems to get the picture. At least, he stops talking back.

"Okay." Blood runs from his mouth and nose, landing on his sweater and forming a pattern that almost looks like a roadmap.

I stand in front of him. "You're a rapist, a predator, and a slimy little shit. You don't deserve to live."

He's not threatened by me. He thinks I'm weak, a nobody. When I talk to him his facial expression turns smug. Like 'okay, I'll humor you, babe.'

"You won't kill me." His words only confirm my suspicion.

"Okay, tell me. Why won't I kill you?"

"You don't have the guts. You're a pussy." He sounds just like Matthew's mother.

"Do you even know why she was in prison, Brad?" Matthew says immediately.

"Why the fuck would I care?" he says, spitting blood on the floor.

Matthew hits him again. On the nose. It must hurt like a motherfucker. "Because if you knew you wouldn't be so cocky right now. You fucked with the wrong person."

"I made a mistake with Thorn," I tell him. "I don't think he understood why he had to die. But you, you will know exactly why I kill you."

"You? You killed Thorn?" His voice shakes. *Finally,* he seems to realize what a dire situation he's put himself in.

I take out the scalpel from my pocket, slowly dragging the back of it along Brad's throat. "He was in the same position as you are now, unable to move and shivering like the little pussy he is." I pause. "*Was.* " I fix my eyes on his - the shade is almost identical to Matthew's, but whereas he is stronger, more determined, and sexier, Brad's are plain scary.

Suddenly, he starts shaking as if he thinks the tape will break. And what would he do if it did? Panic fills his features before Matthew points his gun at him. "Stay still, or this will be a lot messier than it has to be."

"What difference does it make if you're gonna kill me anyway?"

"True. But you decide if it'll go fast or slow. I can be very thorough when I break every fucking bone in your body." Matthew gets in his face. "And I'll enjoy every second of it," he adds slowly before pulling away.

"P-Please. I have a son."

This time it's *me* who punches him. Man, his face is messed up. Blood running from his nose - it's probably broken by now. Is one of his front teeth loose? Probably. "Don't you dare play that card. If you decided to procreate that's your fucking problem. Not mine."

I've never understood the long monologues in movies right before the villain tries to kill the hero. It only serves as a way for the hero or their companions to escape. Now, I can understand that need. The need to tell Brad *exactly* why he's dying. Otherwise, what's the point?

I'm not gonna drag this out, but he *will* know why he dies.

"You have no one to blame but yourself. *You* made me like this." That's not the entire truth - he's not the only one who'll get a visit from us, but it's better if he only blames himself. "You tried to tear me down. Beat me. Fuck me. It didn't work, and now you'll pay for it."

Realization and fear flicker in his eyes when I aim the gun at his forehead. There's a silencer attached to it, so it won't make too much noise. It won't be completely silent, but close enough.

"This won't change anything. You think you can change the system. You won't."

He's right - it won't. But that's not why I'm here. This is not a fucking revolution. This is war. I have nothing more to say to this fucker.

I expected to hesitate in this moment. I've killed before, but this is different. My hand on the gun doesn't shake, and the fear written all over Brad's face does nothing to deter me from this decision. It's the photograph behind him that does.

It must be his son. He's got the same hair color. *Like Matthew's.* I've never wanted to be a mother - why would I? Neither mine nor Matthew's made me want to seek that life. But if Matthew wanted it, I would have gladly given it to him.

But I can't.

And it's assholes like Brad's fault.

So, I pull the trigger.

* * *

I don't remember Matthew pulling me out of the house and into the car. I don't remember the drive back to the cabin. I don't remember him wiping my face.

The only thing I *want* to remember is his warm embrace as we lie on the bed. His fingers run up and down my spine, and I love every second of it. After getting rid of Brad all I want to feel is Matthew's closeness. Letting me know that there's is something good in my world and not only darkness. That's it. That is all I crave.

I press my lips against his neck, feeling his pulse as I trail a path of kisses down his shoulder and arm.

"Thank you," I whisper against his skin. When I reach his wrist, he grabs my chin, pulling me up to his mouth. He pushes his tongue into my mouth, and I open for him. The warmth of his lips catches me by surprise, and I groan into his mouth as we kiss.

I slide my body over his and frame his face with my hands. He's clean-shaven, so my palms graze soft skin as I deepen the kiss. I love him. I love him so fucking much. I want to surrender to this man. Completely.

I don't break the kiss as he slides inside me. This is good. Everything feels so good. That's why I need to make sure.

"You don't hate me?"

"Why would I?" he pants in my ear. In that question, he says everything I need to know. We're the same. I don't know what we are, but that's okay. We might be monsters, but why does that have to be a bad thing?

Instead of answering, I thrust my hips against his. It's incredible. To be able to feel him. For real. I let him take control. Take control over me despite the fact I'm the one on top of him. He owns me. Whatever he wants to do to me, I'd let him.

Using his hands on my hips, he turns us both over so that his weight pushes me into the mattress. He doesn't rest his entire body on me, his chest grazing my nipples as he drives into me. It doesn't take long before we're both panting in a pool of lifeless limbs. This is where I always want to be.

We stay at the cabin for a couple more days, letting the worst of Brad's death cool down. It's difficult to know if the police have connected the dots about me and Matthew, and if so, if they're suspecting us of the murder.

Matthew's listening to the radio in the car, and when he comes back, he's furious. His neck is red, and his eyes convey pure rage.

"What's the matter?"

"They're making him out to be a fucking saint! Like he's a martyr, dying for what he believes in," he spits.

"It doesn't matter."

"Of course, it fucking matters! He should be slaughtered by the media for the raping fuck he was."

"He's dead, Matthew. That's all that matters. That's what we wanted."

I get up from the bed to stroke his cheek. It takes a couple of seconds before he turns his head to me, and then a couple more before his face softens. He leans into my touch. "You're right. I'm sorry."

"Don't apologize."

He doesn't judge me for what I did to Brad - I know he supports me in everything. He's proven that time after time again. It's something else. "Why don't you tell me what's really bothering you?"

He exhales. "I support you in this, Laura. I really do. I won't rest until every one of those guards is dead, or whatever you want to do to them."

"But?"

"It's... I need to know."

"What?"

"Why ah... I need to know why she..." he drifts off.

He needs to know why she hated him so much. He looks broken. Like it's a weakness to want to know why his mother beat him up regularly.

And we both know that there's only one person who might be able to answer that.

"Matthew. Why didn't you tell me sooner?"

"I don't know. I... I haven't... I didn't want to make this about me."

Why can't he see? Why can't he see that this is pointless without him? I wouldn't even be doing this if it weren't for him. If he wants a resolution, I'll give him everything I can to help him. And I don't know what to say to make him understand it.

So, I kiss him. I can't form into words how much I want him to get some form of closure, but I'll do everything in my power to make him get it. It's Matthew I live for. That's all that matters. *He's* all that matters.

The kiss is slow. Our tongues carefully seek each other out, and I press my hands to his cheeks, bringing him closer to me. I hope he'll understand what I'm trying to tell him. *I love you. I'll always be here for you. Whatever you need.*

When we break apart, he presses his forehead against mine. "Thank you."

I don't know why he feels the need to thank me, but I don't fight him on it. Instead, I lock my arms around his neck, bringing him close to me.

He kisses the side of my neck. "Are you ready to go?"

"Yes."

The hob is nowhere near how I imagined it. I'd have thought half-naked women would throw themselves at us, but instead, most people keep to themselves.

Only one person, a woman with a ragged leopard suit and a bad dye job, approaches us. She's not sober, but I can't make out what she's been taking.

"Dear!" she pipes up when she recognizes Matthew. "Where have you been?"

"Had business to attend to," he simply states.

"Can I offer you anything? I know you've never been one for company, but my girls are always a treat." I doubt she even believes that herself. Judging by the looks of this place, most of *her girls* are junkies, hoping to earn a few bucks to score another fix.

"Actually, I'm thinking of that one." Matthew points to a blonde with her head between her legs - she looks like she's recovering from a hangover, but alcohol didn't make her this way.

"That one? You can have her for free. When she's not 'under the influence,'" she whispers the last part, "she's a nervous wreck. You're lucky if she can manage a decent blowjob." She turns her head to me, then back at Matthew. "If you want a threesome, I'd recommend another one."

"Thank you, but I want that one," Matthew says, ignoring the woman's advice.

"Are you sure I can't tempt you with these, sweet buns?" she asks, opening the front of her shirt and revealing a pair of saggy boobs. I think she used to be pretty, but drugs and alcohol must have worn her down, and she seems to be completely unaware of it. It's tragic, really.

"As tempting as that looks, I have plans for the blonde." Matthew smiles at her. It's fake, but whatever she's been taking seems to cloud her judgment.

"She's all yours."

We approach the hungover blonde sitting by one of the dumpsters. I kick her foot, getting her attention.

Her eyes are bloodshot, and her skin looks even grayer than it did in prison. Her cheekbones are more prominent, and I wonder how she's managed to stay on the heroin. I can't see how she'd finance it, because she can't be getting many customers. It doesn't look like she recognizes us, because if she did, she wouldn't look annoyed - she'd be scared fucking shitless.

Instead of saying anything, Matthew unceremoniously grabs her arm and drags her away from anyone's sight. Not that they would care what happens, but you can never be too careful. After we've turned into an alley Matthew shoves her into the brick wall. *Now,* she recognizes us.

"You thought you could get away with it? I fucking helped you. You were *nothing* before me."

Tanisha doesn't seem to know what to say. Good. There is nothing she *can* say.

But an uneven clicking sound approaches from the

street. "Yoo-hoo!" It's the older woman from before, and her face drops when she sees the gun in my hand. She's close enough to see it but too far away for us to stop her from screaming and giving us away.

"Fuck," Matthew exclaims. Before I know it, he takes the gun from my hand.

Three muffled shots. Three growing red stains on the leopard suit. She's dead before she even hits the ground.

Shoving the gun back into my hands Matthew says close to my ear, "We must go. Do it now."

This time I don't hesitate.

I shoot Tanisha point-blank between the eyes.

There's no time to contemplate what we did. We need to get out of here before someone sees us and calls the cops. From what I'd gathered from Matthew, the death rate in this neighborhood is high, and the police usually don't investigate as deep as they should. That's good news for us, but we still need to get the fuck out of here.

The car is parked not far from here, and we dive into it, me in the driver's seat and Matthew behind me. I turn the ignition and pull out from the alley. I can't get out of here fast enough, wanting to put as much distance between us and those bodies as possible.

"Laura, slow down. We don't need any attention right now."

I don't understand how he can be so calm after what

just happened, but I automatically release the pressure on the gas pedal.

"Sorry."

"It's all right. Turn right here," he instructs.

Nothing seems out of the ordinary, so I guess no one has found the dead bodies yet. But that's just a matter of time. If that older lady was some sort of manager, her absence will surely be noticed quickly.

Pulling onto the interstate, I finally let myself relax, but my chest tightens when I look in the rearview mirror. His eyes are cold, focused, and fixated straight ahead. "You had no choice, Matthew. We didn't know what she might have done. Screamed or - "

"I know." His voice is low. Hollow. "She should have left us alone."

I've seen that look before, but not on him. Icy blue eyes, filled with something I can't describe. Then I see it. He did what he had to do, and he doesn't regret it. He knows he's not to blame.

"Right."

We spend the rest of the ride in silence.

By now, there's only one left, and he's not getting off the hook as easily as some of the others. He won't get a clean and easy death.

The surveillance on him is low - we mapped it out days ago. They stay with him to and from work, but other than that he's fair game. It's astonishing really, either how small their resources are or how little they care about the men and women who guard the inmates.

As soon as the familiar car drives away we move to the entrance of his house, and as soon as he opens the door, I punch him right on the nose.

It doesn't hurt the way it used to. I guess it takes some practice before your knuckles grow accustomed to being pressed into other people's faces. Matthew's not long after, giving him another hit in his face that seems to knock him out.

"Good," I say. "Not so much complaining."

With Brad, he needed to know why I killed him. With Bailey, I don't have to tell him. He knows. That's why he's been protected by the cops. If the shithead guards had had the guts to confess what they've been doing, the police might have prioritized their resources where they were needed, but I'm not surprised they didn't. Piece of shit cowards as they are. And now they're paying the price.

Bailey finds himself tied up like Brad and Thorn were. Matthew helped me pull him up to a chair and tie him up, but he's letting me do everything else.

"How much longer?" It's stressful, only waiting for him to wake up. Every minute is precious, especially since we can't be completely sure when his surveillance will be back. We've been tracking them for a while, but you never know when they change their routines.

"Don't know. Should be any minute now." Matthew scratches his nose with the back of his hand, the one carrying his gun. I want to tell him how much I love him for doing this for me, how much I love seeing him like this. This side of him, showing no mercy to my - our - enemies. Unyielding. Unrelenting. Strong. Devoted.

I don't know what to say exactly, but a groan from the chair interrupts me, whatever I was going to say.

"Good, you're awake," Matthew says coolly. "We've been waiting for you."

It takes a couple of seconds before Bailey gains his bearing, realizing what a predicament he's in. His arms flinch as if testing the restraints of the duct tape that binds his wrists, ankles, and abdomen. It doesn't budge.

We've left his mouth free. For now.

Matthew's fists clench at his sides, his breath ragged - it's obvious how much he wants to hit the living daylights out of Bailey.

I make a mental note to let him have his way with this one before we leave.

I put my newly sharpened knife to his throat. "You won't be a nuisance, will you?"

Realization hits when he recognizes us. He knows what's happened to the other guards. Knows that they've paid with their lives, and he's desperate to make sure he won't end up our tenth victim. Or is it the eleventh? Whatever.

Without a word, he only shakes his head slowly.

"Good boy," I say, patting his head for effect.

"Why?" is all he whispers.

" *Why?* " I repeat. "Why are you such a fucking coward? Why are you such a fucking piece of shit?" I scream in his face. "*You* tell me! You tell *me* why!"

I didn't expect to get so riled up about this, but a warm hand - Matthew's - soothes me as I calm down from the rant, I just threw Bailey. His calm spread through me as I try to focus on the task at hand. We can't stay here forever, so we need to make the most of it.

"He can't help himself," Matthew says in my ear, loud enough for Bailey to hear it too. "Whatever whore pushed him out her cunt must have hated him enough not to care what kind of man he became."

This gets Bailey moving, and his arms frantically start shaking, as if the tape is going to break.

Matthew chose his words carefully. Of course, we know that he loves his mother more than anything. She's in the hospital. Lung cancer. Bailey sends all of his extra money to her, so his love for her is his weakness.

"I'm not afraid of dying." A pathetic claim. As if that will take away our power over him. Of course, he's afraid of dying. In the end, everyone is. I've seen it enough times. Matthew's mom. Thorn, Brad, Tanisha...

"Keep telling yourself that."

"What do you want? If you wanted me dead, you'd have done it by now." He's not a total imbecile, I'll give him that. "I'm not stupid. I know what happened to the others."

"Do you?" Matthew asks without a care in the world.

"They're dead. You killed them. Without giving them a chance to fight."

He's got some fucking nerve.

"Not all of them. Did you see the burn marks on Marvel's leg? Did you see the cuts between Brutus's fingers?" Bailey looks at Matthew in disbelief. "No, you didn't, and I doubt they'll be telling you about it if they value their own and their families' lives." Matthew's not lying. We didn't kill all of them.

"The cops will be here any minute."

"No, they won't. We used your tactic." We're not bluffing. It was so easy to pay someone off to set off an alarm in a fancy villa not very far from here, and the cops will be all over that. Rich white people are always prioritized, and we take advantage. Like he used Tanisha to distract me. "She's dead by the way," I continue.

His eyes widen when he realizes that no one is coming to his aid. He's all alone. He's sweating now, small pearls of perspiration covering his forehead. If it's from fear or exhaustion, I can't tell.

Leaning forward, I swipe some of it off. "Are you scared?" I mock.

He doesn't answer. Instead, the fucker spits in my face.

I barely have time to react before Matthew pushes the chair, tipping it backward, and Bailey follows with it. There's a cry of pain when the back of the chair hits the floor, and Matthew's all over him, the gun pressed underneath his chin.

"Do you have a death wish, motherfucker? Do that again and I'll fucking kill you. And it won't be fast."

I quickly dry off my face with the sleeve of my shirt. Putting my hands on Matthew's shoulder, I try to calm him down. I'm pissed too, but we can't lose our temper. Not now. Not when we're so close.

"Matthew. He gets the picture."

He turns his head, looking at me. His breathing is hard, cheeks flushed, and jaw clenched. We stand like that for a couple of seconds before Matthew releases Bailey. But before he lets go, he spits in his face. Without saying a word, he leaves the room.

What the fuck just happened? I've seen him angry before, but it's always been controlled. He's never lost his temper like that. I leave Bailey on the floor and follow Matthew into the other room. He's sitting down, his elbows on his knees and his head hanging.

"He's just trying to get a rise out of us," I tell him, sitting down next to him.

"Well, it's working," Matthew grits out.

"We're almost done. Let's finish this, and then we'll leave."

He exhales. "You're right." He takes my hand and kisses my knuckles.

Bailey is still on the floor, taped to the chair as we come back to the kitchen, and Matthew quickly pulls him up before taping his mouth too. Taking another chair and straddling it, he stares into Bailey's eyes. "Hannah. Frankie. Taylor. Iris. What do all those names mean?" he says calmly.

Bailey snaps his head to Matthew, the names getting his attention.

"It means that their lives belong to us, and their deaths do too."

That's all we need to tell him. Their names. He already knows we have no qualms about killing, and knowing his family members' names is all we need to convince him that we'll be watching him, and that's the best torture in the world. He knows how easily we can get to people. We broke out of prison and killed several COs without getting caught. His family is an easy target. When his mother finally dies from her illness he's going to wonder if we had any part in it, and that's the sweetest revenge.

"Goodbye," I say before we're out of his apartment.

I don't care if he ever gets loose from the restraints. He won't be a problem to us either way. He loves his mother and siblings too much to risk it. Pathetic.

We've already loaded the car, so when we leave Bailey's apartment we're out of this fucking town.

Even if the cops show up at Bailey's apartment, he won't say shit. He'll be scared for the rest of his life, and I can't think of a better retaliation.

Matthew takes my hand in his, squeezing it.

We're almost there.

Chapter Eleven

It's been almost a decade, but this place still looks the same. The house doesn't stand out from the rest, and a bypasser wouldn't have any clue about what atrocities went down in there. The 'a' and 'r' on the mailbox have started to fade, but other than that it's like time stood still.

When we walk up the stairs to the porch, I remember the day that changed me completely. Matthew's birthday. I'd never hated anyone before that. But looking through that window something changed. I didn't understand it at the time, but after that nothing has ever been the same.

I look up at Matthew standing next to me, and I grab his hand for support. Being here is difficult for me, and I can't even imagine what it's like for him. His eyes are hard - unforgiving. Without hesitation, he knocks on the door -

three hard, decisive knocks. If he's feeling insecure, he sure as hell isn't showing it.

It takes a while, and I start to think there's no one home when there's rustling behind the door. It opens, revealing a man in his fifties. Arian's hair is gray around his temples, and the wrinkles around his eyes reveal a hard life. I don't fucking care.

His eyes go to me first, and I'm struck by the intensity of his stare. He doesn't seem to recognize me, and confusion is written all over his face. But when he looks at Matthew his expression softens. It's shock at first and then disbelief.

I look up at Matthew again, but his glare is just as hard as it was before.

"Hello, Dad."

"Matthew." He raises his hand, probably wanting to touch his son, but Matthew rapidly backs away.

"Don't fucking touch me."

He immediately retracts his hand. "Alright, I won't," he says weakly. He looks Matthew in the eye for a couple of seconds but doesn't seem to be able to hold his gaze. Shifting his attention to me, he finally recognizes my face. "Laura? Are you...? I thought - "

Matthew slams his hand against the doorframe in front of his father's face, effectively blocking me from his field of vision. "She's none of your fucking concern."

"Matthew, what - "

"Aren't you going to invite us in?" Matthew interrupts. It's not a question.

He hesitates. I can understand his reaction to me, but denying his son anything at this point is just provoking. He should be on his knees, begging him for forgiveness. For every time he chose to turn a blind eye when Matthew was being physically and mentally harassed. *Especially* the last time. He's pressing all my buttons.

"Ma - " I can't handle him standing there, making himself out to be some sort of victim. Before he has the chance to finish, I take out my gun, pointing at him right between the eyes.

"Cut the bullshit." His eyes flit to Matthew, but he gets no sympathy there either.

"We're going to have a little chat," Matthew says before pushing himself past his father. I lower my gun and follow him. The inside of this house has completely changed-a stark contrast from the exterior. All the furniture has been replaced - the only thing I recognize is the fireplace.

Matthew's dad closes the door and trails after Matthew as he enters the kitchen.

"Sit." He looks at Matthew warily, as if to check that it's him. This ticks Matthew off, and he exhales loudly, getting in his father's face. "Sit the fuck down." Matthew's got a couple of inches on him, and with his physique, he could easily take him down. But the tone of his voice and unforgiving stare are enough.

Arian sits down by the short end of the table, and Matthew and I sit on opposite sides, flanking him.

"I'm going, to be honest with you," Matthew says, putting his gun on the table. His dad looks at it carefully, then back to Matthew. He's afraid of saying something to piss him off. Good. "I've never understood the whole thing about blood being thicker than water." He takes up the gun, examining it as if making sure the safety is on. Of course, it is. "I don't even like you."

He hits just right, and the hurt in his dad's eyes is obvious, but Matthew doesn't flinch.

"So why are you here, then?" Arian asks carefully.

"You know. Hate I can understand," Matthew says, still examining the gun. "She hated me - I can live with that. I hated her too. But do you know what I find worse than hate?" He pauses before continuing. Putting the weapon on the table he finally gives his father the attention he's been craving since we came here. "Indifference."

Arian looks unsure, uncertain of where Matthew's going with this. He should have known the moment he laid his eyes on him.

"You didn't hate me - you just didn't care."

"What do you want, Matthew?" Arian looks down at

his lap, seemingly unable to look his son in the eyes. Is he ashamed? I fucking hope so.

"It's a simple question. Why? That's all it comes down to. Why, Dad?" Matthew's eyes are glistening from unshed tears, but he blinks them away before they spill over. "I spent all my life trying to please you. Nothing was ever good enough for her, and you didn't even care that I tried." He stands up and leans over his father's face, forcing him to look at him. "Tell me what the fuck I did to make my mother hate me and for my father to let her."

"You don't under - "

Matthew slams his fist on the table, silencing his father. "No, I don't. But you're going to explain it to me."

His eyes flit to mine as if hoping to get some understanding from me. He doesn't. Whatever Matthew decides to do, I will support him.

"Why is she here? She killed your - "

"I'm here because I was the only one who cared about your son."

"What's it gonna be? I've got a lot of bullets, but I think I'll only need one. What do you think?" Matthew taunts.

"Probably," he whispers, fear seeping from his voice. He's realizing what kind of man Matthew's become, and it terrifies him. "It's complicated."

It's complicated. You don't understand. He's stalling, and Matthew sees right through it. He takes the gun in his hand, looking his father in the eyes as he cocks it and aims it at him. Slowly. He doesn't waver one bit. "What did I do to deserve it?"

Arian mumbles something barely audible. A cold wave rushes through me because I heard, but Matthew didn't.

"What?"

Arian's eyes no longer show fear. It's determination. Or anger?

"You were born!" he erupts. "You ruined everything. Go ahead. Shoot your father. Prove me right. Prove to me that you destroy everything you touch, including your mother."

Matthew puts the safety back on the gun before hitting his father in the face with it. There's a streak of blood on his cheek from where the gun hit. Matthew is about to take another swing, but I put my hand on his arm. "Matthew. Hear him out first." I have no concern about his father's well-being. I just want to get what we came for.

He takes a breath to calm himself before addressing his father again. "You've got a lot of fucking nerve. Now, my anatomy might be a little rusty, but last time I checked, for a child to be born two people need to fuck."

"You never wondered why you never had any siblings?"

"Guess I was too busy getting my ass kicked by my mother to give it any thought."

"When you came out you made damned sure she could never have children again."

"That's the lamest fucking excuse I've ever heard. She blamed Matthew for not being able to have more than one child. She should've cherished him, knowing he'd be the only one."

"She did."

Matthew snorts. "No, she didn't."

"You're too young to remember. But the knowledge of not being able to have more children put a strain on our marriage."

"Save me the sob story."

"You wanted the truth. I wanted to split up, but she didn't. She threatened to sue me for assault if I filed for divorce. Once, she hit you to show me how determined she was. Said that she'd use it in court as proof of my violent tendencies. I guess she took a liking to it."

Did she take a liking to beating her only child? And he sits there, talking about it like it's the fucking weather. If it were up to me, I'd kill him on the spot. "And you? Where the fuck were you?"

"I tried to build myself a normal life, but it's difficult with a crazy wife, and the cause of it living right under your nose."

"Well, I hope you managed to find a new life for yourself while your son was fighting for *his*," Matthew says dryly.

Silence.

"You're going to kill me now? Now that you got what you came for?"

"We're not done."

"I told you everything. What else do you want?"

"There's this thing that's been bugging me for a while," Matthew says, scratching his temple with the barrel of the gun. "The day I was committed to the hospital someone called 911. I'm pretty sure it wasn't Mom, and it sure as hell wasn't me. That leaves you."

He nods in my direction. "How do you know it wasn't her?"

"Already asked."

"And you believe her?"

"Yes," he answers without hesitation. "Now. You were here. Tell me what happened."

"I don't know what happened. I got here, and she was freaking out. She begged me not to call the police. I called for an ambulance and told her I wouldn't call the cops if she left town. For good."

"You had a golden opportunity to make a change. Get revenge for everything she put Matthew through. And you chose not to. You're a piece of shit."

"And you have the moral high ground here?"

I don't have time to respond before the front door opens. Neither of us has time to react before a blonde woman appears.

"Oh, I didn't know you had - " She stops herself when she sees the guns on the table. She's trying to make sense of what's happening, but I'm out of my chair before she can think. My hand over her mouth prevents her from screaming.

"Sit down, and don't say a word." I take her purse, looking for an ID. Her driver's license says that she's about a year younger than Matthew and me, but it's her name that catches my attention. "Matthew?"

I hand him the ID, and his eyes go wide in realization. The woman sits down in the chair I'd been sitting in, so I take the seat next to her. Matthew puts the card on the table before speaking. "Tell me, Milly *Wright*," he emphasizes her last name. "Why are you sharing a last name with this man over here?"

"He's... He's my father," she stutters, confused.

It didn't take long after Matthew was born that he found another woman to fuck and impregnate. Milly looks frightened, having no idea what's going on.

"Do you have any siblings, Milly?"

"Matthew - "

"Shut the fuck up. You've done enough talking. Let the lady speak."

"N... No, I don't. Why? What does it have to do with anything?"

Matthew shoots his father a look. At least he has the decency to look ashamed. Whether it has to do with Matthew or Milly is impossible to tell.

"You sure about that? We have the same eyes, same hair..."

"I don't know you."

"And whose fault is that?" He turns to his father. " *Dad.* " Realization dawns on Milly's face when Matthew's father doesn't argue. "Are you gonna blame this on Mom too? Or are you gonna grow a pair and take some fucking responsibility?"

"I know you," Milly says carefully, her attention on me. "I've seen you on TV. You're the one who..." She doesn't finish the sentence. She looks like she's about to scream when she realizes who we are. I'm about to take out a cloth to gag her, but she's fast and I don't expect it. She manages to get behind me, pressing a small pocketknife to my throat. It's dull, but it can still do a lot of damage.

Matthew immediately points his gun at her, but she uses me as a shield. The knife trembles against my throat, and I don't want to make any sudden moves. I'd never thought she might have any weapons, and now I'm paying the price. I try to catch Matthew's eye, asking for forgiveness, but his gaze is trained on Milly.

"You don't want to test my marksmanship, Milly." He's right - he's an excellent shot, especially close-range. "If you try anything, there will be at least two bodies here, and I won't have any qualms about it."

She's sniveling behind me - she's in way over her head. "Please just leave."

"That's the plan, but you decide whether or not you'll be alive when we do."

"Dad, leave," she cries.

Matthew's nervous - I can see it in his eyes. This situation's gotten way out of hand, but his hands are still steady.

"No, he stays. I don't know you, Milly, so I don't know what you're capable of. So, if I think for one second, you're about to hurt her, I will shoot you on the spot." He never breaks eye contact with her. "Let her go," he says calmly.

The pressure against my throat lessens, and she lowers her hand. As soon as she releases me, I swiftly move away from her, grabbing my gun in the process.

"You've got guts, Milly. In another universe, I think we could have been friends. We're gonna leave now, but neither of you are gonna call the police. I didn't work at three maximum security prisons without making some friends." He looks at Milly. "Whether or not you want to forgive him is your choice. But if I learned anything from this man it's that he's a pretty good liar. It's up to you if choose to believe whatever lies he'll tell you after we've left." He pauses. "But if you want some brotherly advice, I'd put that knife of yours to good use."

With that, Matthew takes my hand, and we walk out of there. Neither Milly nor Matthew's dad will call the police - I saw the fear in both of their eyes.

Getting in the car, I take Matthew's hand over the console, giving it a light squeeze. At that, he looks at me.

He maybe didn't like the answers he got, but he got them nonetheless, and that seems to be good enough for him.

He doesn't smile, but I didn't expect him to. Instead, he looks straight ahead, focusing on the road in front of us.

We're leaving.

Chapter Twelve

The cold air makes my skin break out in goosebumps, so I pull the blanket over my shoulders. It's that time of the year when the nights are just cold enough to need a coat outside. But I like sitting on the porch like this, with almost nothing but the forest to keep me company.

I'm by myself, and while waiting for Matthew to come home I look through his sketchbook. At first, I'd thought it was too personal, but he doesn't mind me looking through his drawings. His mother destroyed all his sketches when she was alive, and he didn't pick up drawing until about a year after we were out of prison. So, all these pictures are no more than a couple of years old. There's the look on Cash's face when she realized she'd been played, the red stains on the leopard suit, and me slitting Thorn's throat.

In some way, he'd manage to make me look beautiful doing it. I wasn't beautiful. I was angry. Hurt. Ruthless. *Free.*

The sound of the car breaks me from my little trip down memory lane. It took me years before the sound of a car didn't completely freak me out, but now I've learned to deal with it, and I know it's Matthew when I see the headlights through the trees. The left one is slightly dimmer than the other.

We've moved so far away that the risk of recognition is slim to none, but we both always wear some sort of disguise when going to a public place. Matthew usually wears a brown wig and glasses. He says he could just dye it, but I prefer his blonde locks. The glasses on the other hand... are hot.

He takes out the bags from the car and walks up to the porch.

"Hey. You need help?"

"Nah, it's fine. Let me just put this in and I'll join you."

"Okay."

He disappears through the door, but it's only seconds before his head pops out. "Don't you ever get tired of looking at those?" he asks, referring to his drawings in my lap.

"Nope," I say with a grin that he mirrors.

A couple of minutes later he comes back out, carrying a bottle of scotch and two glasses. It's the same one his mother preferred. A shrink would probably have a field day with that.

Sitting down, he laces his fingers through mine. With his other hand, he pours the liquor into the glasses and offers one to me. We both take a sip, relishing the burn in silence.

"Oh, I almost forgot," he says abruptly, getting up from the chair. He doesn't offer any explanation as he half-runs to the car and takes out some sort of magazine. "We made the paper."

"Um, what?"

"Look," he says, giving it to me. It's a monthly magazine that specializes in crime and law enforcement. And he's right. There we are - on the cover. It's my mugshot and the photo from his identification card as a CO. The title says *Captivating Romance*.

"Clever."

"I haven't read it yet."

I flip it open and scan through the pages until I find the story.

The anniversary of one of the most spectacular prison breakouts in modern history is coming up. Five years ago, inmate Laura McKenzie and correctional officer Matthew Radford brutally murdered a guard and the warden of Aurum Correctional Facility. McKenzie was serving a sentence for manslaughter and Radford had recently been transferred to the facility.

At first, the crime made no sense, but when it was discovered that Radford had a different last name eight years prior, the pieces of the puzzle started falling into place. The woman McKenzie had shot and killed was, in fact, Radford's mother.

McKenzie and Radford had a romantic relationship in high school, and the murder took place less than a year after their graduation. There were no witnesses, and with McKenzie pleading the fifth, a first-degree murder conviction seemed far-fetched for the prosecution. Instead, a plea bargain for manslaughter was struck. The motive remained a mystery until news articles about Radford's alleged abusive upbringing began to pop up. According to several sources within the school, Radford was physically abused during his childhood and adolescence. Whether this was the reason for McKenzie's sudden act of violence remains unclear, but the police consider it highly plausible.

After the sentencing, Radford stayed out of the public eye, and directly after changing his name, he began his training as a correctional officer. Although there are no records of him contacting McKenzie in prison until he was transferred there, it was only a couple of months before the breakout.

Radford had never shown any violent tendencies, and, apart from the crime for which McKenzie was convicted, neither had she. But it only took weeks outside the prison walls before the couple gave into their true selves.

Guards and staff affiliated with the prison started dropping dead. Executed. Based on the ballistic reports, the guns used were the same ones that were reported missing after the breakout, leaving McKenzie and Radford as the only suspects.

Since the couple seemed to target correctional officers, the police took measures to protect the rest of the prison staff. But due to limited resources, protecting everyone around the clock became an impossibility, and the murderous couple took advantage.

Zach Brad was the first victim outside the prison walls. His now eight-year-old son barely remembers his father, keeping to himself when we spoke to his mother, Brad's former girlfriend who wishes to remain anonymous. They were not together at the time of his murder.

"I just don't understand why. I know Zach was no angel, but he didn't deserve this. He was a responsible father, and now I've been forced to raise our son all alone."

She says she's had a lot of help from friends and parents, but it's not the same as having the father of her child around. "He was trying to change his shifts, so he'd be able to spend more time with us."

The wounds left by Brad's murder continue to haunt the small family, as is visible by how close she is to tears during the entire interview. Her life has been hard in the wake of Brad's untimely death, and every day is still a struggle.

"I just don't know what to tell my son. He's old enough to ask questions about where his dad is. What am I supposed to say? How do I even begin to explain something I don't even understand myself?"

And so, it goes on. More interviews with surviving family and friends of almost every CO who thought they had a right to my body. Every story is supposed to be more heartbreaking than the next. I guess it's meant to evoke some kind of emotion in the reader. It doesn't. Day by day, those guards broke down whatever compassion I could have felt for them. For every rape, every hit, every subtle grab, my potential pity toward them disintegrated into nothing. I feel nothing.

I skip to the last paragraph.

What caused the formerly lovable couple to turn into cold-blooded killers? According to numerous psychologists, it's impossible to tell what motivated McKenzie and Radford. And, as their latest known crime dates back to almost five years ago, the possibility of that happening gets slimmer, their trail getting colder by the day.

It's possible that Radford's abusive childhood could make him more prone to violence. "Feelings like that can simmer for a long time without manifesting until he's triggered."

"What could those triggers be?"

"It could've been his mother's death, finding out that it was his girlfriend who did it. Or something else."

"What about McKenzie? What drove her?"

"I think she was thinking of herself as protecting a loved one. And then being punished for it would make her blame the legal system. Combined with Radford's troubled background they took everything out on the system. And correctional officers became the faces of that system, and that could have been why they were targeted. Putting Radford in the same place as McKenzie was a recipe for disaster."

I hand the magazine over to Matthew to let him read it too. He snorts a couple of times as I continue to skim through his sketchbook.

Flipping through the sheets I notice one that seems out of place. The material of the paper feels different. I pull it out but don't recognize it. It's drawn by Matthew's skillful hand, but this is a piece I haven't seen before. It's of me in profile, lying in the grass and looking up to the sky. But that's not what catches my eye. It's the date at the bottom right corner. He drew this before I got out of prison.

"Hey, I haven't seen this before," I say, handing him the piece of paper.

He inspects the drawing and lets out a breath before handing it back. "Remember when I asked you what you missed the most?"

"Yeah."

"I promised I'd take you to the stars."

And he did.

His love for me is so unreal I sometimes have a hard

time convincing myself that it's true. I don't know how to respond with words.

Instead, I get up from my chair and curl up in his lap. Steady arms surround me and hold me in place, my knees pushed to my chest, my head against his shoulder. Pulling up the blanket, he tucks us both in. He kisses my hair and I trace my fingers along his collarbone, feeling the ridges and small bumps there. Reminders of life when waking up every morning were a disappointment. My scars are not as visible, but he never forgets. He's the only one I've ever been able to trust, and he feels the same way about me. He shows me every day.

Kissing the side of his neck, and his slow pulse beats against my lips. Taking his chin in my hand, I nudge him to look at me. We've been through so much, both together and apart, and neither of us will ever be what we were before.

Gone are the soft features I remember from when we were kids. Gone is the caring and kind ocean-colored look in his eyes.

They're not warm anymore.

They're icy blue.

Jennifer

Chapter One

Red-soled heels clicked across the barren linoleum hall floor of Corrections. Hips swayed in the expensive skirt suit with the center back slit at the bottom hemline. Hair tucked up in a sophisticated bun as defense attorney, Jennifer Stannis Hannigan was escorted by Private Royce and Lieutenant Mack of the State Police to a room at the end of a long hallway.

The news had covered the case of Dillan Baldwin's death for the past couple of weeks now, Jennifer following every report and printed word closely. She had to, for the man now at the center of it all was a... well, either party involved did not clearly label it.

A brief and exciting encounter that turned into something long-standing and beneficial but never official, a win-win situation for them both. Impromptu meet ups for a release they seemed incapable of finding with anyone else, decompressing after stressful days on the job for her or, in his case to release the pent up energy he quelled when with his rotten family, or simply in want, to fulfill each other's needs. It had lasted like that for a while until she'd met her fiancé. Then it ended and a tango of wicked games and mind-fucking bullshit ensued.

Until *she* needed *him* and everything changed.

However, in the circumstance, Michael Kyle Hansberry was no exception to his own privilege, and that's exactly what led him to where he was today and why Jennifer was where she was. He was cuffed and booked, held on multiple charges that would no doubt led him to see far over twenty-five to life in a state penitentiary. In for a penny, in for a pound.

"You can wait for Mr. Hansberry in here." Lieutenant Mack held the door for her as she stepped into the windowless single camera room.

"I trust once my client is in the room, that will be shut off?" She eyed the security camera in the room's corner ceiling. "Or do you just want to get your attorney-client privilege violation out of the way now?"

"Of course, Counselor," Mack nodded, "it'll be off the moment Mr. Hansberry enters the room."

She nodded and took a seat in the chair opposite where her client would sit. She organized herself, pulling a pen and pad of paper from her briefcase. She sighed and waited, thinking back to when she first laid eyes on Kyle two years ago.

Two years ago

It was a warm and bright one on the day she'd shown up for a summer function, for a charity she couldn't remember, but a function no less. She handed the valet the keys to her BMW 4 Series white metallic coupe and smoothed the non-existent wrinkles of her jungle green, above the knee bohemian dress.

The country club where she held membership since before she was born, and casually at that, was throwing their summer party, a garden party event that kicked off the season with tray passed foods and an open bar.

Deciding she should make face, because it was for charity, Jennifer waltzed into the main lobby in nude heeled sandals and out the double doors where the lush grass spilled over with club patrons crowding around linen cloth-covered tables, while staff in their club polos and tan khakis passed around trays of food and champagne. She caught a tray as it passed by, swiping a long stem glass filled with champagne for herself. Wide and black framed, Jackie-O like sunglasses covered her green eyes as she stepped into the crowd, her blonde hair pulled back into a festive ponytail and off her back in the summer heat.

A few of her father's friends had found her as she moved

through the lawn space, greeting her and smiling at her, striking up brief conversations. She politely spoke with them. She didn't want to be rude, but also didn't care nonetheless. Her father had been gone three years now, her mother since she was a child, his firm in her care, so young, so powerful. At thirty years old, Jennifer was in charge of one of the top defensive firms in the greater Boston area and she was at the top of her game for as young as she was; aptly named one of the top lawyers in the area.

Then, upon finding a garden chair to take residence on, Jennifer pulled out her phone and checked messages and emails. She grew bored as the day wore on, carrying on conversations with people, but those too grew boring and when the champagne wasn't enough anymore, she moved to the bar for something stronger.

Taking reprieve from the heat and growing humidity, Jennifer stood between chairs at the bar next to a seated, tall man with broad shoulders covered by a dark green polo shirt and black designer pants, Sperry's on his feet. She gave him a once over and turned her attention back to the bartender, ordering herself a scotch sour and moved her attention to her phone.

"That's a tough drink for a lady."

She thought the man sitting to her right, the man with the broad shoulders, was the one speaking up, but to her surprise it was someone else, the man to her left. Red polo, plaid golf pants and a greasy-looking mustache.

"Well, I'm not your average lady," Jennifer raised her brow.

"Hardly," the red polo leaned in. "I'm Lee. How about you put that drink on my tab, and we take a seat outside."

A snort sounded from Jennifer's right.

The bartender set Jennifer's drink in front of her and she slid over to him a large tip. She bit back the smirk she wanted to share and inhaled, "Well, Lee... it is an open bar, so there is no need for the tab. And as far as the seat outside," she leaned forward just a little, "I'll pass. You see, men like you, with your greasy mustache and horrible plaid golf pants, I eat men like you for breakfast. No one with tact tries to pick up a woman at an open bar with not one but two failed lines on being a lady and buying her a drink."

A dejected Lee grabbed for his drink and left the room, leaving Jennifer to take up a seat at the bar and sigh with a deep roll of the eyes. The bartender snickered as he cleaned a couple of high balls for an order. The man in the green shirt smirked as he brought his beer to his lips, not once looking at the interaction but simply listening. It was silent for a bit, Jennifer sipping her scotch sour, taking in the air conditioning and the lack of company. Now and then, she'd catch the man in green looking at her from the corner of his eye. She had to admit he was hot and had a great boy hiding under his clothing. It was either the booze or the heat, but she felt a pooling between her legs.

It was then a clearly ditzy, brassy brunette dressed in a

white sundress, huge brimmed hat and ghastly chunky heels giddily called out to the man in green from the doorway and Jennifer could have sworn she heard him groan in annoyance.

"Kyle! There you are!"

"Fuck me," he grumbled before he barely turned his head to acknowledge the brunette. "Liss, didn't think I'd be seeing you here."

"Oh Kyle, you're so funny," the woman giggled and looked at Jennifer, "he's so funny."

Jennifer bit her lip back and feigned humor in her eyes, "hilarious," she said, scrunching up her nose.

"So, I just won in the silent auction a trip for two to Barbados, and I think you," the brunette pressed into the man at the bar, touching the tip of his nose with her fingertip, "should go with me. I'm going to go powder my nose and be right back so we can chat."

As quickly as she entered, she was gone, and Jennifer couldn't help but say something.

"That girlfriend of yours, she's..."

"Not my girlfriend," the man, now known as Kyle, shook his head. "She's a fucking gnat." Kyle looked up at the mirror behind the bar. "She's a whore I can't shake."

"So she's stalking you?" Jennifer wondered.

"Many do," he replied with a smirk and raised brows, a cocky tone to his words.

"I'm Jennifer," her lips mimicked the smirk on his own,

almost subconsciously. She liked him. Already she could tell he was fun, a little dangerous, but fun.

"Kyle," he nodded, and sipped his beer. "So what do you do that gets you in here? I don't think I've seen you around."

"Attorney. I've been a member here since I was in diapers," Jennifer replied, sipping her scotch. Her body was turned to his in her chair, slender legs crossed at the knee.

He gave her a once over, his eyes trailing up her legs, eyes narrowing at the hem of her skirt line and up to the way her breasts curved against the bust of her dress. "Hmmm, well, that explains the scotch."

"Scotch is synonymous to legal work for you?" Jennifer quipped.

Kyle rolled his eyes. "Hardly, you just don't look.... I expected..." he paused, "I don't know, just not that." He could see it now though, tight button down blouses tucked expertly into pencil skirts, hair pulled back and neat, he bet she wore glasses too from time to time. She probably needed a good fuck. She seemed like she could use one. Her legs were long and lean, and she had sexy skin and green eyes. He was quick to assume she did yoga or pilates.

"Hmmm, well, what do you do?" She asked with a quizzical look, then gasped. "Wait, let me guess, trust-fund entrepreneur playboy?" Jennifer licked at her lips, taking that last sip of her drink. She glimpsed Liss on her way back

from the ladies' room, quickly catching the eye of what seemed to be a friend of hers. "I think your gnat is back."

Kyle's eyes catch the mirror again and sees his former one-night stand in an animated conversation with someone. "For fuck sakes," he groans.

"Seems like you need an out. If she's stalking you, running will not help," Jennifer pointed out.

"You got a better idea?" Kyle couldn't help but wonder.

"Well, clearly subtlety won't work. You're going to need to be more..." Jennifer thought, "aggressive."

"Oh, it's not been subtle, I don't do subtle," he pointed out.

An odd idea struck her quickly, always thinking on her toes, "Then a more visual approach, perhaps?"

Kyle grunted, "You offering?"

"Depends," she shrugged, "what's in it for me?"

The sexiest of sly smirks crossed his plump lips and his eyes danced with a little danger as Kyle replied, "It's not about what's in it FOR you, but what could be IN you."

Jennifer didn't even need to think about it. She needed a little mischief in her life, an escape from the stressful career, the late nights and long weekends. She needed a release that she hadn't felt in ages, a proper good all senses igniting release. And who else to get it from than a trust-fund fuckboy who, in his own words, didn't do subtle? "Deal." She put her hands on his smooth jaw, pulling him in for a deep and desperate kiss.

Not one to turn an offer away from an attractive woman, Kyle kissed her hard, his tongue dipping into Jennifer's mouth, neither having a care of the venue they were in. He was a great kisser, and he smelled delicious, woodsy like mahogany and teakwood with a hint of oak. Her fingers gripped his shirt as his hands dropped from the bar to her hips.

She tasted like scotch and vanilla, no doubt from her drink and lips. Her taut waist fit perfectly in his huge hands, and he heard the faintest squeak emit from her as she relaxed into their kiss.

Then came the shriek of disappointment, and he smirked against Jennifer's lips before breaking away.

"Kyle, what the hell?" Liss whined. "I was just telling you we were going on a trip!"

His eyes were still on Jennifer as she leaned in to whisper, "Coat room, out to the left, three doors down on the right," before grabbing her clutch and walking away from him and the scene they caused. A wink from the bartender sent her smirking as she headed out of the room.

Minutes later, Kyle was opening the door and finding his way in the dark. He needed little light as Jennifer's hands were quick to find his belt and flies, a clank coming from the buckle as it hung down where her hands were already looking for what she wanted. His lips found hers and she was quickly backed into the wall by the door. He moaned as she stroked him, lips dragging across her neck and back up her jaw. She smelled expensive, sensual even, warm and strong, but had this hint of floral softness. A heady mix of jasmine, cedar, and amber. A scent that was driving his senses wild.

"You don't waste any time, do you?" he whispered against her skin, nipping at her. His body caged her in as a hand moved for the bottom of her dress.

"Not when I know what I want," she panted against his assault, her hand full of his hard, thick cock pulling him free.

He palmed her cunt, feeling her already wet panties, and somehow Kyle knew this was well worth the antics. His first two fingers swiped over her panty covered folds and pressed against her clit and she moaned against his lips, all the while still stroking his dick.

When Kyle moved her panties to the side of her folds, Jennifer hitched her knee over his hip as she lined his tip against her slick. She guided him up and down, wetting him, and then, with a thrust forward of his hips, he slid right in.

"Fuck," she purred against his ear, a ground out groan coming in reply. He was thick, stretching her pleasurably.

Kyle felt the warmth depths of her walls around him, snapping his hips forward while in the same motion he lifted her to seat inside her. Jennifer's ankles locked at the small of his back as he fucked her into the closet wall. He used the wall as a brace to carry the shifting weight from his pounding into her, her cries of heat in his ear urging him on. Her voice dripping in ecstasy, encouraging him.

"Oh yes, right there," she cried, "so fucking good."

"Fucking so tight," he ground out. He could feel her bubbling around him, imagining her coil tightening. When she snapped, he pounded into her harder, chasing his own rush and when he was near, he pulled free, dropping her to her feet harshly, losing his load on a coat nearby.

As Kyle fixed himself, Jennifer fixed her panties and made sure her breasts were properly in her dress. She pulled her pony tail free from its mess and fluffed her hair a second before opening her clutch and dropping the hair tie in and removing a card.

With his back turned to her, Jennifer slipped the card into his pocket. "Call me when you want a good fuck," she said with confidence and walked out.

The opening of the door interrupted Jennifer's thoughts, and Kyle entered, cuffed, looking smug as ever, dressed in a blue sweater, tweed pants and his loafers. His hair looked as if he'd run his hands through it a few times during his booking and processing. Mack cuffed him to the table, allowing the man to take a seat comfortably.

Cold blue eyes, vibrant from his current attire, looked back at her, still a smug smirk across his lips, hands folded together on the table. He moved to speak, but she held up a manicured finger at him. Her eyes moved to the camera in the corner, waiting for the light to go off. As she waited, she took him in again, seeing the man behind the facade. The man she knew hid beneath the smug and arrogant exterior. He looked stoic, but she read the look of deep plotting behind those cold blue eyes. His jaw was clenching, flexing under grinding perfect teeth, fingers pressing into one another as his hands were clasped in between them.

Then she spoke, "watch what you say, they're still listening."

There was no way they wouldn't be. She knew with a case like this, there was every foreseeable ear listening in if they could.

Kyle's eyes automatically flicked up to the camera before his attention turned to hers, watching as her nose wrinkled up in disgust.

"Why do you smell like vomit?" Jennifer balked.

"Because I was puked on," Kyle deadpanned.

"I don't even want to know," she sighed, her tongue poking the inside of her cheek before she shook her head. "Jesus, Kyle, I don't hear from you for three weeks..."

"What were you expecting? Flowers? Exploding hearts from a box of chocolates? We've gone longer without so much as a text." His expression was arrogant as he interrupted her, cockier than when he'd walked in, knowing damn well he'd cornered her.

Her eyes narrowed at him and she locked her teeth, the back of her tongue peeking just between her lips. "Then the news pours in about what happened to your father and

I find out you're arrested in connection to it all and that's when you decide to call me?"

"Who else would I call? You're the best defense attorney around, and I obviously need defending." Kyle rolled his eyes as if the answer should have been obvious.

"You're damn right I am," she agreed. "Shame, no one told your uncle."

"My uncle?" Kyle frowned.

"Yes, I headed him and one of his attorneys off in the lobby." Jennifer shrugged snuggly as she unbuttoned her jacket and slipped her arms out, tossing the fabric over her chair from her sitting position. Kyle snorted. "He clearly didn't get the memo that you'd organized your own attorney. And, speaking frankly, I've seen the guy he had with him in action. The previous ADA ate him for breakfast. You wouldn't stand a chance, especially not now..." she stopped and took a deep breath, refraining from mentioning the person she'd been about to and instead she straightened up and drew her shoulders back. "Well, it goes without saying."

As she turned back to face him, the strained buttons of her blouse gave him a peek at something he'd missed the last few weeks. Her body pressed against his, his mouth on pert nipples.

"You know, I love it when you get all feisty." Kyle smirked, an air of tease to his words as he caught eye of her breasts peeking through the opened buttons of her blouse. "Careful counselor, I might ask for a conjugal,"

"Focus, Michael," she scolded. His eyes narrowed, and she stared back. "What? You hired me the minute you picked up that phone."

A cold staring contest continued. They were one in the same; calculating, smug, downright vile with words and demeanor when necessary. Never one to outdo the other without it turning into some game of foreplay.

Then, in a change of character that inwardly surprised Jennifer, Kyle sighed as he leaned in as best he could, "I didn't think you'd come," his voice was deep but quiet while his eyes softened.

"Why wouldn't I?" She sighed, knowing full well he was wrong in his assumptions. She leaned forward, pen clicking in her writing hand, the other tilting her notepad so she could take notes. "Now, tell me everything that's happened since your father's birthday. In as much detail as you can."

A sky, devilishly sexy smirk crossed his lips. "Should I start how I fucked you in my bed that morning or how about in the Beamer after breakfast at the club or how about when I fucked you again against the window of my bedroom before I left for that bullshit party?" Kyle raised his left brow curiously, leaning forward against his forearms, propped against the cool table. The softness he'd had about him gone just as quickly as it had appeared.

"I'm well aware of those incidents, and how they could impact your case if it leaves this room, so why don't we start from the party itself?" Jennifer pointed out. She didn't have the patience for his games, especially now, when she was doing him a solid by at least keeping him out of orange scrubs and maximum security.

* * *

For nearly an hour, Kyle carried on, no doubt loving the sound of his own voice, recounting the events of his life since his father's birthday. Jennifer took comprehensive notes the entire time, glaring at him as he reached certain points like when he was questioned initially at the station with no attorney present, how he wasn't aware of being recorded as he was questioned again after he was cornered in the study with Dione and the authorities, and the antics he recalled about when Dione puked on him.

It oddly made sense why he hadn't called her for their typical rendezvous the night of Dillan's party. Rendezvous, that had interestingly become more frequent since September. He didn't want to make her an accomplice to what he'd done.

"Well, you've certainly got my work cut out for me. Thanks for that," Jennifer sighed deeply. "I'll call down to the courthouse and find out when you have your arraignment. For now, you're stuck here. Keep your nose clean and stay out of trouble."

"What's the plan, Jennifer?" Kyle asked lowly, eyes locked onto hers, using her nickname reserved only for him.

She licked her plump lips and leaned forward. "You let me do my job and keep your mouth shut."

She packed up her things and knocked on the door for the guard to open it and collect Kyle. They exchanged a look between them as he was un-cuffed from the table and escorted out. When he was gone, Jennifer pinched the bridge of her nose and exhaled deeply. The feeling in the pit of her stomach was ready to bring up her late lunch. She swallowed the bile down and gathered her things, leaving the jail.

This case was going to be the most difficult one she'd ever have to defend. It would test her professionally, beyond the course and scope of her talents.

"God damn it, Kyle," she cursed as she pulled away and towards traffic back into Boston.

* * *

In the darkness, night having descended upon the jail, Kyle laid awake in his bunk. Given the circumstances of his case, the high profile of it all, Lieutenant Mack made sure Kyle was in a cell by himself. It was cold and damp, yet his predicament hadn't fully weighed in on him. All they had was a confession, under duress and a semi-confused state. Surely, it wouldn't hold up in court. Especially with Jennifer in his corner. She was good, damn good. He'd seen her close regular 'Joe Schmoe' cases, and he'd seen her keep some of the most crooked out of a place like this, all on technicalities. He knew she'd make it work for him.

He sighed as he thought about his attorney. She was something else. Unlike so many women he'd come across, and he knew plenty of women. He thought back to how their arrangement began.

He'd looked at that business card for days. How dare she just drop it into his pocket and leave him, limp-dicked and cum-stained, no less in the coat closet of the Country Club? The sex was hot, a quick fuck he had enjoyed. And the lawyer, she was hot, smart and witty. She could think on her feet and he appreciated that. He also appreciated the way her pussy hugged his dick, tight and sinfully wet. Initially, he was soured, wondering who the hell did she think she was to pull game on him like that, but it sparked a bit of a challenge in him as well. And Michael Kyle Hansberry never backed down from a challenge.

"Alright, let's play," Kyle stood from his couch and grabbed his keys to his vintage mint condition BMW and headed out. He knew exactly where the address on the card was located. He often frequented the upscale bars

and shopped at the high end shops in the same neighborhood.

It was near eight, well after the workday, but something in him told him she'd be there and if she weren't, he wasn't far from a regular place. He knew he could go to quell his thirst.

As he drove, he imagined her in her office, what she was wearing, if she wore sexy black-framed glasses over her green eyes. He was growing more feral with each passing mild.

Soon enough, he'd pulled up to the building and parked rather haphazardly in a stall. There was a security guard at the front desk behind the locked glass windows.

"Can I help you, sir?" A pudgy, aging man asked as he opened the glass door.

"I have business on the 60th floor," he remarked, not even stopping for the guard. The short, pudgy man tried to track him to the elevator, but Kyle's saunter was purposeful and the doors had closed before the guard could get more information.

The elevator was quick and its doors opened on the expansive 60th floor, no one around to greet him. He looked in the open offices and found them unoccupied. Until he got to the door at the end of the hall, reading the nameplate on the wall beside it. 'Jennifer Hannigan, Senior Partner'.

"Jackpot," he twitched. With force he flung the door open, surprisingly not startling the woman inside.

She was looking out the floor to ceiling windows of her office, hair down and straight, a starched white pin tuck shirt tucked into a gray pencil skirt, black stiletto pumps on her feet.

"Took you long enough," she quipped.

In fewer strides than he was tall, he was on her, lips over hers, pressing her against the glass while her fingers curled into the lapels of his cardigan. "You're a fucking tease," Kyle rasped against her lips as his tongue dove into her mouth to quell his hunger. His hands pulling the material of her shirt away from it tucking.

"Only if you want me to be," Jennifer moaned as his lips found that spot he seemed to remember from the closet, where her jaw met her ear and neck. A sound emitted from her chest that had Kyle pulling at her top, busting nearly all the buttons off, some pinging against the glass, as he exposed her breasts and cream laced bra.

Before he could decide his next move, Jennifer was sinking to her knees, breasts spilling out of the top of her bra. She released his button and zip of his flies, a thick bulge freeing from the confines. The grunt that he gave at the feeling of more space in his pants made her insides twitch. She palmed him over before flipping through the waistband of his underwear, fully freeing his dick. She wrapped her lips around the tip and gave a little suck like one would a lollipop before taking him in her hand and titling the erection upward, licking the underside from his balls to his tip.

She kitten licked at the pre-cum leaking out, then took him all the way in, gagging a little as he hit the back of her throat.

"Fuck," he ground out, falling forward, and used a splayed hand to brace himself against the glass.

Her head bobbed against his shaft, deep at first, then shallow and deep again, her one hand wringing his cock at the base when she didn't take him fully, the other hand rolling his sac in her palm. Her knees were set in the carpet, between his feet.

He grabbed a fist of her hair and gave it a little tug. "Feels so fucking good." At this rate, he was going to cum fast, but he wanted to feel that sinfully wet pussy around his cock before he did. He tugged at her hair again, regretfully pulling her away from his dick. "Get on the desk."

Jennifer smirked as she stood at the command, a look of lust in her eyes that matched his. There was something feral about the way he'd looked at her, on her knees, lips swollen and wet from sucking his cock.

Kyle stepped nearly a half step aside, freeing her from the way his body caged her in, making her have to step around him. He watched as she propped herself up on the edge of her desk, legs long and lean, heels barely skidding the floor. Her eyes bored into his as if she were asking him 'what now?'

"Turn around," he deadpanned. She obliged. With his dick still straight, he stood behind her, foot parting her

heels just a little more. He pressed into her, his chest against her back, hot breath in her ear, "I'm going to fuck you raw." His lips twitched into a blink and you'll miss it smirk as the sound of her quick gasp filled his ear. He peeled back her shirt, allowing it to fall to the floor, and used his hands to flip her skirt from her knees to her waist. He salivated at the smooth, firm skin of her round ass, eyes trailing up her back to her neck. The head of his cock slid along her covered slit as he watched. Fuck, she was soaked through her cream lace panties already. The rough material scratched sinfully at his tip. Long, thick fingers curled around the waist of her panties and pulled the material down to her knees. Kyle felt at her slit with a middle finger, feeling the way her honey stuck to his digit. He spread the arousal over the head of his cock, ready to slip.

Aligning himself with dick in hand, he ran it up and down his prey's opening before sliding into home base.

They both moaned in pleasure, his thick shaft stretching her, her walls tight around him. There was no need for adjustment, for he just started thrusting, hard and fast. When she curled her body up and away from her desk, a long arm pushed her back down, grasping at her neck, thumb pressing into the inked Sanskrit in the center.

A deep moan elicited from her as he pressed and goose flesh covered her skin, her insides coiling tight and fluttering around him. "Oh, fuck," Jennifer moaned.

"Shit, yeah," Kyle ground out, continuing his fast pace, perusing his release.

With one hand gripping her hip, the other pressing her down at her shoulder, thumb pushing into the back of her neck, the sounds of her impending release, Kyle fucked her hard. The heat of the moment was feral and wild, loud with grunts and moans, pants and gravelly sounds, skin slapping against skin. And when she broke over the edge, she took him with her, Kyle pulling out in time to shoot hot streams of white across her tight ass.

When he was through, he tucked himself back in his pants and zipped up. Using her shirt to clean off his hands and tossing it to her desk, he walked to her drink cart and poured himself a glass of scotch, sitting down on the couch across the room, slouching a little as he sipped. "So, what's the deal here? We fuck any time we want? Because I don't do attachments."

Jennifer took her dirty shirt, wiped the streams of cum away from her skin and pulled her panties up, tossing the shirt in the garbage can under her desk. She fixed her skirt back to its rightful cut and made sure it was on straight, seem at the back before moving across the room to Kyle

She took the glass from his hand, taking a pull from it and handing it back. "It's simple," she sashayed away to her en suite bathroom, pulling a fresh shirt from a small closet inside, "we have needs and we have a means to release those needs. No strings, no attachments, just convenience." She finished the buttons on the top and tucked it back into the skirt as if he'd never just dicked her down at her desk. "We each get what we want."

"How do you know what I want?" Kyle smugly sneered, tossing back the rest of the scotch and set the glass down on the coffee table in front of him, standing but firmly staying put, hands on his hips.

"Because you like to play games just as much as I do, otherwise, you wouldn't have come." Jennifer raised a brow.

"Hmmm," he huffed. Damn, was she interesting and the two times he'd had his dick inside her have proved to be well damn worth it.

"I'll call you." Jennifer turned on her heel and walked back to her desk. "Shut the door on your way out, will you?"

He stared briefly at her retreating form, then turned on his own heel and headed out of her office with a smirk, leaving the door wide open.

Kyle smirked to himself as he stretched out on his bunk. That was an interesting day, to say the least. He cracked his neck a little, adjusting to the most uncomfortable pillow and mattress he'd ever laid on. He took in the boring white painted brick and concrete walls around him, the rusting, shabby barred door at the foot of his vision. This was a fucking state of inconvenience if he'd ever seen one. He thought to himself briefly how much he'd thank Jennifer when she got him out. How grateful he could be.

He was already in an aroused state, and if he played nice and she did her job, he could hold out for it. He just had to wait. While patience wasn't his best virtue, in fact he lacked it all together, Kyle Hansberry found himself waiting on the one thing he never had to, a woman.

Chapter Two

Jennifer didn't have to wait long for Kyle's arraignment, for it was happening first thing on the next morning's docket. She showed up after working all night gathering what she could from his arrest and list of charges being brought down on him.

And there were quite a few.

She knew that to have any chance of fighting his corner successfully; she needed to get her hands on a copy of his confession, but that would have to wait until after the arraignment. For now, she waited in the courtroom for Kyle to be brought in from holding.

She picked at her notes, looking over them and glancing around, near boredom really, as the Assistant District Attorney, Damien Gilbert, stepped into the courtroom.

He was a tall drink of water of a man, dark hair, piercing

brown eyes, cocky and overly confident. He was always on the other side of the aisle from her, vying for the seat he now held, Assistant District Attorney. He'd been awarded it a few months ago, unceremoniously earning it when the former ADA had resigned because of familial reasons and a murder trial involving his son prior. It was a case that had shocked the legal community, and one Jennifer steered clear of. Roger Rosamond had been well respected, someone that Jennifer had quite liked, although she'd often fought cases against him. He'd been clear, articulate and whilst he had an air of calm confidence bordering on arrogance in the courtroom, he'd done it with grace and dignity, unlike Damien who was cutthroat and ruthless, with no concern about who he trampled over to get the results he wanted.

Damien shot Jennifer a glance from across the aisle, a snarky smirk playing at his lips, "Counselor!"

She nodded back with a devilish hello of her own, having already expected his arrival, and turned her attention to the door opening alongside the judge's chair and bailiff.

An armed officer was escorting her client, now tastefully dressed in a pewter suit with a white button down complimented by a steel blue and white polka dotted tie. Jennifer couldn't help but wonder who sourced the suit from his closet as he looked cleaned up, but uncomfortable. Suits were not in his wheelhouse unless it was absolutely mandatory. Kyle's hair was styled back and while his face was not cleanly shaven, there was not a look of concern to his conceitedly handsome features. He still wore handcuffs, but had them cuffed in front of him instead of behind his back.

The officer instructed Kyle to take a seat next to Jennifer and then proceeded to uncuff him with the promise that if he tried anything, they would go back on or he would get a bullet to his chest.

"Little harsh around here this morning, aren't they?" He joked once the officer was out of ear shot.

"You could try to look a little less inconvenienced, *Michael*." Jennifer rolled her eyes. "And you still smell like puke, despite the wardrobe change. Which, by the way, where'd it come from?"

"Jennifer, please don't," he shot back, ignoring her question and instead honing in on the fact she'd used his given name, not his preferred one. He didn't want her to call him that. Never did, never would.

"Kyle, everyone in this room is watching you. Including that asshole over there," she slightly nodded in Damien's direction.

Kyle followed her gaze, and Jennifer heard a little growl roll in the back of his throat.

"Oh, for fuck's sake." He mumbled as he eyed Damien from across the aisle. "This douchebag?"

Jennifer shot Kyle a look. "He's the ADA. Who did you expect? Santa Claus?"

"Jesus Christ, I hate that lanky streak of shit."

"I know, just like everyone at the Country Club knows," Jennifer licked her lips and stuck the tip of her tongue back between her teeth in annoyance, "but the people in this courtroom don't, and they don't need to either. Keep your mouth shut and try and leave the pissing contest you two had going on at the door, okay?"

"He going to be a problem, Counselor?" Kyle asked, leaning in towards her.

"In what way, Kyle?" Jennifer raised her brow, and he matched her inquisitive expression. "No," she answered with a snort.

"Good," he nodded.

At that point, the bailiff called out to the courtroom that the judge was entering and for them all to rise. The Judge called upon the court officer to call out the docket number after he'd settled into this chair.

"Docket Number MSC-S-07-3847-CR-8942, The People versus Michael Kyle Hansberry."

"Thank you. Everyone bar Counselors and The Defendant may take a seat. For the record, we have Assistant District Attorney Damien Gilbert representing The People." The Judge looked up and Damien confirmed with a 'yes, Your Honor' and the introductions then continued, "and representing The Defendant, Michael Kyle Hansberry, Miss Jennifer Hannigan."

"Yes, Your Honor."

"Miss Hannigan, do you and your client wave the reading of Mr. Hansberry's rights and charges?"

"No. We'd like all rights and charges read, Your Honor," Jennifer replied for her client.

"Very well," the judge looked at his notes read, "initial charges filed against The Defendant, Michael Kyle Hansberry, are as follows: 1st degree murder in the death of Sasha McKinnon, attempted 2nd degree murder on the life of Dione Alda, conspiracy, obstruction of justice, blackmail and theft. Do The People have any additional charges to be filed at this time?"

"Your honor, The State also motions to file charges of Attempted Patricide, given the circumstances surrounding Dillan Baldwin's death," Damien added on public record.

"Well, when you put it that way," Jennifer mumbled to herself as she stood next to Kyle and took a deep breath. "Objection, Your Honor. Dillan Baldwin's death was ruled a suicide, therefore the prosecution has no grounds to file a motion on attempted patricide, by way of recommendation of private investigator, Mr. Wesley Clinton."

"Overruled, The State will be allowed to file," the judge said, siding with Damien. "I will read the full list of charges now as motioned and filed, once again the charges filed against The Defendant, Michael Kyle Hansberry, are as follows: 1st degree murder in the death of Sasha McKinnon, attempted 2nd degree murder on the life of Dione Alda, attempted Patricide, conspiracy, obstruction of justice, arson, blackmail and theft. How does The Defendant plea?"

"Not guilty," Kyle replied. Murmurs erupted in the court and Damien looked like he'd been slapped, he was in such shock.

Jennifer smirked to herself and spoke up, "Your Honor, my client enters a plea of not guilty by way of temporary insanity and emotional distress placated by the shock and post-traumatic stress of hearing the news he's no longer receiving the monetary contributions his father had promised and willfully managed."

Kyle stood smugly, despite being painted a spoiled and arrogant rich "kid", as Jennifer further explained his plea. She was there to play ball, no question about it. And the scoff she heard from Damien made her smirk. Game on.

"At this time, The Defense would also like to go on record by stating my client is not a flight risk and should be granted bail."

The look of shock still hadn't left Damien's face as he turned to look at Jennifer when she'd suggested a bail be set for Kyle to be freed upon until his trial.

The judge took a moment, jotting some notes down. "Alright, the plea stands as not guilty by way. Miss Hannigan, Mr. Hansberry, you may take a seat. Mr. Gilbert, let's hear from The People."

The Assistant District Attorney adjusted his jacket, his shock morphing away as his usual smugness resumed, and began his statement to the judge and members of the courtroom. He carried on about Dillan and while evidence based on the investigation by Clinton, Mack and Royce showed Dillan committed suicide, "Mr. Hansberry should be held accountable for his death as well, given the premise that he switched the labels on the vials of medication and had he not done so, Dillan Baldwin would be alive today."

Jennifer rose from her chair. "Objection, Your Honor, I strongly point out that my client should not be charged in Dillan Baldwin's death. It was officially ruled a suicide and the death certificate was signed off by the medical examiner. My client, Mr. Hansberry, therefore, by means of already established legal fact, should only be charged with what Mr. Clinton, Detective Mack and Private Royce have filed with the court. Any involvement in Mr. Baldwin's suicide by my client is pure speculation at this point and unnecessary for this arraignment hearing, as the prosecution is well aware of."

"Counselor, your objection to the charge of Attempted Patricide is denied and is granted to The Prosecution as a formal charge against Mr. Hansberry. Now, Mr. Gilbert, how says The People for bail?"

"Your Honor, The People set a petition for no bail in

this case. The People feel it is necessary for Mr. Hansberry to remain in custody until the end of his trial as he poses a flight risk."

"Very well," the judge turned his attention to Kyle and Jennifer. "Mr. Hansberry, with a no bail-no bond set, you are to remain in custody upon further review of your trial. Bailiff, please escort Mr. Hansberry back to his cell, this hearing is adjourned. Counselors, my chambers in ten minutes."

Before the bailiff cuffed Kyle, he remarked, "in it to win it, huh?"

"Don't," she chopped back. "And the very least you should be right now is concerned. This isn't going to be easy, so don't act like it is."

"But you can do this, right?" A sudden look of realization crossed his features as it registered he might be in a bit more trouble than he'd arrogantly assumed.

"Yes," Jennifer deadpanned while in the back of her mind, she wondered if it were even possible.

* * *

In the slowest ten minutes to have passed, Jennifer entered the Judge's chambers. Ever the ass kisser, Damien was already in there, making himself comfortable.

"Jennifer," he nodded with a twitch of his lips, crossing his legs and adjusting his tie.

“Damien,” Jennifer’s reply was clipped, and she didn’t take a seat. Instead, she simply set her briefcase in the chair and stood behind it.

The judge, a graying tall, broad man, entered the room, shucked his black robe and took a seat at his desk and, with a quick nod to them both, he got straight down to why he had called them in.

“Alright, you two, let’s have it out now. Is your personal relationship going to effect this case? It’s no secret in this courthouse that the two of you were personally and romantically involved, having since gone your separate ways. And truth be told, I’d rather not facilitate a soap opera in my courtroom. So should we sign Substitutions of Attorney now, or can we act like adults?”

“Gary,” Damien spoke as if he and the judge were golf partners and friends. Jennifer couldn’t hide the smirk that crossed her lips as the judge shot him a pointed look. Suitably chastised for his overly informal nature, Damien cleared his throat, "No, Your Honor.”

The Judge then turned to Jennifer. “No, Your Honor,” she replied as well, with a small shake of her head. Jennifer was professional enough and took too much pride in her work and reputation to allow anything personal to interfere in the courtroom from her end. That said, she didn’t trust some sort of challenge or dig not to come her way from Damien. But that would be on his head, not hers.

“Okay, I’ll run with this for now, but the first sign that

either of you are using this case to air whatever issues the pair of you have, I'll pull the plug and the fallout will not be pretty." The judge stated, to which both of them gave an incline of their heads to say they had understood. With a wave of his hand towards the door, the judge dismissed them both. "I'll send a Notice of Hearing when I close my docket for the day."

Jennifer left calmly, but her calm was quick to break when Damien grabbed her by the arm in the hall.

"What are you doing?" He frowned. "Temporary insanity for a spoiled, rich pick? Come on, Jen. You're better than that."

"I'm doing my job. And besides, what about you? Attempted Patricide? Really?" She shook her head before she scoffed, folding her arms across her chest. "Oh, and how's the intern, by the way? Still fucking the same one, or have you got another?"

"I thought we were keeping personal business out of this?" Damien countered.

"Oh, I am," Jennifer replied, before she smirked. "In the courtroom."

"Really? So defending Kyle, that's not personal?" Damien raised his eyebrow.

"Fuck you, Damien," Jennifer leaned forward snidely, "He's hired me, he's paying ergo, he's a client, nothing more. I know how to separate my personal affairs from my job. You should really try it sometime."

"This will not be easy if you fight this Jen," Damien's voice dropped, clearly trying to give her an out, a way to change tact and keep Kyle where, if Jennifer was being honest, he should be. "It's clean. Evidence is there, and a confession."

"You can't peg him for Dillan. At best, the caretaker. The initial confession was nothing but bluster - him confessing because it amused him. And as far as that confession in custody goes, it was completely under duress and you know it. So, game on. You do your job, I'll do mine." Jennifer spat. "You want to play hard? We'll play fucking hard. I've cleaned up a lot bigger messes than this, so don't come at me like I can't do my job and win."

"It's clean cut, Jennifer," Damien pointed out, with a laugh of disbelief. "You can't win this one. It's stacked against him. Don't throw your career, your father's name, your entire life away for some low-life, murdering, trust-fund prick."

At the mention of her father, Jennifer lost her control, "It's Jennifer, you bird dicked lanky piece of shit. And you're going to be sorry we played this game."

Jennifer turned on her heel and walked away, the tightness in her chest nearly constricting from stress. She had to get down to the adjacent building and meet with Kyle. She didn't have time for Damien and his bullshit petty games.

Despite her frustration, she focused on what Damien had pointed out - it was stacked against her and throwing around self-assured declarations she could win was currently immature. Given everything in its premature stage, the surmounted evidence that would no doubt be presented, and going toe to toe with Damien, didn't assure her she could. And to make it worse, this had only been Kyle's arraignment, and she'd allowed Damien to rile her. She'd already allowed it to become personal and there was no going back. Fuming, she headed across the street to where Kyle was being held.

Of course, she had to be kept waiting for a decent twenty minutes until he was reprocessed and he was in a room waiting for her.

She walked in, and her annoyance at the entire situation was further compounded by the sight of him lounging back in a chair, as if he had no care in the world. With an angry snort, she took in his relaxed demeanor and shot him a look. At her expression, Kyle at least had the good grace to sit up and frown.

"What?" He asked.

"Life plus fifty-six years. You're looking at nearly two life sentences here, Kyle, one without the possibility of parole."

"Yeah, I did the math."

"Funny, did you do the math before or after you tried to kill Dillan? Or was it when you drugged Sash hoping she'd died before care got to her?"

Kyle rolled her eyes before shooting her a downright

warning look, which would most likely make anyone else quake in their boots. Jennifer merely scoffed, not in the slightest perturbed by his expression.

"This is serious."

"Funny, who's the one actually doing the time here, Jennifer? Certainly, not you." Kyle's voice was steely and low.

"For fuck's sakes, Kyle! That isn't my point!"

"Then what is?"

Jennifer paused, licking her lips, fingers pinching the bridge of her nose. "You know what it is. It's not just my reputation here." She looked him dead in the eyes. "As good as I am, it will not be enough. It's your life on the line. They won't seek the death penalty. Your case is too bland for that, but you won't see outside these walls again."

The guard knocked on the door. "time's up, Counselor. We must take him back."

"Yeah, we're done anyway." Jennifer shot back. Kyle looked at her, raising his eyebrow.

"What, no goodbye?" He asked sarcastically and Jennifer simply shook her head as she turned towards the door.

"I'll see you in a few days."

"Jennifer..." The tone of his voice when he spoke her nickname made her stop. It was softer than it had been, loaded with some unstated meaning, and she took a deep breath, turning to face him.

"What?"

"Nothing." He gave a quick shake of his head. "It doesn't matter."

With a roll of her eyes, Jennifer left Kyle with his escort and made a hasty exit from the jailhouse.

Chapter Three

Try as she might, as she sat in her car, traffic getting the best of her, Jennifer couldn't get Kyle out of her head.

It was unsettling to her to see him so flustered. His usual arrogant, narcissistic demeanor and continuous belief that because of his social status he was untouchable, that he could do anything and consequences be damned, had unraveled quite easily in front of her behind closed doors. But it was that same asshole attitude that put him in the current predicament he was in. A very compromising situation where the stakes were high, and the consequences were damn well life altering. And this time, there was no trust fund, no whining Mommy and Daddy to bail him out.

Simply put, he was about as deep in the shit as he could get.

Michael Kyle Hansberry was going to face the courtroom and judgment of his peers one way or another, and it had clearly dawned on him when they'd been sitting in the small room together. She'd sensed it in the way he'd called to her by her nickname, the nickname that only he could get away with calling her since her father had passed.

And the look on his face, well, she'd seen that expression before. Seen the concern, the worry, the sadness even. It boiled down to defeat. And the last time she'd seen it was when she'd walked out of his life, at the time she'd thought forever, for good...

* * *

Jennifer was waiting for Damien to pick her up for dinner at the country club. He'd said he wanted the night to be special, and he knew she enjoyed spending time there. Why exactly, it hadn't mattered, and she knew he didn't really care. He'd called her upon his arrival and she met him in the lobby of her building, dressed in a black, mid-calf pleated maxi dress with a boat neck collar. Her black stilettos tapped across the lobby floor, a nude manicured hand pushing the door open as the doorman was talking with Damien.

"You look beautiful," Damien complimented.

"Thank you," she accepted his kiss to her cheek. "Don't

wait up, Bobby," she'd joked with the doorman, giving him a wink.

The doorman laughed as Damien opened the passenger door for her, closing it once she'd sat inside his Mercedes Coup, much like her own.

The entire drive to the country club, Jennifer listened to Damien drone on about his day, not once taking the time to ask about hers, but held her hand and kissed the back of her fingers from time to time. Upon their arrival, the warm summer air had cooled a bit and Jennifer's choice in attire was just enough to keep the cool breeze at bay. They were shown to their table, a stone's throw from the fountain and lake separating the eighteenth hole from the main clubhouse restaurant. Under any circumstances, it was a breathtaking view, all lit up and glowing. The veranda wasn't as stuffy as she'd known it to be during the summer and she smiled, warmly accepting the outstretched cloth napkin from their host.

Damien coughed to clear his throat and flagged down a waiter.

"Yes, Mr. Gilbert," the young man smiled.

"A bottle of Krug, please, two glasses," Damien ordered. With a nod of understanding, the waiter disappeared.

Small talk between the couple ensued, Jennifer finally getting her chance to get a word in when something out of the corner of her eye distracted her.

A face that had been off her radar for half a year had just been seated behind them, Damien not taking notice. Kyle, looking as handsome and smug as ever in a light blue linen long sleeve and Dockers, took his seat facing her, his deep blue eyes boring into hers from over Damien's shoulder. There had been a long-standing feud between the two men for a better part of three months prior to the ADA winning her over, ending their little arrangement. From parking lot quarrels to pissing contests over items at silent auctions. And in the end, Damien felt he'd won, given Jennifer had agreed to a date with him and they'd been together since.

Jennifer swallowed hard and tried to keep her attention on Damien, but it wasn't easy. Every time Kyle's date, some bottle blonde with fake boobs and silicon injected lips so much as twitched, her eyes were staring just beyond Damien's shoulder, inconspicuous enough he hadn't caught on. By the time dessert had come, Jennifer wasn't sure if Kyle had stopped staring at her through his entire meal. It made her palms sweat, her heart race, and her stomach flop. She was thankful all she'd ordered was the summer strawberry salad.

She'd not realized what was happening before it was too late and Damien was already on a knee before her. It was as if she was underwater and everything he'd been saying was muffled. Her eyes flicked around the room as onlookers took notice and waited for her reply.

Kyle's eyes were on her, watching her with a glazed over look, a completely deadpan expression on his face. His date was trying to get his attention, but his gaze never faltered. Jennifer was sure Blondie had shrieked when the woman looked at her, pure excitement on her plastic face at Jennifer's expense. The slew of emotions visibly running over Kyle was hard for her to see and a motion distracted her.

The black velvet box was opened, and she looked down, seeing the most god awful looking yellow gold and diamond encrusted ring glaring back at her. When her eyes drew back to Damien's and ultimately over his shoulder, she saw Kyle exiting the table in a hurry, his date chasing after him.

In a barely audible sound, she said, "Kyle". But all Damien's ears heard was the 'I' and he grinned, looking at her.

"Yes?" He wanted to confirm.

"Yes," Jennifer answered softly.

It pained her to remember. It pained her to think she'd played herself at her own game. She'd had said yes, and didn't even know why, for reasons she still, to this day, couldn't completely fathom. She supposed it felt like the 'done' thing to do. To finally grow up, so to speak, and be seen as a woman, despite having already garnered respect in her field of work. Of course, at the time it had looked good in front of the board, the remaining senior partners taking her more seriously as a professional woman. Once word spread around that she was 'off the market' so to speak, she knew she would be viewed more on merit as opposed to how likely she was to spread her legs for someone. It truly was a sick, sad state of affairs, misogyny alive and well even in this late day and age, but she'd said yes, anyway. Deep down she knew all along Damien wasn't in it for her, necessarily, at least not in the end. She understood full well that part of his thinking was that if he could snag one of the top defense attorneys in the state as his young wife, chances of securing the DA's slot looked particularly good for him.

And Jennifer didn't have much chance to contemplate any of this. A week later, Damien was gone. A trip with his guys to Miami. She didn't question that either. Nor did she comment much when she took a night out with her girlfriends.

While they gabbed and gawked at her "stunning" ring, had Jennifer's heart been in it, she would no doubt have questioned her motives there and then. But it wasn't. Her mind was elsewhere. Since the night of the proposal, she'd been plagued by visions of Kyle leaving like he had. It woke her late at night, it clouded her thoughts in her office, it filled every non-concentrating moment she could think of.

What was she doing?

Jennifer drowned her questions with little to no answers in drink after drink, some bougie cocktail after another before hitting her scotch. By the time she left in her cab, she was to the point of thoughtlessness. Or rather, acting on impulse over rationale. So, instead of asking the Uber to take her home, she gave him another address.

Within the hour, the Uber pulled up to the house with its 1950s modernist design, large windows along the front of the house, dual balconies and that vintage Beemer sitting in its drive.

Jennifer sighed and stalked up to the front door. She raised her left hand; the diamond glistening off of the light from the porch as she knocked.

There was no immediate answer, and she wondered if this was a ridiculous idea. Maybe he had someone with him. Maybe it was the girl from the Club last week. She didn't care. She just kept knocking, glimpsing at herself in the window panel that ran along the door. Her hair was down and sporting a messy look seeing as she'd been running her fingers through them a lot since leaving the bar, her eyes were wide, and carried a certain vibrancy against the smoky shadows of her makeup and the way her outfit of choice, a heart-shaped strapless jumpsuit, clung to her curves. She knew she looked good. She'd chosen the outfit for a reason.

Maybe she'd known she'd end up here all along.

She knocked again and again. Finally, a bereaved looking Michael Kyle Hansberry answered the door. He didn't say a word. He just stared at her, taking her in. Then he moved aside, a silent 'come in' spoken between them.

One heeled sandal in front of the other, she stepped into the foyer. The instant the door clicked shut, her lips were on his, tasting the scotch he'd been partaking in. Or was that her own? It didn't matter.

She broke away from his tongue, melding into hers in that way only he knew how to do and she whispered, "tell me to leave."

"I can't," he panted.

"Why?"

"You know why," came his reply.

Without wasting another breath, Jennifer's lips crashed into his, tongues clashing with teeth. She felt his hands move from her waist to her ass, and with a moan she was lifted from the ground, her back against the foyer wall as her ankles wrapped around his lounge pant covered hips, her heels digging into the small of his back.

Pressing her into the paint, Kyle's hands reached behind himself and pulled her heels off her feet before bracing her against him, one arm behind her back, hand tangled in her hair, the other around her midsection. He moved through the first floor of the house, ravishing her with his tongue and nips to her neck and jaw. They'd made it to his room, across the living space on the far end. Soon, her feet touched the floor and Kyle had his hands on the zipper of her back. In a swift motion, the jumpsuit had pooled at her feet and Kyle groaned, seeing she'd nothing but panties on underneath.

Jennifer wasted no time. She had the hem of Kyle's white tee over his head, disheveling his hair more. She kissed him, her tongue in his mouth and deep while her hands palmed at his hard and waiting cock from inside the waistband of his pants. Her face was cupped in his large hands as he guided the pace of their kiss, fingers tangled in her hair all the while, backing her up to the full panel windows of his room.

Her bare back and ass hit the cool glass as a thick thigh spread her legs apart. She felt pressure against her panty covered clit as Kyle pressed his thigh against her and Jennifer couldn't help but roll her hips, seeking a much needed release. His hands gripped at her hips now, letting her roll against his still dressed legs while his lips nipped and locked on her exposed neck, collarbone and the start of her sternum. When his tongue flicked over a hardened nipple, Jennifer cried out, causing a moan to escape from Kyle's lips, vibrating against her flesh.

Open-mouthed kisses back up her chest and a long lick up her neck had her whining against him and as his lips sat right at her ear, he whispered, "You're so fucking needy, drunk and needy."

Chills spread over her skin despite the fire burning inside her and a hand dipped below the waistband of her panties, taking over the job that she was doing on his thigh.

"You're soaked, Jennifer," he growled against her ear. "I'm going to make you cum so hard."

He pressed into her clit with his thumb as his first two fingers entered her and now, rather than riding his thigh, she was riding his hand, slightly bouncing with the movements of his thrusting fingers. Her walls were beginning to flutter and Kyle knew she was only going to last a mere few more seconds. Nails bit into his shoulders delightfully as she mewled, riding out her first of many waves to come. And before she was fully recovered, he'd pulled the crotch of her panties aside and slipped his solid, thick cock from his pants. He was deep inside before she could take a grounded breath, both of them moaning at the feeling of him stuffing her full, pressing her body into the glass. His hips bucked into her, sliding her up and down against the window, her ankles locked as she rolled into him. Their mouths were on each other, again all tongues and teeth.

It was filthy; it was messy; it was desperate, but it was needed.

The glass rattled with each hard fuck of his hips, his cock continuously buried to the hilt, yet he tried to go deeper and deeper with each thrust. As her next orgasm showed its face, Jennifer's body started shaking against his hot skin.

"Oh my God," she cried out as her whole body seized up around him, clenching and gripping, clawing at him like a vise.

And in a very un-Kyle like move, he came with her, his body letting go of all he had, spilling his seed deep inside her.

It wasn't the last time he'd given her what she needed and sought after his own selfish needs that night. After the windows, came the floor where she rode him, her hands flat against his chest, his hands holding her in place while he filled her again. And then it was his bed, already in a euphoric state and still drunk on one another, he took her again. First with her on all fours from behind as his hand gently gripped around her neck, his thumb pressing against her tattoo, deep moans emitting from her chest as he did so, and then again with her led on her back, his body caging her in.

Each time she came, he was right along with her, their bodies in perfect synchronization and pure bliss.

Dawn rattled them both awake, Jennifer first, as she felt the pounding in her head start to dull her sore body. She looked down at the man in bed with her, as he still rested against the mattress, his head on the pillow. They said nothing as they stared at one another and when she opened her mouth to speak; she didn't trust her voice, for it came out in a broke whisper.

"Tell me to stay."

Kyle looked at her with a look she'd never forget. One of defeat, confusion, heartache and sadness. "I can't."

"Why?" she whispered.

"You know why," he swallowed.

With a silent tear and a lick of her lips, she left the bed, dressed, and waited for her Uber outside. He never chased after her, never said goodbye.

Jennifer felt something warm on her cheek as she pulled off the beltway. A glance in the mirror proved it to be a tear, and she wiped it away. She had her work cut out for her, but she owed it to herself to do the best she could. She had to. No matter the consequences.

Later that evening, after pulling files and books, case reports and notes, Jennifer was left alone in her office, in fact, her entire floor. She'd dove straight into research the moment she had returned from court, halting all calls and communications within her office and asked her assistant, Riley, to delegate her cases to other partners and clerks, having them file Substitutions of Attorney papers within the court system. The Hansberry case would be her sole charge for the time being.

Seeing Damien that afternoon was a hard blow to her ego. Sure, she'd somewhat expected it, but the irony of her protecting Kyle from him and the law wasn't lost on her. The worry that Damien would drag what he knew to be personal information about she and her client into the record was an actual threat.

Jennifer sat at her desk, heels kicked off and Kyle's file tossed about over her desk. She had an open bottle of scotch on her desk, a short glass with two rocks in it. She eyed the papers and unofficial transcript from the arraignment before eyeing the bottle of tequila on her trolley near her sitting chairs. It was tempting and given the company, even more so.

The day had started just fine and, like she'd passed in thought a moment ago, Damien had shortly ruined it.

Jennifer knew the man was out for blood. It was a given. Damien had it out for Kyle the day their little pissing contest started at the country club, all over a damned parking stall. From there, it had only escalated.

And all things between Damien and Kyle aside, there was his job to protect, the deserving proof necessary to further seal his appointment as ADA after Rosamond had stepped down. This was his big break, a chance to redeem himself for getting it so wrong with the Rosamond trial and what better way to cement his worth than now. Taking down one of Boston's most prolific bachelors and defame someone whom most thought to be one of *THE* best defense attorneys in the region.

This would be a double win for Mr. Gilbert, and career suicide for Jennifer.

There was the problem within itself. On one hand, this case wasn't just about her reputation. She was good and had gotten half the Irish mob out on a technicality, a procedural error. But this, well, it was about Kyle. His freedom and life rested in her hands and despite their complicated arrangement, if one were to call it that, she cared. She wasn't in this for the money. God knows she could summon his parents for her legal fees, but Jennifer truly cared. She cared about her clients and fair justice. It was why she followed in her father's footsteps, as it were.

But how 'fair' it was to aim to keep Kyle out of jail was a gray area. A very gray area. Just another way she was allowing her personal feelings to compromise her professional standards and beliefs. And her feelings were what could complicate each step she made. Right now, she could separate her feelings from the situation. However, being truthful to herself, she didn't know for how long that would last.

Jennifer huffed and moved through her research, hoping to find anything she could to set up her defense. Even with the judge trying to fast track this case to speed through the holidays, she needed days of preparation. And at some ungodly hour in the morning and an optical migraine later, she packed it up and headed back to her penthouse in downtown. No doubt her work was cut out for her. She knew that. She just needed sleep, even for a few hours, before the hard work would start again.

Chapter Four

In the three weeks that followed Kyle's arraignment, they gave Jennifer all the requested pieces and files of discovery. She poured over each piece of paper, each letter on every document. She'd fielded her client's calls, her assistant ensuring Kyle that Jennifer was diligently working away and would be sure to set an appointment with the warden when she was ready to meet with him. She'd foregone her Thanksgiving break, cooping herself in her office and relinquishing familial obligations, to read each piece of evidence carefully and listen to the recording that was taken and submitted as Kyle's supposed confession.

Immediately upon hearing the recording, Jennifer let out a frustrated "fuck", slamming her hands on her desk. There was absolutely no way a jury would hear the smug indignation of his voice and think his words were under duress. She just lost her biggest argument to win a Motion to Dismiss or even a Motion to Suppress, she knew it, but fuck if she would not try.

A few days later, she sat in a room, within the jail, waiting for her client to enter. Her heeled foot tapped along the linoleum, pen clinking on the table. She buried her chin in her turtleneck sweater.

In Kyle traipsed, a typical smug look to his face but a nice shiner to his right eye. He was growing facial hair by now, the rough start to a beard, his hair a bit longer than a month ago. He sat with a huff in his seat and sighed. "Thought you forgot about me."

Jennifer licked her lips and sat straight, tugging her sweater down. "Purple's not your color, Kyle."

He popped a shoulder. "I always liked you in a sweater."

Ignoring his remark, she snorted. "That shiner is going to look lovely in front of the judge tomorrow."

"Maybe I can play the sympathy card." Kyle shrugged, and Jennifer sighed.

"Okay, focus." She shook her head, "so, I've finished going through the evidence from the prosecution. The biggest issue we have is your confession."

"How so?" He leaned forward on his elbows and scratched at his ear.

"Because you sound like a smug asshole. I wanted to file for a motion to dismiss or suppress because it was taken without myself or any attorney present, and imply duress, but no judge in the world is going to swallow that. I'm going to try but don't expect it to wash. So it's likely tomorrow they'll set a date to proceed to trial."

"When?" She had his attention now.

"Best case scenario, the spring, worst case, first part of the new year. But that's not what I'm concerned about, Kyle. I'm concerned about what this recording is going to do to your case."

"I told you they had it, Jennifer."

"Yes, but you didn't tell me you sounded like an arrogant asshole, mind you, that shouldn't come as a surprise." Jennifer scoffed.

Kyle's jaw ticked and Jennifer reached into her bag and pulled out a copy of the transcript of the recording. "I transcribed it so you can have a copy." She slammed it down in front of him, mainly in annoyance. "Just in case you forgot what you actually said. But now, I think our best course of action following when they dismiss my motion to suppress is to pursue the temporary insanity angle."

"That's all you've got?" He scoffed. "Huh, I'm paying you to work for me, aren't I?" He watched her pop a brow up. "So work for me, Jennifer." Kyle's words were laced with emotion, venom, and if she cared at the moment, fear, but she didn't.

Her face turned to stone. "For the record, I have been working my ass off this last month, you prick. Your case is the one only I've got right now, the rest given away to partners and associates because this is a pain in my ass to even handle. Why the fuck do you think I haven't been here? Huh? I've been in my office, I've been slaving away at home until late at night, researching and working to win this case. I've been in court, I've shown up to file motions. So just because you don't see my ass in here to sit in front of you and look fucking pretty, does not mean I'm not doing what I can."

Kyle blinked at little at her outburst and Jennifer glared at him, "but yes, that's all I got because you fucking killed your father's caretaker and confessed to not only that but also attempting to kill your father using his damned nurse to do it for you, all because he cut you out of his will."

She was met with more silence. "So you want me to work for you, then you do this my way."

"Fine," Kyle popped a shoulder. "So what do I do?"

"Pray for a goddamned miracle. Because if a jury hears that recording as it stands, you're going down in hell fire. Failing any divine intervention in our favor, I'll arrange a psyche evaluation. Tomorrow, you keep your mouth shut. Speak only when addressed and be polite."

At that, Jennifer looked at him before she scoffed, "and try to look like you give a shit about the fact you killed someone and inadvertently caused your father's death.

Because your blatant indifference is going to do nothing to help."

Jennifer collected her things as she railed at Kyle, slipping her coat on as her punctuated remark. She knocked on the door for the guard to open it and out she went, leaving Kyle to stew on her words.

* * *

"Your Honor, The Defense motions for all charges to be dropped based on the fact that my client was questioned and confessed under duress, when, unbeknownst to him, a recording was taking place of this confession without the presence of counsel." Jennifer had been at it for the entire morning before lunch recess, arguing about discovery submissions and misleading information. And now she was grasping at straws.

Damien turned his head to look at her, completely dumbfounded, jaw slacked in shock. "Objection!" He shouted, standing to his full height. "The Defense is reaching to delay the inevitable. She's already made such claims to which The Court denied her objection. Her client committed murder..."

"Allegedly," Jennifer interjected.

Damien looked at her like she had two heads, his rage building. "Allegedly? Allegedly? Jesus Christ, Jennifer, he killed his father..."

"Dillan killed himself..."

"Because he thought he was dying, because your client fucked with his medication! The same client who confessed to all this, along with the murder of another woman, when he was backed into a corner and you want to embarrass this court and its Judge by denying the facts?"

"Order! ORDER! ORDER!" The Judge called out before anything else was damaged or unprofessionally executed. "That is enough, Mr. Gilbert. Both of you, approach the bench"

Both attorneys approached the judge as whispers in the courtroom continued. Damien's assistant, the same then intern he fucked behind Jennifer's back, sat at their table, scrambling at notes and papers while Kyle sat back in his seat, a smug smirk across his lips, watching the scene unfold before him. He'd never seen Jennifer so worked up and despite this being his own case, he was highly impressed, and very turned on.

The Judge eyed the two and sighed, speaking in a low tone, "I suggest the both of you tone down whatever pissing contest you're vying for in my courtroom or I'll throw you both out in contempt and expect substitutions on my desk by tomorrow morning. We made a deal that this wasn't going to get personal. Keep it." Damien and Jennifer eyed each other, and the judge checked his watch and continued, "the charges still stand, and defense's renewed request for a motion to suppress is denied."

Damien smirked, like the cat that ate the canary, but the judge was quick to slap it off his face. "I suggest you wipe that smirk off your face and you hold your temper in my courtroom, Gilbert. This is not your first murder. But it will be your last if you continue this act." Jennifer remained neutral as Damien took a lick from the judge. "Now, back to your seats."

As both attorneys returned to their desks, the judge cleared his throat.

"Miss Hannigan, do you have anything else you wish the court to consider?"

With a deep sigh, Jennifer shook her head, "no, Your Honor."

"Does your client wish to consider his plea?"

"No, Your Honor."

"In that case, I declare we are ready to proceed. Jury selection will begin on Monday, January 13th. Mr. Hansberry, you will receive a formal summons via your attorney." The gavel slammed down. "Adjourned."

Damien was still thoroughly annoyed at his opponent as he stood, loosening his tie while he gathered his papers and whispered harshly to his assistant. He glared at Jennifer as he walked by, daggers boring into her frame that only Kyle could see.

With a deep breath, Jennifer gathered her papers, and Kyle was ordered to stand for the bailiff.

"What now?" He asked as he was cuffed.

"I'll arrange that psyche evaluation for next week." She looked at him. "In the meantime, I suggest you read that transcript and think carefully about it, if you get my drift."

Kyle nodded, and without another word, he was led away. As he reached the door, he cast a quick look over his shoulder, his eyes meeting hers, and Jennifer kept her face as straight as she could.

But each time he left, a piece of her broke even further, leaving with him. The walls of their predicament closing in on them.

* * *

Jennifer wasted no time. As soon as she left court, she drove back to her office and searched the contacts on her computer for another one of her father's long-time friends, Dr. Brad Peterson.

She dialed the number and waited for an answer.

"Brad, Jennifer Hannigan, do you have a moment?"

The call took all of fifteen minutes and when she was through, she was scanning and sending the documents via a confidential server to the good doctor's office.

While waiting for Dr. Peterson to conduct his initial analysis, she met with Kyle and explained how this would work. The best outcome they could hope for was a ruling that he was not of sound mind when he committed his offense. Kyle would then have the option to decide if

Jennifer put a plea bargain into Damien's office in an attempt to lessen the charge from murder to manslaughter on the ground of diminished responsibility, or gamble on the evidence totally acquitting him when heard by the jury.

Once more, she urged him to read the transcript of the recording and did her best to coach him, as much as she could, exactly how he needed to appear and come across.

But she was worried. And if the way he had scoffed when she mentioned a plea bargain was anything to go by, his arrogance was really going to fuck him even more.

* * *

A few days later, Dr. Peterson called Jennifer to arrange an expert examination.

So, now, in the second week of December, the good doctor and the attorney sat in a private room at the jail, awaiting her client's arrival.

In he swaggered as nonchalantly as ever and Jennifer had to suppress the groan she felt. She needed him to play the game, no matter how wicked, and she had a horrible feeling this was all about to go desperately wrong.

Kyle sat down in the chair without a word and Jen glared at him, "what, no hello?"

"Kyle, this is Dr. Peterson. He's going to interview you today and I need you to answer as honestly and genuinely as possible. He's going to play back the recording that the DA's office has submitted as evidence, and the two of you will discuss it. If at any point I feel the interview is not going professionally, I'll step in. But until that happens, I'm a fly on the wall."

Kyle sat back in his chair, the clink of his cuffs sounding as he rubbed his ear, a nervous habit he had as long as she knew him. With a lick of his lips, his eyes met Dr. Peterson's, and the interview began.

The doctor asked general background questions, all of which Kyle begrudgingly answered with his typical asshole snideness. With each petty and childish remark, Jennifer inwardly groaned, her veins coursing with frustration, at one point telling him to tone it down. He wasn't making his situation any better and was completely ignoring everything she had taken great pains to spell out to him.

In the two hours that Dr. Peterson had spent with Kyle, Jennifer felt like absolutely nothing had been helped. What made things worse was the look on Kyle's face as the recording played back for his own ears to hear.

Jennifer paced the floor like a caged animal, for she'd heard it enough and it grated on her nerves each time.

As they listened, Dr. Peterson noted every single twitch, glance and glare the selfish bastard gave in reaction.

When Jennifer walked Dr. Peterson through the door upon the interview's completion, she stepped into the hall and ask, "so...." She crossed her arms over her chest as she looked at the doctor.

Dr. Peterson shook his head, almost apologetically. "Jen, I can't in good conscience side with you. Nothing I saw or heard today leads me to conclude Mr. Hansberry didn't know what he was doing. In fact, quite the opposite."

"That's what I was afraid of." She sighed and crossed her arms over her chest. "No sliver of a bone you can toss my way?"

"Mr. Hansberry is narcissistic. That much is clear, possibly bordering on narcissistic personality disorder. However, that won't wash either. Narcissists more or less fully control their behavior and acts at all times." Jennifer sighed as Dr. Peterson took a deep breath, "that said you might have an angle. You see, narcissists don't feel responsible for their actions. They believe that they are victims of injustice, bias, prejudice, and discrimination. If you can successfully argue that this was exacerbated by the shock of being cut from his father's will you might, and it's a very thin might, have a case for diminished responsibility due to Self-Worth Dysregulation Dysphoria."

"What's that?" Jennifer frowned.

"A narcissist reacts with depression or anger to criticism or disagreement, especially from a trusted and long-term Source of Narcissistic Supply, in this case, being his father." Dr. Peterson explained, "they fear the imminent loss of the source and the damage to their own fragile mental balance. The narcissist also resents their vulnerability and extreme dependence on feedback from others. This type of depressive reaction is, therefore, a mutation of self-directed aggression. And, in this case, Mr. Hansberry took it out on his father. And the caretaker was self-preservation as she knew what he had done."

"So basically what you're saying is drop the insanity angle and go for the 'poor Kyle, he was never loved by his family and is a consequence of his circumstance'?"

The doctor shrugged, "that's for you to decide. But if you want my personal opinion and not my professional one, I'd see if the prosecution is open to a plea bargain. Drop the patricide if he accepts a manslaughter charge for the caretaker on the back of my report."

"Alright, thank you, Brad. I appreciate it. I know my father would too."

"And again, personal opinion only, there's no way a jury will feel sympathy when they hear that dammed recording." Dr. Peterson gave Jennifer a small smile. "I'll write up an official statement which, of course, I will stand by in court and do my best for you but..."

"I get it, Brad. I'm right there with you. This case is hard, toughest one I have ever taken on and it's a little personal. I'll see what I magic I can do. I look forward to your report."

"Anytime, Jennifer. Try to enjoy the holidays huh, and give your godfather my wishes."

"I will." She shook the doctor's hand and watched as he was escorted down the hall and away from where they'd stood.

With a deep breath, Jennifer popped her neck, unbuttoned her suit jacket, and stepped back into the room with Kyle. She paced the room as he watched her, her Louboutin heels clicking against the dirty linoleum.

The pacing and her quietness were making Kyle uncomfortable.

"So, you just going to pace the floor all day or..."

"Or what? Did you hear that? What did you sound like to yourself on there?" She ran a frustrated hand through her long blonde waves and seethed as her eyes met his.

"I sounded like I sounded." He replied as if it were nothing different. "How'd I do with the doctor? What did he say?"

"Really, Kyle?" Her hands flew to her hips in a huff. "Not well."

"So we find another one."

"No, you don't understand. If anyone in this fucking city was going to side with us, it would have been him. Sitting there acting like a petulant little child, who was indirectly responsible for the death of his father because he took away his allowance, doesn't make you crazy, it makes you a spoiled little asshole."

He kept his mouth shut as she carried on. Her eyes looked down at the recorder, and she snatched it off the table.

"And this.... This fucking thing is your undoing. I did everything I could, everything to stop these braggadocios and damning tape from being admitted and guess what, Kyle... I failed." She tossed the device on the table again. "So now, a jury is going to hear that next month and they will not even think twice about convicting you and sending you to county in orange scrubs where you'll be in gen pop." She leaned forward on the table, in his face, "and let's face it, your smug pretty boy ass will end up being some hairy, burly bear's bitch for the rest of your life all because you... you fucking crowed like the high school quarterback that fucked the head cheerleader on prom night."

When he had nothing to say, no quip or demand for more justice, Jennifer collected her things and slipped into her winter coat.

"We have one option left, and it's a thin one. We go for a plea bargain on the back of Dr. Peterson's report, which states that your father's rejection tipped you over the edge and you were temporarily out of character. We ask them to drop the charge of patricide if you plead guilty to manslaughter instead of murder regarding the caretaker."

"I'm not going to do that, Jennifer."

"Course you're not," Jennifer shook her head, "because

you're a narcissistic asshole and none of this your fault, is it?"

He popped a shoulder and cocked his head. "I hired you to keep me out of prison. Not put me in for some lesser charge."

"Fuck you," Jennifer scoffed and shook her head. "I'm going now. Over the holidays I have things to do and people to see. I suggest you take the time whilst you're stuck in here with whatever shitty form of festive dinner they give you to consider whether you'd rather take this for fifteen to twenty years or fifty." She shook her head, her voice wavering as she stood in front of the door, her hand on the handle. "I always knew you'd ruin me one way or another. But I didn't expect it to be from all sides."

* * *

With a groan, Kyle shifted on his uncomfortable cot. His mood was as dark as his cell. Staying in this place, at first, had seemed unlikely; he had Jennifer fighting his corner, but now, having had time to digest the meeting they'd had earlier in the day, he was understanding this could realistically become his life.

The fact Jennifer had basically said they were as good as beat scared him, because he was depending on her.

He needed her.

He'd always convinced himself, from their past

liaisons, that she needed him. She called him more often than not when she was feeling vulnerable, in need of a release, and in typical Kyle fashion he never refused and never pried or ask why, except for one time...

Outside Boston, at the Baldwin estate, Kyle was enjoying the company of Dillan Baldwin. His phone chimed next to the chessboard. Dillan glanced down at it and then back to his son, who was concentrating on his next move.

"Are you needed?" Dillan asked.

Kyle made his move and smiled, winning the game, picking up his phone and looked at the message.

He slid the app open. It had been months since he'd heard from her, not since the needle-dick-parking-lot-diva got down on one knee. Yet, he found himself intrigued.

'With Dillan.' He sent a quick response before he looked back at the game in between him and his father.

"I'm not sure yet," he answered the older man honestly. A couple of months ago, Kyle had received his last text from her. It simply read, 'Neil and I are over.' And even now, in recollection of the event, Kyle couldn't help the smirk that crossed his lips.

That said, if Jennifer was texting him after this long, something was off. What was it and why? And did he actually care?

'I need you.' Came the reply a few minutes later.

"I need to go," Kyle said, standing tall and grabbing his

long camel colored coat from the back of the chair in Dillan's study.

"Is it a woman?" Dillan asked. Typically, his son, much like him in many ways, only stormed off if his parents were en route or he'd had enough of the-typical Baldwin family gathering. But never usually during their one-on-one time together.

"Goodbye," he stated with a smirk and walked out, touching Grandma Lily on the forearm where she sat in her wheelchair by the front door, her favorite spot, on his way out.

He sat in his minted BMW and floored it off the property towards Boston, but not before replying, 'Where are you?'

'Judges.'

A couple of months ago, Kyle had received one text from her and nothing until tonight. It simply read, 'Neil and I are over.' And even now, in recollection of the event, Kyle couldn't help the smirk that crossed his lips.

When he arrived, Jennifer was sitting at the bar, her back to him. And, as he strode across the bar in his usual arrogant manner, he immediately spotted exactly why she had called him.

Her lanky prick ex occupied the table to the side and was clearly cozying up to the plain looking brunette next to him.

He drew his shoulders back and continued towards her,

like a lion stalking his prey. As if she could sense him, she turned her eyes, licking onto his. A few seconds later he drew up by her side, and without so much as a word, his lips were over hers as his enormous frame caged her in with one hand on the bar top, the other on the back of her chair. She moaned in the back of her throat as his tongue lolled against hers. Associates around them be damned.

God, she tasted so fucking good, Kyle thought when he pulled away. The notes of her scotch and just 'her' lingered on his tongue.

"Is he watching?" He asked with a smirk as he sat next to her.

Jennifer's eyes flicked towards Damien, and she smirked. "Definitely,"

"Perfect," Kyle winked and ordered a beer from the bartender.

One round down, complete with touches of his hand against her cheek, tucking back that foreign strand of fly away hair or his hand resting on her thigh over her pencil skirt, the ruse of laughter at some joke or story he told, and that was all it took to finish the game. Kyle paid the tab, Jennifer finished her scotch, and the two walked out, not missing the chance to saunter by the newly minted assistant DA and his intern.

Damien glared at them, clearly hot under his collar at the arrogant playboy. Kyle Hansberry just beat Damien Gilbert at his own game, and he hated it.

"Fuck that guy, man," Damien mumbled, but just in ear shot of the duo, a disappointed look on the intern's face.

"She will," Kyle quipped as he kept on walking, his hand firmly planted at the base of Jennifer's spine. He didn't need to see her face to know she was smirking.

The second they entered the space, his eyes followed Jennifer as she shed her jacket. Untucking her button down, she made her way to the drink cart, fingers undoing the buttons on her shirt as she went.

Kyle shucked his camel colored coat and tossed it over the back of what he'd deemed the world's most uncomfortable and stiff couch as he sat down. Soon, Jennifer stood before him, two short glasses in hand, amber liquid swirling just a little in them. Her hair was pulled back in a tight bun at the nape, but her eyes, a multitude of shades of green and yellow, stared back at him.

He licked his lips as he looked at the swells of her breasts, peeking out over her black bra, and he knew the matching panties were under her pencil skirt.

"What did he do to you?" He asked carefully, slowly.

"I caught them in his office, just before his ADA appointment, fucking on his desk," she answered, placing one knee against his thigh, then the other. She straddled his hips, towering over him as he sat under her. "I threw my ring at him and walked out."

"Why did you text me?" Kyle asked. He knew why, but he wanted her to say it. He took the drink she offered him

and the two tossed back the expensive liquid, forgoing any rules on how to drink good scotch. Jennifer took the glasses and set them on the table, running along the back of the couch. Her breasts were right at his nose, and Kyle inhaled her heady scent. He was already hard, and he wanted payment for his rescue.

"You know why," she rasped.

His hands pushed up the form fitting skirt above her hips to her waist, palming her ass. He silently relished in the way her skin felt under his touch. Kyle slid his hands from her ass to then up her back and over her shoulders, pushing the fabric down her arms, trapping her elbows behind her just enough. His mouth was on her, his tongue inside her mouth. He felt her try to work out of her blouse, but he smirked against his assault, hearing her whine in irritation. He sensed her wanton desires and relented, pulling the shirt free of her arms, flinging the fabric to the floor at his feet. Her hands flung to the hem of his sweater, pulling quick at the bottom, lifting it over his head and tossing it away. Manicured nails scratched at broad shoulders and down a bulky chest, over sculpted yet not defined cut abs and fiddled with the thin belt he had all the while, she panted in his ear breathy moans, his lips on her neck.

Kyle nipped into her at the base of her neck and shoulder as he worked expertly at the clasp of her bra, letting the garment fall away from her chest, only to give her an unexpected sound from his throat. Jennifer had freed his hard dick out of his pants. A devilish smirk split her lips when his eyes met hers. He gave a small scoff and twitch of his left brow before giving her exposed ass a quick slap, smoothing over the skin and running a long finger under her panties, slipping the material away from her and sliding it to the side, opening her to him.

She sank down on him; her swollen clit, looking for friction against his pelvis. Kyle grunted, feeling her wet depths swallow him. Big, firm hands and forearms posed as brace for her back as she rolled her hips against him. He sucked at one of her breasts, a pert nipple between his teeth caused Jennifer to loll her head back, arching her body into his more. A long flat tongue moved upward along the valley of her breasts before it flicked over the ignored nipple.

"Make me forget," she whispered.

Devilishly he smirked, gripping her ass with both of his hands and lifting her just so slightly and slamming her back down on his cock. "He never fucked you like I can," Kyle baritoned in her ear and nipped at her neck, just where her jaw connected, right at the bottom of her ear. Jennifer purred with a deep shudder that Kyle felt as he buried himself deep with a thrust. "I know what you like," he thrust again, "what you want," he thrust a third time, swiveling his hips as he did so, "what you need."

"Oh, fuck," came from her lips, in a voice she didn't even recognize, but he did, and oh, did it sound so sweet.

He lifted her, bearing her weight in his arms and laid

her on the ill fitting, stiff couch. The leather was cool on her back. His pants slipped to his knees as he railed into her. He could feel her coil tighter, a look of euphoric lust to her face.

"Harder," she moaned as his fingers bruised her hips.

"Fuck yeah," Kyle grunted with a thrust, increasing his speed.

She moaned and quipped as he buried her into the couch, practically softening the furniture. He hated the fucking thing, anyway. It was never comfortable.

"Kyle," she let out a breathy cry as she came hard, pulling his climax from him.

"Fuck," he ground out, chasing his orgasm, his hot seed filling her. Sweat beaded at his hairline, a sticky glisten over his chest and shoulders. It felt so good to cum like he had, a buildup of months and months with no proper release, a relief of sexual contentment only coming from being with her. He's had others in their time apart, not even a handful, but none gave the gratification he felt after giving Jennifer her undoing.

He watched as her chest heaved, trying to regain control of her breathing. Sad eyes looked back at him. "Jennifer," he said, "what's wrong?" He felt a lump in his throat. Had he hurt her? She wanted what she knew he could give. They've gone harder before. She sat up, his softening cock slipping out of her as she moved her back to the arm of the couch, nearly cowering away from him, and he wondered if he was the problem.

"I hate him," she swallowed. "You make me forget. I needed that."

"He's a prick," he said, reaching to wipe the silent tear that was escaping down her cheek, black with mascara.

He stood to dress, handing her her top, the bra somewhere he didn't care to look for in the moment. She stands from the couch and pulls it over her arms, not bothering for the buttons. As he slipped his sweater over his bare chest, honied dick now back in his already buttoned pants, she looked at him, as if she wanted to say something. He raised his brow, and she kept her thought to herself.

If she'd asked, she was afraid he'd say no, so her request for him to stay the night with her was left unsaid.

"I'll call you later," she said instead and walls away, down the hall toward her room. Kyle gave a quick nod and let himself out.

Kyle groaned, the raging boner in his pants at the memory doing nothing to ease his he feeling of discomfort. Whilst back in September, she might have called him for help. The truth was, he depended on her just as much when he needed a release.

And it had been her he had called to help him out of his current predicament.

Because, despite all their pretense, all their bravado and refusals to admit it, there was something deeper there. Some form of connection that made them turn to one another without so much as a second thought.

Kyle sighed and turned onto his side. Maybe he should have pushed it, stayed, provided her that friendship that he could see she needed instead of merely being a fuck, but he was too selfish.

He let out a loud exhale as his hands picked at the scratchy blanket he was laid upon. Maybe, if he had given her the comfort she needed, had the courage to call her out on the fact that things between the pair of them were getting a bit heavier than either had intended, he might not be where he was now.

Because she would have answered his call when he left his father's that night after their argument.

But instead, he'd walked away. He'd he left on his own accord, unlike today when he'd been led back to his cell.

The more he thought about it, the more he realized what a shit position he had put her in. It wasn't just his life on the line, but her professional reputation. Which she had willingly offered up to scrutiny when she took his case on.

And now that bothered him.

"Fuck," he groaned, turning back onto his back, his eyes locking onto that thin chunk of light which streaked across the gray ceiling.

He wondered where she was right now. She said she had things to do over the holidays, people to see, but he did not know who she'd be spending Christmas with... maybe it was the uncle, no, Godfather she had mentioned in passing one time.

It was kind of ironic, really, how little he actually knew about her, although he was placing all his trust in her.

But trust he did. And for that reason, he decided. If she was telling him a plea bargain was the only chance of getting out of here before he was a decrepit old man, then that's what he would do.

Chapter Five

Mid-shin high duck boots covered determined strides as Jennifer hiked through her godfather's property deep in the country on Christmas morning.

She'd driven through the night from the city, getting in at a rather ungodly hour after nearly three whole days holed up in her office, after Kyle had done a u-turn and said he would consider a plea-bargain. As such, she'd been working tirelessly to get everything in order, holding discussions with Dr. Peterson about how they could possibly fashion a case to keep Kyle's inevitable stretch in an orange jumpsuit down to a minimum.

The issue was, she didn't have any faith that Damien would go for a plea bargain. Not least because he hated Kyle, but this was, on the face of it, a cut and shut case and an easy win for him. Kyle had confessed. So, she needed to be prepared to convince the jury he had been temporarily blinded by circumstances, hopefully throwing enough reasonable doubt out there that he was guilty.

But she was at a loss. She knew they wouldn't side with him, no person in their right mind would. So now she was rapidly facing up to the fact that she was already going to have to think about her mitigation statement when it came to sentencing.

Terribly overwhelmed with a sense of defeat, she'd decided to take refuge in a hike along the property as the staff inside prepared for the dinner feast.

Strolling beside her was a man in his sixties, with dark green, kind eyes and a stout frame. He kept warm dressed in a similar fashion as his goddaughter. A matching camel colored fedora adorning his head of full gray hair. Joseph Flanagan, a big boss in the Boston Irish mob. Her father and Joseph had been friends for years, Jennifer's father working cases for Joseph and lower-level men from nearly the start of his career.

"So, are you going to tell me what's on your mind, or..."

Jennifer took a deep breath and exhaled, her breath fogging the chilled air in front of her.

"You don't have to tell me, but whatever it is, no matter what it is," Joseph stopped walking and took her by the shoulders, "I'll take care of it. All you have to do is say the word."

Jennifer nodded. She knew he'd help. She just didn't

know how he could. "Thank you," she sighed. "I don't know what it is yet. This case, it's...."

"Ah, that pretty boy who killed his father."

"He didn't, not directly. It's... complicated," she bit her cheek.

"Well, we have a long walk back. We've got nothing but time."

"It's personal, in a way." She started.

"How so?"

"He's... a friend. We've known each other for a while and he needed this as a favor."

"And you don't think you're going to win." Joseph took a deep breath.

"No. Not at all." The defeat was heavy in her voice. "What's worse, it's Damien is who I'm up against and he's not letting up."

"Lanky, piece of shit." Joseph wrinkled his nose. "I could have him killed?"

"No," she chuckled. "I don't know what to do. I have done everything in my absolute skill set to change this. Damien is fighting me hard. The judge doesn't play nice, and despite my best work and painstaking hours, Kyle is guilty."

"Having a guilty client has never bothered or stopped you before."

"He confessed." Jennifer shrugged, "and yeah, I've

managed to work that before, but this... everything I've tried has just not worked." She bit her lip, "he's going to go down and hard, for a very long time, and honestly, if I didn't know him, I probably wouldn't have touched this case with a fucking bargepole."

"But you did, because you care, right?"

Jennifer shrugged. "Like I said, it's personal. I've known him for a while and as shitty and abhorrent what he did is... I kind of get it."

At that Joseph chuckled, "you understand why he did what he did?"

"In a fashion. I mean, I'm not making excuses. He killed a woman and caused the death of his own father. But, I don't know, Kyle... he's a product of circumstance. I know that doesn't excuse what he did but I can't help feeling had anyone in his family even showed him a shred of compassion or care, taken the time to show him right from wrong, he wouldn't have grown up as a damned narcissistic sociopath."

"Well, that's a heavy description, dear," Joseph chuckled.

"Well, it's the truth. He is! I've not met anyone with such a sense of entitlement."

"Oh, I don't know," Joseph smirked, "I'm sure I could point you to a few who you know, who hold a similar gray moral compass."

"That's just it though. That's why I get it." She kicked at a twig. "I'm about as gray as the sky and I learned it from the two most important men in my life."

"How desperate are you to keep him out of jail because, well, there are options? It just depends how dirty you're willing to fight."

She thought for a moment. It hadn't occurred to her as an option. Just getting him a lesser sentence or no death penalty had been her main objective... Until now.

"Desperate might not exactly be the word but, I'm open to options."

Joseph looked at her, "you need to think carefully about it, once you cross that line there is no going back as your dad well knew. So far you've kept your nose clean, done everything by the book. But before you can decide if you're willing to go bent, there's a more pressing question you got to ask yourself."

"What's that?" She wondered.

With a slight twinkle in his eye, her godfather chuckled a little. "Have you broken your own rule?"

Before Jennifer could answer, they'd reached the house and one of her uncle's men approached, whispering something in his ear. With a sympathetic look, he excused himself, "I'll see you at dinner. Take some time, use the study if you need to, there's already a warm fire inside."

She watched him go, temporarily floored by his question, knowing full well what he was implying. She nodded and licked her lips, heading upstairs in the grand countryside mansion. Changing from her boots to her house slippers, Jennifer set about grabbing her briefcase from her room. She found the fire-lit study and began scouring through the file for the umpteenth time.

She pinched her brow and ran her hands through her hair before tucking it back up in a disastrous bun atop her head, the tension in her neck tight. She ran her fingers down the back of her neck, massaging small circles to gain relief. Her eyes fluttered closed a little as her mind wandered a bit. A flash of Kyle's thumb pressing into the ink there.

Her phone rang, startling her. She looked at the ID and sighed. It was him. It had to be. The number flashed as '*Unknown*'.

She slid her thumb to answer and waited as the automated recording told her an inmate from the facility Kyle was housed in was calling and if she wanted to accept the call. She did.

"Kyle?"

"Merry Christmas, Jen."

She blinked, "erm, Merry Christmas to you, too. Are you... are you okay? Do you need something?"

"*No, I just wanted to,*" he cleared his throat, "*to just say Merry Christmas. See how you were.*"

Jennifer shifted a little in her seat. This wasn't like him. In all the time she had known Kyle, she'd rarely seen or heard any sentiment from him at all.

"I'm okay. I'm upstate, working while visiting my godfather. Did you have your meal time yet?"

"Not yet, although I'm not getting too excited over it."

"Well, nothing like a turkey roll and some slop on Christmas, huh?"

Kyle chuckled before she heard him take a deep breath, *"suppose I better get used to it. I mean, even if you pull this plea bargain off, let's face it. I'll be fed it about twenty times over before I see the light of day again."*

"It's better than a lifetime of them, right?"

"Yeah." His tone was despondent, defeated. This was nothing like the cocky asshole Jennifer knew, and she was feeling extremely worried.

"Kyle..."

"I'm sorry, Jennifer."

She blinked, "what? Sorry? What for?"

"I shouldn't have put you through this. I should have called someone else."

Jennifer sighed, "Kyle... look, if you had called someone else, you really would be looking at a lifetime inside. Now, I can't promise that isn't what's going to happen, but I'm trying my hardest. That's more than anyone else would have done."

"I know, and thank you. You've done more for me than anyone ever has."

Jennifer felt a lump in her throat. This almost felt like a goodbye. He wasn't... surely, not...

"You're not... not going to do anything stupid, are you?" she whispered.

"No."

"Why are you apologizing, Kyle? What's going on? You're scaring me."

There was a pause, before his soft voice replied, *"you know why."*

Jennifer gasped as the words she hadn't heard in a long while spilled from his lips.

"My time is up. I have to go. Merry Christmas, Jennifer."

"Merry Christmas, Kyle." She whispered before the line went dead.

She tossed the phone onto the desk, blinking back the tears that had filled her eyes.

Kyle Hansberry apologized to no one, so the shock of that alone would have been enough, but the utter defeat in his voice had killed her.

Because she cared. She cared about the asshole.

You know why...

Three words. Three words that had been used by them both in the past, because neither of them could face up to the fact they had both broken their rule, both taken things beyond a simple fuck and duck relationship.

Three words that replaced an unspeakable three more.

She wiped her eyes and stared at her laptop before she snapped it shut with a loud sob.

She couldn't see him stuck inside. No matter what he had done, or how vile a person he was. She fucking cared too much about him, and logically, she knew she shouldn't. But she did, as abhorrent as that might appear to other people.

She cared enough to make her want to cross that line, to fight as dirty as she needed to.

But mere bribes and threats weren't going to cut it here. They needed a drastic solution. A solution that meant she might never practice law again... but that was a consequence she was willing to take.

And there was only one person she knew that could see it through. One person who would bend the world flat for her.

She stood up, wiped her eyes, and made her way out of the study. She stopped the caretaker, who told her that her godfather was in the lounge, so she headed straight there.

"Clover?" He frowned as he saw her and she sniffed and then swallowed.

"I need your help."

* * *

Kyle was escorted to his meeting with Jennifer by his usual guard. After his call to her at Christmas, she hadn't spoken to him until three days prior, saying she needed to meet to discuss a few things before his trial was due to start in a couple of weeks.

But instead of meeting with Jennifer, Kyle walked into the room to find a tall man, built a lot like he was, with a thin beard and goatee and spiky hair. Alarm bells began ringing in his head as he took in the man's tailored pinstripe suit and gaudy red colored shirt, suspenders peeking out from his jacket as he gestured for Kyle to enter the room.

"Mr. Hansberry, I'm Nick Mole. I'm going to be taking over your case."

"Where's Jennifer?" He cut right to it.

"Mr. Hansberry, Kyle," Nick tried again.

"Michael." He corrected the man standing before him.

"Michael," Nick sighed. "Look, it's with deep regret that I am the one to tell you this but, Jennifer's dead. She was murdered three days ago."

Kyle blinked, the words echoing round his head as he swallowed.

"I... murdered? What the fuck do you mean?"

"She was killed. She's dead."

"I know what it means, you brainless shit. I meant how? I just talked to her three days ago about meeting today. She can't be dead."

"She didn't turn up for work yesterday morning," Nick shook his head, "while she might work from home occasionally, she always calls in. When her assistant hadn't heard from her by lunchtime, she called to her penthouse."

"And found what?" Kyle demanded.

"A crime scene. There was a lot of blood and broken items. When the cops viewed the security footage, it showed a suspect dragging her into the elevator and out the utility door. If you spoke to her three days ago then, it can't have been much before she was taken. I'm sorry."

Kyle sat back, trying to process this new information. It made little sense, and he felt the insides of his chest ache like he was growing short of breath. "I don't understand. Did... did they catch the guy? Fuck!@#"

"They're holding someone in connection with her murder, yes."

"Who?"

"He's a former client. I don't know the exact details, but it appears that he took exception to the fact Jennifer only got him a reduced sentence instead of a not guilty verdict. He was released last week. The police suspect this was retribution."

Kyle bit his lip, casting his eyes downward.

"I'm sorry you had to find out this way," Nick said.

Inhaling deeply, blue eyes met blue eyes and Kyle raised his left brow, brushing his feelings to one side. "So what the fuck are you going to do for me, given the best lawyer I knew is no longer available?"

The rest of the meeting lasted only another five minutes, as Nick had somehow enraged Kyle enough that he yelled at him to go fuck himself and was escorted back to his cell.

He refused his dinner, refused anything from the library cart, and did nothing but lay in bed. And as night fell over the chilly space, he continued to lie there, tossing and turning.

Kyle couldn't sleep. All he could do was think. And for him, that wasn't a good thing because every thought led back to her, to Jennifer, and now she was gone.

It was a ridiculous night with his parents. A forced dinner to discuss plans for his Father's birthday next week and he had left halfway through, a care not given about what the menu was or the seating arrangements. Kyle was now finding himself in the elevator to Jennifer's penthouse, with his security key card to enter. He was trying to figure out why he was there, but he couldn't put it in words. When the doors opened into her space, he sighed, seeing her sitting on that God forsaken couch, her fireplace roaring. She looked up from her papers, highlighter and pen in hand, humming at the distraught look on his face, hair slightly disheveled.

He stalked across the space, camel coat, her plum and floral scarf around his neck, blue sweater and tweed pants, fire burning in his eyes. His lips were on hers forcefully, pressing her back into the cushion. She let the papers and pens fall into her lap as she now pushed the coat away from his big shoulders, the heavy material falling to the floor. He'd already kicked out of his loafers as he kissed her, one hand balancing himself into her, gripping at her waistline, the silk of her robe cool against his fingers, while his other held the back of her head, pressing her against his lips.

Kyle broke away for merely a moment, just enough time to reach behind his neck to pull at the collar of his sweater over his head and dropping it to the floor. Then he was back on her, tongue delving deeply into her mouth, a tuft of a moan escaping from the back of his throat. He couldn't help the rut of his hips as he felt her hands unclasp his tweed pants, her fingers touching his fiery skin. Soon after, Jennifer was running those same hands over the waistline of his pants and silken boxers, nails scratching at his firm ass before taking her hands and squeezing his cheeks. He shuddered as his skin met with the air of the room, his pants and boxers falling to his thick thighs, his dick springing free. He wanted her mouth on him and she was ready to give him just that. He stood tall, breaking their kiss, and for a moment, Kyle took her in.

Her lips were swollen and pink from his doing, her chest heaving to catch her breath, her frame covered in a deep burgundy silk robe, her blonde hair wild and still in its curls from the day. Her eyes, however, it was her eyes that drew him in. They were bright, the specks of green and yellow flickering in the warm light of the fire against the lights overhead. But something in them made him feel safe, like he mattered. A lick of her lips brought him back to reality, his head lulling back as her mouth enclosed around the head of his dick.

At first, his hands remained still but soon he had his fingers in her hair, resting on the back of her head as Jennifer sucked him hard, one of her hands rolling his balls, the other wrapped around the base of his cock bringing it to meet her lips as she swallowed his length.

She worked him over, feeling a burn build in the pit of his stomach, his abs flexing as he tried to hold back. She could feel the throb of his dick against her tongue and roof of her mouth. He pulled back on her hair a little, his cock slipping from her mouth with a wet pop. Kyle bent forward, kissing her heatedly, himself sinking to his knees as he pushed the silk robe away from her body, pulling the tie so it fell away, pooling at her knees.

"On your back," Kyle croaked between heavy breaths. A thick tongue licked her own lips as she gave a long blink in reply. Kyle watched as she crawled just a few steps away, his eyes eating away at the image of her on all fours, until she laid at the stretch of rug between their current spot and the fireplace.

He too followed the same way, kissing at the inside of her knee, to her thigh and up to her opening. It made his mouth water because he could smell the sweet arousal that dripped from her. He nipped at soft flesh of her thigh just before her outer lips, bruising her but gave a healing kiss quickly. With a flat, long tongue, he gave her a taste, and she curled her body inward at the feeling, a sound leaving her that was high-pitched but gravely at once. "You taste so fucking good," he hummed against her clit.

"Fuck," Jennifer moaned as he expertly ate her like he was cleaning his plate.

His tongue lashed at her insides, cleaning her of her sweet and sticky honey from her inner most places to her outer folds, tongue fucking her and humming against her clit. He left dinner early and now he was famished, devouring her like she was a fucking five course meal. But he was edging her, keeping her just at the throes of her bursting coil so that when the time came, he knew how she'd let go. His tongue curled around her clit just as two fingers interned her, spreading her, stretching her, preparing her for his next assault. When he turned his hand palm upward, hooking his fingers at just the right angle he'd memorized, he looked up at her.

Her eyes were hooded, long thick lashed not unlike his own were fluttering against her blushed cheeks, plump pink lips were being licked by the tip of her wet tongue before bright teeth pulled in her bottom lip. Her breasts were perfect mounds on her chest with nipples pebbled and hard at their peak, moving up and down as she tried to maintain decorum in her breaths. A sheen of sweat covered her tight abdomen as his left hand splayed over her hip, keeping her close to him. Her hands were busy, one in his hair, keeping him right where he was while the other combed through her hair and remained at her crown, a handful of blonde curls in her fist.

"Let go," he hoarsely whispers and she snaps, her walls pulling his fingers in with her pulse, his hooks dragging away at her most sensitive and deepest spot. A strangled cry emits from her throat and Kyle swallowed the lump in his throat. He allowed her to ride out her wave, back arching away from the floor, watching as her hands shift to the rug, fisting the fabric in her palms before settling between her, caging her in with his hands at her ribs. His body sunk low, the head of his cock right at her slick opening, and with a thrust, he slipped right in.

The glow from the fire cast across their bodies like a warmth irradiating from the outside in. Jennifer laid beneath him, Kyle's body caging her in against the lush throw rug at her back. His lips kissing after each nip he gave to her skin. Nose brushing against the crook of her neck as he gave a hot, open mouthed tongue-kiss to her collarbone. Her fingers were in his hair, her breath hot in his ear. His thrusts were deep, long and slow, calculated. As he thrust, his hands ghosted along her sides, up her arms and pulled her hands free from his neck and hair. He held her wrists as he guided her arms to lay above her head. He caged her in again, his eyes searching hers, his hips never stilling.

Jennifer's legs moved from wide hips to her knees bent and now her legs were around his thrusting waist, ankles locked at the small of his back, heels pressing into his ass. He could feel that familiar knot building in his belly again. But something was happening in his chest, constricting it tight. Their eyes locked and his dick twitched inside her near throbbing core. His hands traveled up the soft skin of the underside of her forearms, open palmed before closing around her hand, entwining his fingers with hers, the veins and tendons of his firm hands flexing and showing as he squeezed her hands with his.

"Kyle," Jennifer gasped with a cry as came.

His throat gave out a guttural moan as her orgasm set off his own, her grip like a vice, his thrusts long and languid, drawing it out so slowly, his entire body rolling against hers as his seed settled deep within her, his lips on hers, tongues slowly rolling with their tide against one another. And as the rolling tide of ecstasy ebbed back, Kyle collapsed above her, gently laying over Jennifer, his weight evenly distributed so he didn't crush her. His mouth remained on hers for a while, kissing her, his chest heaving in deep breaths against her own rise at the swell of her breasts. Then, he broke free, stood back on his knees, slipping away, Jennifer suddenly cold at the missing warmth of his body. He stood to his full size, naked body towering over her as she lay there, awaiting what would come next. She saw something there, something hidden behind his still lust blown eyes, but she couldn't name it. Maybe she was afraid to, maybe she was unsure. But something had changed within him.

"I'll call you," he said lowly, voice dry.

Jennifer sat up and nodded, taking her robe from the floor and covering herself with it as she watched him dress and then he was gone.

The feeling of something wet against his face broke Kyle free of his memory. He reached up and wiped away the... What the fuck? A tear? Angrily, he sat up and threw himself off his bed. He was shaking. He was so engaged. He swiped everything he had sitting on the metal table drilled into his cell wall, what little items were there crashed to the floor. Kyle walked to his sink and gripped the sides, white knuckled. Then he looked up at his reflection in the mirror. What he saw was not himself.

Tear-streaked face, red eyes, wobbling lip. His skin was pale, and a sheen of sweat coated his skin at his hairline. Kyle Hansberry had just realized he'd lost everything he ever cared about and didn't have the balls to admit it before it was too late.

With a heavy fist, he shattered his own stare; the glass falling away and into the sink, never feeling the sting on his skin. It wasn't until his blood ran in streaks down the steel sink and down the drain had he realized he'd split his knuckles and gashed his arm badly.

It was then the guards seized upon him to control him. Belly to the ground, knee in his back and cuffed.

"Take him to medical, clean his ass up." The head guard spoke brashly.

He spent the night in medical, cuffed to the hospital bed, reduced to complete numbness and on a 51-50 hold.

Chapter Six

The news of Jennifer's death spread like wildfire through the legal community and left most reeling at the tragedy, including the ADA himself. Damien made sure to make any and all public statements he could on the matter and a fully grieving Kyle watched from the side-lines as it happened. His trial was pushed back nearly a month, mid-February, now the date set for opening arguments.

When the morning of that day finally came around, Kyle met with Nick, whom he'd come to loathe, not really caring how this associate from Jennifer's office was going to handle his case. The guy stood zero chance against Gilbert, and Kyle knew that. And he wasn't Jennifer. No one was Jennifer.

But it didn't matter, not really. Kyle had a plan. He was going to let them do their thing, and he was going to do his.

He fully intended to wind Damien up, probably tell him to eat shit, maybe to go fuck himself too, before switching his plea following his own testimony to guilty. He was done. Either way, he was going down, he'd come to terms with that, and at least this way he got to do it on his terms.

"I'm going to step out while you get cleaned up." Nick said, watching a shaven Kyle sit in his cell. "There's a new suit there, one I suppose was set out from your former counsel for you in her office."

Kyle said nothing, only glared at Nick as he left his cell, leaving a guard behind to supervise. He stood up and slowly made his way to the garment carrier. His fingers unzipped it and he took a deep breath as he looked at the smart black and gray pinstripe inside. His hand skated over the woolen material of the jacket, and he wondered if Jennifer had touched it in the same way he had. He wondered if she took the time to think of how the fit would go, if the tie matched, if it all coordinated right down to the socks and shoes.

But he knew the answer. Of course she would. Because nothing Jennifer did had ever been left to chance. With a last sigh, he set about getting himself dressed.

He changed and was cuffed, a heavy weight upon his shoulders, as he was escorted to the squad SUV to take him to the court in downtown Boston, Damien having won a change of venue verdict two weeks after Jennifer's death. He caught Nick's eye as the attorney gave a slight nod before getting into an awaiting town car just behind them. Kyle glanced up at the clear blue sky before he climbed into the awaiting car and was locked in the back.

The caravan neared downtown in less than thirty minutes. And, as the SUV began their back street approach to the parking garage, a larger SUV running a red light. sideswiped it. Kyle was flung around in the secured cage like a rag doll, his head colliding with the metal side of the vehicle as it flipped onto its edge. Dazed and confused, the sound of screeching tires and the smell of break smoke and burned rubber filled his nose. Sirens were muted in the distance as feet shuffled outside his window, the integrity of it shattered but still intact as it was bulletproof. Before he had time to register what was going on, Kyle heard gunfire, followed by screams, and the back of the vehicle was wrenched open. He was hauled out by his shoulders as he grew further in and out of consciousness. Quickly the cuffs were gone, and he was heavily thrown into another blacked out SUV.

Bleeding from his head, he caught a glimpse of Nick sitting in the captain's chair next to him. As the vehicle sped away, Kyle looked around, his mouth hanging open as his eyes fell on those of his substitute attorney. "Okay, what the fuck?"

Nick said nothing, but shoved a duffel into Kyle's lap. "You have seven minutes to change. No questions."

"Bullshit, no questions. Who the fuck are you?"

"No questions, Mr. Hansberry."

"Oh, eat shit! I'm not changing until you tell me what the fuck is going on!"

"You're being taken to an airfield. From there, you'll be flown to an undisclosed location that I've not been informed of. That's all I know." Nick checked his watch. "Six minutes, Mr. Hansberry."

Kyle glared at him, "who—"

"Look, asshole, you might want to spend your life in prison, but someone is paying me a lot of money to make sure you don't." At that Nick opened his jacket pocket to reveal a gun in a holster just inside and Kyle took a deep breath, "so get changed because one way or another, you're getting on that flight, because I want my money."

With a snide glare and award-winning side eye, Kyle began slipping out of the expensive suit and into the change of clothes provided in the duffle. He looked at the bottom of the bag and found nothing as he stripped and changed.

"So I just get on the plane, and that's it?" He asked as he pulled the gray button down over his arms. "What then?"

"Four minutes. You better hurry."

"Fucks sakes."

The SUV had been speeding through alleys and around traffic, nearing the back of Logan Airport and flying through an opened gate into a darkened hangar as it hauled to a stop. Kyle did up his shirt as he pulled on the jeans as well, stopping a moment as he saw the designer label. This was all high-end gear, and perfectly in his size. Whoever was behind this knew him well enough to know. His mind pondered this as he did up the belt and sat down, slipping his feet into the tan Louboutin boots.

But he didn't have much time to think on it, as just as he'd finished fastening the zips on the side of the smooth leather, a movement above him caught his attention.

"You'll need this." Nick handed him an envelope as he glanced up. "Do not open it until instructed."

Kyle took it from him before he shoved it in his pocket as the door to the SUV opened. He was yanked out, the whir of a private jet engine filling the outside space. Men with guns stood at the ready, lining the way to the open ladder door. Kyle put one foot on the steps before he paused and glanced around for a sign, any sign, of someone he knew.

But there was none.

He climbed until he was inside and was met with unfilled space. Not even a stewardess or steward to see to his needs. The pilot poked his head from the cockpit. "Take a seat, buckle up. We leave now."

"You going to tell me where we're going?"

"No questions, Mr. Hansberry."

Kyle rolled his eyes and sat in one of the soft chairs, pulling the seat belt round his lap. His head hurt and he was in no mood for this bullshit. Not to mention he still was bleeding from the gash in his forehead. Just after the private jet leveled out, he took it upon himself to find the bathroom and, hopefully, a first aid kit. He stopped dead as a short, curvy blonde walked out of the door to the cockpit and he blinked, momentarily dumbfounded, as for a split second he thought it was Jennifer.

But it wasn't. Because Jennifer was dead.

"Mr. Hansberry, once you've sorted yourself in the bathroom, I can tend to the wound on your head and check you over. Then we'll get you something to eat and drink."

In the bathroom, he splashed cold water on his face and shook his head. He wondered, well and truly wondered, what the fuck was going on and who the hell was behind this Hollywood escape. It had to be his family. His mother, specifically, because there was no one else it could be. He had no friends, mere acquaintances, and none of those would put themselves out like this for him. The only real friend he had ever had had died a few weeks ago. No, it had to be his mother, and for a split second, he felt a surge of gratitude towards her. That was, until he realized her motives wouldn't have been completely selfless. No doubt unable to face the shame of having a son in prison, she probably thought this was a preferable option.

Out of sight, out of mind. Just like he had been when she'd palmed him off on nannies through his childhood and then shipped him off to boarding school as soon as he was old enough.

He sat back in his chair, and the blonde appeared again. He said nothing as she looked over his wound, examined him and confirmed he at least had a concussion.

"Right," he said, his voice devoid of emotion, "is there anything to drink on this plane?"

"Scotch, coming up."

When she returned, he took the glass a flick of his head in thanks. The first sip rolled over his tongue and he sighed, savoring the taste. It was even more good as it was the first drink he'd had in months, but it was smooth, yet crisp. Burning delightfully as it hit his throat. But there was something else.

It was... familiar.

And then, he realized. It was Nelson Reserve, Jennifer's favorite brand.

Once more, he found himself on the verge of tears. His left hand curved under his nose and ran the length of his face. Ruefully, he looked out the round porthole window at his seat and cried.

* * *

Kyle wasn't sure how long he was in the air, but quite some time later, the wheels were screeching to a halt in a deserted airstrip. It was only then he was told to open the envelope that Nick had thrust into his chest back in Boston. In all honesty, he had forgotten about it, but he leaned forward a little and pulled it out of his back pocket. With a long finger, he tore the flap open. It was a large sum of cash, not US dollars, but bill notes he didn't recognize. Then he pulled the passport from under the bills.

"So, now I'm Canadian." He rolled his eyes and opened it, flicking to the identity page. The picture of him was cleverly doctored, so he sported a thick beard.

"William Randall Jackson." He scoffed, rolling his eyes. "Suppose it could be worse."

His date of birth was the same, so that would be easy to remember if he was asked. And his place of birth was cited as Toronto. *Again, simple.*

"Welcome to Cape Verde, Mr. Jackson."

Kyle blinked as his eyes flicked to the stewardess. "Cape Verde?"

"Islands off the West Coast of Africa," the blonde answered.

"I know where... you know what, never mind."

"Welcome home. Enjoy your new life."

He could that was a dismissal, and he rose to his feet as he was handed a new duffel bag. "Your essentials. Enough to get you through until you're settled."

"Where do I go?"

"The Marina. They'll find you."

"Don't suppose there's any point in me asking

who th*ey* are?" He grumbled as he thought what the fuck else could honestly happen. He figured he'd spent the last seven or eight hours in a somewhat hostage situation, only to be dumped near Africa with absolutely no idea what was going to happen to him.

But he was free...

As the realization washed over him for the first time since he'd been 'liberated', he paused at the steps to the plane and turned to the blond. "Hey, I know you can't tell me who's behind this and, you probably don't know, but... well, if you can, tell them thank you for the concussion."

Nothing was said, just silence and the closing of doors as the jet was refueled and prepared to turn around. On foot and with plenty of swearing, Kyle hoofed it to the marina. As he walked, he learned he was, in fact, in Boa Vista, one of the popular tourist islands, which made up Cape Verde. There were plenty of people, bars, hotels... which meant, he supposed, plenty of crowds to blend in with and get lost in. But he was too exhausted to pay much more attention than that. He was confused as to what the time was too. He swore when he left Boston it was early morning, his trial had been set to kick off around nine. A seven-hour flight put his arrival in Cape Verde at, what, three PM back on the east coast, which meant...

Oh, fuck it, he was asking.

"Hey, what time is it?" He grabbed a bystander to ask.

"Just after eight," the man replied.

Kyle nodded and then asked for the direction of the marina. The man obliged, and with a curt thanking, he set off the way he'd been pointed in. He walked for fifteen minutes, and his mind was wandering once more about the events of the day. He expected now that his face was plastered all over the news back home and wondered if he'd landed on America's Most Wanted list yet.

And then a smirk curled over his face as he thought about Damien's reaction to finding out he'd gone missing. A snort escaped his nose as he could picture the look of utter horror and disgust on his rat-like face.

After another five minutes, he reached his destination and found another man in a suit waiting for him. "Mr. Jackson?"

Not even bothering to ask questions this time, Kyle nodded.

"Follow me please, sir."

Kyle followed the man down the lit boardwalk where he stopped in front of a small but luxurious looking yacht.

"This will take you to your final destination. It's a bit of a long way round but, well, take no chances, huh?"

Kyle grumbled, "whatever, man."

He headed up the ramp and sighed as the comforts of his previous lifestyle came into view. Kyle glanced around the inside cabin which sported a couch, coffee table and a stand up wet bar at the back, all in matching mahogany wood. He could have cried at the thought of a soft bed, comfortable sheets, a proper shower with decent toiletries where he didn't have to watch his back with every lather, rinse and repeat.

"Mr. Jackson?" another voice spoke and he spun to face a man who must have been the same age as his father, give or take. He sported a thick beard, which was graying like his hair and he was dressed in a pair of dark denims, a pale t-shirt and deck shoes.

"I'll be your captain for your trip. We're heading to Santo Antao. It's an overnight journey. We'll be anchoring up just off the coast for a few hours and docking just after ten thirty in the morning."

Kyle frowned, "fourteen hours? Seriously?"

The man shrugged. "I'm just following orders. I was told to keep you off radar, so a night at sea it is."

"Yeah, yeah," Kyle sighed before he looked around once more.

"Bedroom is through there, bathroom to your right and this door behind me leads to the deck if you want to take in the night sky."

Despite himself, that appealed to Kyle. He'd never been one for nature or any shit like that, but after months of being locked away, the thought of sitting in the fresh air with a decent drink was, frankly, heaven.

"There are snacks and a few pre-prepared meals in the fridge. Galley kitchen is through there." His Captain nodded to his left. "Help yourself to whatever you want and don't mind me. I'll be invisible unless you call for me." At that, he tapped at a switch on the wall. "This is the intercom. There's one on deck and one in each room. Just hit one and I'll be with you."

"Okay. Thank you," the phrase felt foreign on his tongue, despite him having uttered it several times in the last hour or so, but he was *t*hankful. But to who, he still had no idea. "Hey, can I ask who's doing all this?"

"Goodnight, Mr. Jackson."

"Take that as a no, then." Kyle snorted. Dropping his bag to the floor, he walked straight to the bar and poured himself a huge measure of scotch before he went in search of the bedroom, intending to dump his bag and then head up into the night air and drink enough to quiet his mind.

Chapter Seven

The stilling of the engines awoke "Mr. Jackson." The boat had taken forever to reach its destination, an agonizingly slow journey out to sea, around some islands and back, stopping just offshore. Captain had left him alone to drink his evening away, a hot meal in his stateroom when he came back in. But Kyle wasn't in the mood for eating, so much was sinking in.

Despite his lonesome nature, he'd never *truly* been on his own. Never had to fend for himself. Even in prison he had a bed, meals three times a day. Now... well, he had no fucking idea where to even start.

Dressing quickly, he'd just pulled on a clean blue polo shirt, which had been in the bag he'd been handed on the plane, when there was a knock on his door.

"Mr. Jackson? No rush at all, sir, but would you care for breakfast before we shuttle you to shore?"

"Uh, yeah, sure." He groaned.

"Of course. It'll be ready in the galley when you see."

He cleared his throat, "thanks."

Kyle took a moment to shake his head and stepped out onto his private deck, the glittering sea below him and an island off the horizon. "What the fuck now?" he said aloud.

"Don't worry," the captain spoke, chuckling. That's where we have come from. Port side is where you're heading. Ten, maybe fifteen minutes or so in the speedboat."

"And that's it? It's over? I'm where I'm just supposed to live and let lie. No one is coming for me?"

"You'll be taken to Porto Novo, the biggest city in Santo Antão. Plenty of bars and hotels for you to find what you're looking for in."

"I doubt that," he mumbled. "I'll eat, now, thanks."

With a nod, the older man nodded and headed off, returning momentarily with a few plates upon which a selection of pastries and cold meats and cheeses were arranged.

"Coffee and champagne are on the way up," he nodded as Kyle sat at the table. "We'll need to get you on the sand by mid-afternoon."

"Sure, whatever." Kyle shrugged.

He ate. He watched the water and ate some more. He sipped his coffee and sipped the fizz, but none of it gave him fulfillment. When through, he showered and changed, a white tee over his body and dark denim over his legs. He fished the cognac colored work boots out of his bag but not before thumbing through the stacks of cash. He wondered exactly how much was all there, where it came from. With his new Aviators on and slicked back hair, scruff from a day or so of not shaving dark on his jawline and cheeks, he descended from his stateroom, duffel in hand.

"Ready?"

"As I'll ever be." Kyle nodded as he was led to the back of the boat. Carefully, he descended off the platform at the back into the waiting speedboat, where his travel companion handed the driver an envelope.

"This is where I leave you, you're in good hands. But if you will, permit me one last piece of advice?"

"Can't hurt," Kyle shrugged.

"Porto Novo is huge, full of tourists and locals alike, but it isn't the biggest of most frequented holiday destination. That said, you want to stay off radar, then stick to the local bars and inns. There's a good one just ten minutes from the chief port along the beach. They should have rooms for a short while until you get your bearings and a chance to figure out your next move. It's called Parley. Doesn't look like much, but it's a safe bet."

"So it's a dive?" Kyle snorted. "Can't say I've seen one of those places."

"Maybe that's the point, besides, they do a damned good scotch. Grab one or two and stay a while." The Captain gave a last nod before he tossed the rope line into the speedboat and pushed them off, the driver pushing the throttle.

Not long later, Kyle was disembarking at the end of a long jetty and blended into a line of people that were snaking their way through the harbor from a ferry which, he assumed, must have arrived from one of the other islands.

And that was it. He was through.

No stumbling blocks at the checkpoint, nothing. It all felt too easy, but he was done worrying about things. Keeping his head down, he followed the crowd away from the small harbor and headed towards what he assumed was some form of town or village square set just back off the shoreline. From there asked a local the direction of Parley, who pointed the way.

He found the inn the Captain had mentioned. The sign was nonexistent and shutters hung off their hinges at the main building. The paint was a sun faded blue and had a thatched roof while the building itself ran along the beach. The whole thing had a dilapidated-looking entry with tiled floors and chipped stucco walls. He stepped inside and immediately went for the bar, slugging his duffel under the sticky wood surface and taking a seat on a creaky, rusted out stool. A small man of African descent approached him and, heavily accented, asked what he'd want to drink.

Kyle hesitated and then shrugged, "I've been told you do a good scotch."

The man nodded and took a moment to speak to another patron before he started Kyle's order. He slid the amber liquid over to Kyle, who picked it up and sniffed it suspiciously. Then, with a loud exhale, he necked it in one.

It burned his throat, pleasantly he may add. And he made a noise of appreciation.

"Good?" The bartender chuckled.

"Uh, yeah," he shrugged. "I'll take another."

"Want me to leave the bottle?"

He thought for a second, "yep."

The bartender placed the bottle down and Kyle picked it up. "Hey, I was told there might be a room available?"

"There was, but someone took it this morning," the man replied apologetically. Then, as Kyle placed a pile of notes in the bar, he licked his lips and leaned forward a little, "let me see what I can do."

"You do that." Kyle replied, pouring himself another finger of the spirit he'd been served.

He only saw her profile, at first anyway. But it was enough to make him look twice. The curve of her nose and chin, high set cheek bone which was visible as her bobbed dark hair curled behind her ear.

With a hard blink, he shot back more. Then, as he glanced around the worst bar, he'd probably ever stepped into, he caught the glance of a woman at the opposite end.

The woman he stared at watched him, raised her own glass to salute him and threw back her drink in one go. He continued to stare as she stood and turned to go. He noticed the way she looked back at him over her shoulder, then carried on.

His heart was beating so fast in his chest. But, until that moment, he'd convinced himself he was seeing things.

He necked that and then, he frowned. He looked at the bottle, the weight of it in his hand. The label. It was familiar, the taste again more so. It was the same scotch as the plane. The same he'd shared with....

And then he saw it.

That Sanskrit ink stood out like a beacon and he felt his chest constrict, a feeling he'd never experienced washed over him and he fought back whatever it was as he tossed back the last of his drink and nearly leaped from the stool to chase her down.

It was forceful, angry almost, bruising even, pushing the two of them inside with a kick to the door. His hands grabbed her face, holding her to him as he aggressively dipped his tongue into her mouth, savoring her, as if he were gentle she'd vanish. When her hands wrapped around his forearms, he snapped back and pulled away, heavy breaths between the two of them.

He followed her across the dingy bar and through a small door at the back, over which a shabby sign was hung, telling him this was for residential guests only.

"I thought..." Kyle swallowed hard, his voice thick with emotion, "they said you were dead."

"You're free," Jennifer replied, her own voice cracking.

He grabbed her when he caught up to her, the palm of his hand closing over her bicep, turning her to face him just as she opened the door to a room. She spun, green meeting blue, and he gasped before instinct took over and his lips were on hers.

"Jennifer, I don't... why?"

"It had to be this way or the consequences would have been far worse," she implied, standing in the same spot.

"Tell me why," he begged in frustration, turning to her, caging her in, both his hands against the wall at her shoulders.

"You know why," she said, eyes scanning his.

This had become their ruse, neither able to say the words directly. He'd started it, saying 'she knew why' years ago. But until now, he couldn't even admit to it himself. He couldn't say it, yet he felt the words strangling him, so instead he just latched onto her lips in force. His weight pinned her to the wall, her hands fisting in the white tee that clung to his body in the humidity. The sun was setting outside, but neither paid any mind to it. An enormous hand cupped her face, fingers splayed through her hair, thumb pressing into her cheek as Kyle kissed her. He wanted her, but he hated her, angry at the plot that unraveled beneath his watch, but sheer need was gripping him from months of deprivation. His knee pushed between her legs, spreading them apart, his thick thigh pressing against her to keep her there in his assault.

"You lied to me," he ground out as his lips painted across her neck.

"I had to. There was no other way."

"I thought you were fucking dead," Kyle stated angrily, pulling away from her.

"I am, officially..." she shrugged, "just like you. By now, your body is burned to unidentifiable..."

"How? Who?"

"I know people too, Kyle. People who want me to live a happy life. With people I...."

She stopped dead and looked at him. Kyle's eyes searched hers, still not daring to believe this was true. That it had been her all along.

In desperation to feel her, be sure this wasn't a dream he was about to wake up from, finding himself back in that shit hole cell, he kissed her.

She was petite under his grasp, ways so light but never frail. She was fierce, mighty, and one hell of a good time. He enjoyed that about her. She could be just enough of a vile fuck when he needed it or soft and caring when he was suffering. She knew how to gauge him, even from the beginning. It's what made their arrangement work for so long, right until the end. Now, it was a free for all, nothing to weigh them down or tear them apart. No circle of friends, no pressing matters or obnoxious family. No obligations, just them.

"Kyle," Jennifer gasped as he hit that spot only he knew about, where her jaw connected at her ear and neck. He bit down on her skin, where he'd normally kiss or suck away at her sensitive spot. "I... I had..." she tried to manage, but his lips silenced her.

His free hand gripped the back of her knee and hoisted her leg around this hip, his weight pressing even further into her. She had nowhere to go, to get free, and she didn't want to. Something in her snapped, breaking open a dam wide enough to swallow the sea. Her hands grabbed his face, trying to control something, and he growled at her advance, releasing her leg and pinning her hands above her against the peeling paint of the old hut. Her hands were easily cuffed by one of his. She didn't struggle, she never did. He pulled at the shoulder ties of her sundress and then her panties, what thin material there was, it all pooling at their feet. His free hand then undid the button of his jeans, pulling free his desperate and throbbing cock. The whole time his lips were against hers, tongues violently clashing, a mix of anger and pain coming from him and she took it all in stride, fully aware and capable of stopping him if she chose.

Jennifer felt the breath leave her lungs as he thrust hard and deep into her. Kyle expressed a deep, guttural moan as he felt her already constricting around him. His cock pulsed inside of her, the feeling of being so full still leaving her struggling for breath. Her back scratched against the rough stucco of the wall. Kyle let go of her hands he'd pinned above her and Jennifer gripped his shoulders as she tried to move against him. His head was collapsed against her chest, deep nose breaths inhaling her scent. She pulled at the fabric of his shirt and he slipped it over his head and to the floor, all while still pinning her against the wall, cock balls deep inside her. He thrust his hips upward, sliding in and out of her just a little, and she mewled. Again and again he moved like that, eyes boring into hers, less angry with each passing thrust.

It was months since they'd done this, and whilst Kyle felt that time, he hadn't. Her hair was different, skin more tan, but she was the same. The same sassy, strong, take shit from no one woman he'd first fucked in the cloakroom at the country club.

She felt so good against his body, the way her smooth skin slid against his.

Kyle raised his head to look at her, his heavy arms holding her up against the wall, still fully seated inside her. The look on his face broke her. Never in their entire relationship had she ever seen what she saw now. The hard lines of his face were smooth, eyebrows slightly raised in what appeared to be fear or worry. Stunning and nearly always cold blue eyes stared back at her, pooling in salty tears, red from the sting of emotions he desperately tried to hide. Even his breaths shuddered against her touch as her thumbs ghosted over his strong cheekbones. A flare of his nostrils and a blink and you'll miss its quiver of his bottom lip left her near speechless.

Their moans were filthy with each hard go. He was close, so fucking close, and if he went any faster, they'd both fall through the wall and spill out into the hall.

"I know," she said.

And the damn broke, Kyle Hansberry sobbed for what could have possibly been the first time since childhood. Their bodies sank to the floor, her body running along the wall, his still with her. She kept her legs wrapped around his waist as he kneeled, her hips situated just over his, his weight pinning her against the barren wall. His hands curled into her flesh, sobs wracking his large build, while her delicate hands ran over his shoulders and into his hair, cradling him, soothing him.

About the time her fingers grazed at the hair at the nape of his neck, she was writhing, just ready to spill over the edge of desire and again Kyle latched a rough bite to her spot and she came hard, him spilling into her right behind her. Both crying out in release, bodies shaking from an invisible chill between them. Her chest heaved against him, silence filling the room aside from deep breaths. His forehead was pressed hard against the swell of her breasts, sweat glistening off of them both in the setting sun filling the room.

After a while, his body became heavy and Jennifer had thought he'd cried himself to sleep while still holding her, but as she moved to unsheathe himself from deep inside her, to allow her body to recoup fully, he squeezed her frame. She leaned back only a little and held his tired face in her hands. She pressed her full lips to his forehead and brushed away the strands of hair that were astray. Kyle took a deep breath, conscious of the tears streaking down his face. He gave a little huff and jerked out of her reach a little, causing Jennifer to arch her brow.

"So, is this flea pit where you've been living since... you 'died'? Because, not being funny, Jennifer, I bet even the cockroaches have given up and moved out."

She tearfully snorted, "Yeah, no. It was just for the night to find you."

"Right."

"I wasn't sure what time you'd be coming ashore, and... well, it's a brief drive into the hills."

"The hills?"

"Yeah, it's... my place. It's a long story but, I'll explain on the way. I promise you it's safe, well guarded."

"Who are you?" He touted.

"Yours." She whispered, brushing back the strand of stray brown hair that hung over his eyes.

Kyle swallowed, "Jennifer, I..."

"I know. You don't need to say anything."

He wanted to, he really wanted to. But the words just

wouldn't come. Instead, he kissed her again, holding her to him.

She didn't need to say anything, she stood, albeit on shaky legs and moved toward the decrepit bathroom in her room, the door hanging off its hinge and all he could hear was the shower running. As Kyle stood, his body felt like it weighed a ton, his mind throbbing, his eyes stinging against the remnants of his emotional outcry. He kicked off his boots, stripped away the remaining clothes he had on, and joined her.

Their shower was silent, Jennifer taking care of him, standing on her toes to run her fingers through his wet hair, long fingers and delicate hands massaging soapy lines into his back. He kissed her, slow and soft. He kissed her lips; he kissed her neck, his thick fingers traced his own lines across her skin, in places like from her shoulders down to her hands where he joined his with hers and wrapped their arms around her frame, pulling her close to him, his bare chest against her back, her ass lining up with the top of his endowment.

Emotionally exhausted and bodies drained, they ended up in bed, not a thing in their bellies, but the scotch consumed at the bar and Kyle's patisserie breakfast.

* * *

It wasn't planned that way, but Jennifer had pointed

out driving in such an emotional state wasn't a great idea for either of them. Kyle fell asleep first, his bitching and whining about the state of the scratchy bed covers fell silent after about sixty seconds as they lay wrapped up around one another on the lumpy mattress.

It was some hours later she woke, alone. The room was silent, the only sound the waves hitting the rocks and shore of the nearby cave.

Slipping back into her dress from earlier, Jennifer followed the breeze and found Kyle slouched against the stucco wall, the night sea behind him.

Jennifer traced lines on his skin, soothing her own heavy eyes into sleep, her mind clear for the first time in absolute ages.

Kyle's side of the bed was cold, like he'd been gone for a while. And Jennifer's mind was half right to play a trick on her, wondering if she'd dreamed about their reunion. She sat up and looked around, finding remnants of him nearby.

It was then she noticed the dirty, tatty curtains flapping in the night sea breeze, the doors to the little balcony area open.

"Kyle?" Her eyes slid to the near empty bottle of liquor in his hand, which he must have gotten from the bar.

He didn't speak, hell he barely looked at her. His face screwed up as he drunkenly sobbed, not so silently anymore as she'd found him.

His boots, his shirt, the duffel the bartender had dropped inside the door while the two of them were occupied in the shower. But where was he?

"Oh, Kyle.." she dropped to her knees next to him, "what... I thought we were okay? We went over why I did it, I told you how and who... what's-"

He shook his head, "I did it." He sobbed. "I did it. I'm... I'm so sorry. I'm sorry. I did it. I killed him. I killed Dillan. I did this."

"I know, I know you did." Her right hand settled between his shoulders. Her left reached for his, which was hanging in front of his knee, his elbow and forearm resting on his thigh. "I've always known."

"What?" He grimaced a little as he took a drink from the bottle in his right hand.

"Selfish, I'm such a selfish bastard. I killed my father. Because of money."

"Faced with the same revelation you were that night when Dillan told you he was cutting you off, I don't believe for a second anyone else in your family would have behaved differently."

His expression barely flickered a change, but his eyes softened a little and his nostrils flared. He closed his mouth to take another pull, but she stopped him, taking the bottle and setting it down. Then he whispered, "I hurt you."

"Yeah, you did." Jennifer looked at him. "I will not sit

here and sugarcoat what you did, because you did it. But I will tell you one thing."

"What do you mean?"

"I let you go. When that prick slipped a ring on your finger. I should have told you to stay that morning. If you had, then... maybe I wouldn't ... I'm so sorry. I'm sorry for Dillan, for my family, for putting you through all this. I ruined your life." He broke.

Jennifer moved and wrapped her arms around him, holding him to her. As his face pressed into her neck, her hand cradled the back of his head. "Shhh, it's okay. It's okay."

"I'm sorry. I'm sorry." The words repeated over and over as he cried. Thirty years of ignored and pent-up emotions, repressed feelings and circumstances all because he was a spoiled little rich kid who became the grown up trust fund prick and didn't have to ever care to do anything or live for himself, all came pouring out of him.

Jennifer could do nothing but hold him, soothing him as he sobbed, his body shaking as he clung to her.

"I love you," the words spilled from his lips in a broken cry.

Jennifer stilled, swallowing as the words registered. She pulled back to look at him, her hands cupping his face.

"I know," she whispered, because she did. She knew, although he had never admitted it out loud. She knew, because she had never said it either. But she did.

"I love you. I'm so fucking sorry." His hands came to cup her face.

"I love you, too."

"Shhh, it's okay. I know..." her lips brushed his before she reiterated her earlier declaration. "I love you."

"Please forgive me," he replied against her skin.

He pulled back as far as he could to see her face, the sincerity, the warmth. A caring comfort that exuded from her he felt deep inside him.

"I do, I do." She repeated. "I always have."

They watched the sunrise that morning, the warmth of its dawn rays on their skin. And when he felt tired again, Kyle helped Jennifer up, pulling her by his hands into his arms.

His eyes burned, his throat itched, and he felt clammy, like he'd broken a fever sweat. His tee and jeans clung to him, his bare feet pressing into the cracked ground.

"Let's change and go home," Jennifer whispered. "We'll figure it all out from there."

He merely nodded, "home."

A nice car came to collect them thirty minutes later. With his duffel in the trunk, his eyes roamed the scenery, taking in the situation. They said nothing as the black car meandered through the narrow roads along the coast, winding inland and upward towards the cliffs.

After an hour drive, it came to a stop outside a set of large, steel gates. The driver punched in a code and they swung open to reveal a large, modern, glass sided house built into the hillside.

"Okay, what the hell?" His voice rasped, tired from the day before. The strain of it all. His brain hurt, and not just from the hangover.

Jennifer smiled a little. "This is home, for me, for you... If you want it."

She climbed out of the car, and Kyle followed, looking around. She's explained to him already about her godfather and he assumed this was also by his hand.

"So, err..." he moved behind Jennifer, who was standing, shielding her eyes against the sun as she looked out over the ocean, "it got a pool?"

"Yeah," she sighs. "Infinity, out back. Third floor master suite looks out over the cliff."

"Suppose I could get used to it." His hands dropped to her hips.

"If not, we'll arrange something anywhere you want."

"Jen," he sighed, "that was a joke."

"I know, but..." She turned in his arms, "Look, I'll be the first to admit, I don't know how to do this relationship stuff, if that's what it even is. And Kyle, you can always go. You don't have to stay here with me. If you want a life of your own, because you tire of whatever..."

He cut her off with a deep kiss.

"Can we just not? I don't want to think so far ahead. I just..." his arms wrapped around her as he smiled, a soft and genuine smile, "I just want to live. Be happy, make you happy."

"Make me happy?" She chuckled, "careful, Kyle, you're losing yourself."

He shrugged. "I lost myself a long time ago, sweetheart."

"A day at a time then," Jennifer didn't know what to say to his admission. But she quite liked the 'sweetheart'.

"Well," his hands pulled her closed, "why don't you show me around, so I can make myself at home?"

Chapter Eight

It was late, that much Jennifer knew. She'd woken when she realized Kyle wasn't in bed and his side was barely warm. Padding down to the second floor of the house, the main living space with the wide open floor plan, Jennifer found him in the kitchen, standing at the stove with the hood light on.

"Kyle..."

"Princess?"

"It's late, what are doing up?"

"Couldn't sleep, and I was hungry."

"Real food will do that," Jennifer wrapped her arms around him, her hands splayed over his chest while her cheek pressed into his back after she kissed his spine. "Why couldn't you sleep?"

"Don't know," Kyle replied, "maybe I miss the clanging

and drips coming from hundred-year-old pipes or the concrete slab that masqueraded as a mattress."

Sarcasm laced through his tone, and Jennifer chuckled against his bare back. She then stepped away to lean against the counter's edge. "You're burning it. The fire is too high."

"Oh, shit."

She giggled and took over, "what do you want to eat?" She turned and dumped the burnt eggs down the sink.

"Now you're awake... you."

"Kyle!"

"What?"

"You said you were hungry."

"Well, now I'm hungry for something else."

"Yeah?"

"Yeah..."

"Like?" Jennifer turned off the burner and pushed the pan away from the edge.

Kyle gripped her hips and pivoted so she was between him and the counter. "Hop up there and spread 'em, sweetheart, and I'll show you."

Jennifer licked her lips as her mouth dropped open just a little. She palmed the edge of the counter and hopped up backwards, the thin strap of her silk nightgown falling to drape over her shoulder. Kyle's hands fell to her knees, pushing her legs apart. Her skin, now more sun kissed than ever, was so smooth under his touch. His lips met hers, noses brushing. "I love you."

The words still made her heart beat wildly and her insides twist in delightful knots, "I know," her breath fanned his face.

He chuckled a little before he dropped to his knees and pulled her to the edge of the counter.

"Oh, you're just going to.... Oh." Jennifer slowly tossed her head back as her eyes rolled closed. "Fuck," she squeaked while Kyle wasted no time in licking at her folds.

"I told you," he muttered in between laps, "I'm hungry."

"Oh fuck, right there... Yes," the little scruff he'd grown out in the last few days felt delicious against her soft inner thigh skin and outer petals. He kept at her, relentlessly, the way he always did. Her heels dug into the blades of his shoulders. "Shit baby, I'm going to, oh yeah, Kyle..."

Kyle groaned as he felt her cum, her legs jerking, knees clamping round his ears. "Fuck, sweetheart, you taste so good," he kissed into her as she rode out that high.

"Fuck, Kyle..."

"Oh, we're going to," he nipped at her knee. "I need you, Jen. I'm so hard, sweetheart."

"Come here... "

He stood, pulling himself out of his gray sweatpants and stroked his hard cock a few times before lining himself up, his tip and leaking head rubbing against Jennifer's clit. With a tilt of his hips, he buried himself straight to the hilt. His forehead fell to her shoulder as her nails raked up and over his neck, into his hair. Both groaned at the fit, her tightness and his girth.

"Fuck," he pulled back and thrust again.

"Again," Jennifer whimpered.

Kyle sunk into her shoulder as he resisted just railing her there. He was already throbbing inside her. He looked down at where they were joined and watched himself slide out and fast thrust forward. His hands gripped at her thick hips.

"Jesus fucking Christ," he groaned, "fuck, you take me so well."

"Turn me around," Jennifer moaned. "Soft later."

"Fuck..." Kyle pulled out and grabbed her, yanking her off the counter. Spinning her around, he gripped the back of her neck and pushed so she was bent over in front of him. Giving her ass a good rub, he spread her cheeks before sliding fast back into her warmth.

Jennifer's hands splayed over the Italian marble as he piled drove into her. Then she arched her back and the change in angle made Kyle's cock rub against her soft spot. His big hand grabbed at her hair, pulling her back just a little more.

"Don't stop," Jennifer begged.

He kept going and going, the warmth in the pit of his

belly and balls becoming hard to ignore. "Jen, baby, I'm close."

Jennifer reached down to palm her clit, and in doing so opened her two fingers over where his dick slid in and out of her hole, adding extra friction to his shaft.

"Holy..." he choked on the curse, "I can't... I can't last much longer."

The heel of her palm pushed harder at her own nub as she squeezed her fingers against him. "Please."

"I'm going to... fuck, Jen, I'm going to cum."

"Oh fuck yes, please," she squeezed at him again.

With a growl, Kyle bit down on the back of her shoulder as he blew, his knees trembling. She went on the cusp of his, her second overtaking her with a cry as Jennifer dropped her weight to the counter. Kyle's chest heaved against her silk clothed back, but she could feel his heartbeat against her.

"Jesus," Kyle breathed out against her shoulder, kissing his bite mark with good intentions.

"Still hungry?" She panted.

"Nope." He chuckled. "I'm going to take you to bed, then we're going to go slow."

"Good, because we got all night."

"No, we have forever."

His lips kissed up her neck, nipping at the hinge of her jaw as she sighed, "yeah we do."

He carried her to bed, the moon dancing on the ocean

below. The night, however late it was, glistened with stars. And Kyle kept good on his word, taking things slow with pure delight.

* * *

Jennifer was up first the next morning, Kyle clearly exhausted from the last forty-eight hours. Leaving him be, she wandered into the kitchen and set the coffee going, whilst she moved to the large windows and looked down at the view below her.

It was set to be a beautiful day, a little on the cooler side and breezy, but it would make for a good chance to head to the market and show Kyle around a bit.

It was important that they kept their cover stories up. Jennifer Hannigan was now known as Vanessa Barrowman, a wealthy socialite who had inherited this house in the hills from an uncle who died. She had recently moved here to escape her family trauma, her Canadian Boyfriend to follow soon. To keep things as normal as possible, Jennifer had made sure she had been to the little villages and towns around the area, so as not to appear aloof. She knew that if she stayed hidden away, it would attract more attention; locals would make up their own stories about who she was.

She had to admit to herself, as she looked out over the ocean, she was shocked this had all worked. It wasn't that she hadn't trusted her godfather, far from it as clearly she'd trust him with her life. But the fact that she had Kyle with her and that part of the plan, as wild as it was, had actually worked. Now they just had to navigate how they settled in to life with one another.

It made Jennifer smirk, living a life with Kyle. In fact, it made her laugh. That man, no doubt, had never lived with anyone outside his parents in his entire life. A revolving door of women and staff, country club bunnies and memberships, high end clothes and cars, a life of a privileged bachelor, a trust fund prick. He was in for a rude awakening if he hadn't already noticed. And the only thing that worried Jennifer was if he could cope.

That said, he had no choice. They had staff; a security team and a housekeeper- a local lady by the name of Mrs. Renley - who worked Monday to Friday and did the cleaning and general housekeeping chores. But other than that, no one. There was no chef, no regular driver, no personal assistant. Just them.

"I can hear you thinking all the way from our bedroom upstairs," Kyle rasped as he approached her from behind. His shadowed stubble beard rubbed at her bare shoulder as she kept her gaze forward.

"How much Portuguese do you know?" Jennifer wondered aloud.

"The total of fuck all."

"Better learn," she sighed. "It's hard, like a dirty Spanish, but you can do it."

"Why the fuck do I need to learn? Everyone speaks English."

"Not everyone, it's the primary language here, and we're fitting in," she turned in his arms. "Kyle, this life is not like the one you're used to. I told you, no staff outside the security team and Mrs. Renley, our caretaker." She smirked. "I cook, I shop, there's no personal assistant, we hardly drive...." She sighed. "So, like I said, if this isn't what you want, I can arrange for more suitable options for you. But this is our lives now."

"Yeah, I get it, no more spoiled little rich brat." He rolled his eyes, almost as if he was bored with the statement.

"I'll spoil you when and where it counts." Jennifer leaned up on the balls of her feet and pressed her lips into his. "I can get used half naked you walking around the house every morning. Just, maybe, keep the beard." She rubbed her palm over his cheek before stepping back towards the kitchen. "Grow it out a little."

"The beard? Why?"

She just smirked over her shoulder. "I like it."

"It itches," he groaned.

Jennifer popped a shoulder and passed a mug of coffee his way. "Go check out the rest of the house. You've seen most of it. There's a gym off the pool deck and I'll have breakfast ready soon."

"Okay." Kyle took the mug and watched her head off before he strolled over the pale tiles that spanned the entire open plan downstairs of the house and headed out to the pool area. He shivered a little. It wasn't as warm as it looked, but still a damned sight better than Boston had been.

He sipped from his mug as he looked around. The infinity pool stretched the length of the patio, its edge spilling into the view. His gray sweatpants kissed the stone under his bare feet and he made a note he needed slippers. He ran his free hand over his longer locks and scratched at his beard. He smirked, thinking quickly of Jennifer's comment about liking it. Maybe he would grow it out. Just maybe.

The last forty-eight hours were a blur for the man in his thirties. He was broken out of prison, escorted across the world in a plane and on a yacht and now he was sitting pretty and free in a hillside mansion, so to speak, with the hopes of a carefree rest of his life.

He knew he should feel freaked out. Freaked out at having to take on a whole new public personal, at having to leave his entire life and home behind. He should also feel sadness, guilt even, at what his family would think, and that he would never see them again.

But he didn't.

For the first time that Kyle could ever remember in his entire life, he felt free. Free from the stresses, expectations and assumptions people made about him and his life. There was no one weighing him down, no asshole friends offering him a line, no gold digging dolly birds warming his bed for a night before he kicked them out, no family telling him he was a waste of space or time.

It was only now he could see that life for what it was-toxic. He'd thought it was what he wanted, acting like a playboy with no cares in the world.

But he *had* cared, which was what had driven him to do what he did. He saw that now.

And understanding it was liberating.

He gave a shake of his head and walked back towards the doors off the pool deck. He slipped into the gym and found all the basic needs, from weights and machines, to bikes and ellipticals, two each. There was even a boxing bag and balloon. He could see himself spending time here. In fact, he could see himself spending time anywhere now. He wondered if he'd get bored, not having enough to keep himself occupied.

But that thought flew from his mind when he realized he could do anything he wanted, within reason.

No one knew him.

Hell, he could even write if he wanted to. A secret passion he never devoted much time to before, as he'd never seen the point. Everyone would have just laughed. Well, everyone bar his dad, maybe.

The thought of Dillan closed his throat up and pulled at his chest. There was pain there he was going to have to learn to deal with, guilt that would eat at him until he knew how to displace it and cope, but that would take time.

And, in a twisted way, he almost welcomed it now. His penance for the shit he'd done it made him feel human.

"Kyle?" Jennifer's voice echoed off the bare walls. "Breakfast..."

"Coming," he called back, and after a last look around, he headed back into the house.

After breakfast, the two showered and changed. Kyle wondering if Jennifer would ever go back to her blonde hair again to which she smiled and said "maybe in time".

Dressed in denims and lightweight jackets with tees, sunglasses and a hat for Kyle, Jennifer forced him down the drive and out to the road for a walk into the small village where she frequented the outside market there.

"I don't suppose this market sells laptops?" He sarcastically questioned as they walked along the path.

"Uh, no, but if you need or want one, we can get you one. We have no phones either, in case you haven't noticed." She smirked. "Why?"

"Promise not to laugh?" He asked, his hand taking hers.

Playfully, Jennifer smirked, relishing in the way his fingers locked with hers, a gesture from him she wasn't used to, "not entirely." She giggled.

"Then I'm not saying."

She squeezed his hand. "Hey, lighten up. I'm just kidding. I can be a sarcastic brat, okay?"

"I want to write." His voice was a little quiet, childlike even, as he spoke the words in a hurry.

"Write? About what?" She inquired, her voice giving a hunt of intrigue as her eyes couldn't express it.

"Don't know, whatever takes my fancy, grabs my imagination. I err, I took a creative writing module when I was at college. Thought it might fill my days a little."

"Okay," she nodded. "Let's see what we can find."

"You know, after you died, they made me see a shrink." Kyle kept his eyes focused forward. "Old bastard wanted me to start a fucking journal of my feelings."

"How did that work out?"

His face shot her a glare. Through his shades and cap, she could sense his blue eyes. She smiled, "we're almost there." She nodded towards the village as it came into view.

"So, what are we buying?"

"Hope you like fish," she laughed. "Just some simple stuff. It's more just to show you around, give us something to do for a while."

"I like fish, actually." He chuckled.

"Good. It's a staple here. This village has a lot of the staples of the island, but if we want more of the imported goods, we'll have to head to the port."

"Steak?"

"We can track it down," Jennifer chuckled.

Kyle gave a nod as they rounded the corner, and Jennifer led him through many little streets until they reached the market square.

Stands were set up with fares and offerings, from produce to seafood, chickens and eggs, spices and herbs, and various knick-knack offerings and handmade items. Kyle let Jennifer lead him round, as she examined various pieces of fruit and veg. She handed him a handful of some random nut and dried fruit mix, which was actually pretty good. He nodded, and she smiled, buying a bag before they moved on to the next.

However, it didn't take long before annoyance set in and sighs began. An hour into it and a heavy bag later, Kyle was leaning into Jennifer's ear and whispering, "when can we go? My feet hurt."

"Stop it!" She chided him, "I just need the ingredients to make the pasta for the ravioli you requested and then I'll take you for a frozen margarita."

"They have a bar?" He said.

"Oh, this is going to be a rough first few weeks," she joked with a sigh. "Yes, they have a bar. A snappy little one here and several in port."

"Hey, I'm trying, okay?"

"It's only been half a day, but I know you are," she cupped his cheek and sighed. She turned back to the cassava and flour purveyor and spoke in Portuguese about how much she needed in weight and when she was handed back her items, she paid and they walked on.

"How do we get expendable cash?" Kyle asked.

"We have a safe, an allowance. Inside the safe, just in case we need it, is an envelope like the one they gave you on the plane. Two new identities and an undisclosed location. I'm told we won't need it. It's just in case."

"So, we're still rich?"

"For this part of the world," she looked at him, "filthy. But we have to live with means. Budget. Nothing extravagant."

"Define extravagant."

"You won't be seeing the yacht again," she snorted. "Outside of the staff and house, we're well off. The staff are paid well, very well. And we don't have to worry about anything, I'm told. Don't ask questions, don't draw attention."

"Oh, okay."

"Why?"

"Just wondering. What I'm supposed to do, for clothes and stuff... taking you out, dates and all that romantic shit I don't know."

Jennifer laughed. "You have a closet full in the house,

as you know. Like I said, we get an allowance. Cash shows up on the counter each week. What's in the safe is for emergencies and if we have to split for any reason. Don't worry about the romantic stuff, I know that's not you, it never has been. There's no country club to bill or fancy restaurants. The Port is where all the tourists go, so we'll figure it out. There's places there for things if we want. I know you don't know how to date any more than I do. But I think we're sort of past that now, don't you?"

Kyle gave a shrug. "I guess."

"What?" Jennifer took his hand this time, while her other passed the canvas grocery bag off to him.

"Nothing doesn't matter. Are we done now?"

"I hope out of all of this, you find yourself, Kyle, that you learn to open up. And you can open up with me." Jennifer dropped his hand. "We're done. I promised you a drink. Come on."

Kyle sighed as he followed her across the square, "hey, Jennifer, sorry I'm just... I don't know what I am, other than shit at all this."

She popped a shoulder, "me too. So leave it at that."

She led him to the opposite end of the village, a literal shack on the edge of the road where it sat looking over the cliffs like their house did. A few machines of swirling, icy liquid sat on a makeshift counter like they did at mini-marts and gas stations stateside.

"Ah! I see Mr. Jackson has finally arrived." A thin man

with mixed skin smiled at her from behind the counter. He spoke with a Portuguese-English accent and a bright smile.

"Hi, Sam."

Sam smiled and held his hand out for Kyle, who shook it.

"Can we get two please, Sam?" Jennifer ordered.

"Absolutely, with the extra special?"

"Sure." She smiled.

"What's the extra special?" Kyle asked.

"More tequila." Jennifer smiled. "They're weak coming from the machine."

"Oh..." Kyle chuckled

"There's a great bar round the corner too, local joint, popular, has all these Portuguese liquors. A few brandies you'd like."

Sam passed their margaritas over and left the two alone.

"Sounds good. Maybe we can take a trip there one evening then." He nodded, smiling as he took a sniff of the frozen drink in front of him. "Okay, I can smell the special."

Jennifer grinned and took a dip. "Perfect as always, Sam."

Sam chuckled and tipped her a wink before he moved over to serve two other customers.

Together and calmly, Kyle and Jennifer sat at the bar,

looking out at the water and horizon. They said nothing, each lost in their own thoughts.

Jennifer had her hands resting on the table, her glass between them when fingers danced across her forearm and pulled her right hand away from the drink. Those same fingers laced with hers and gave a squeeze. She turned her head with a smirk, but Kyle wasn't looking at her.

He was looking forward still, "not a word." He whispered.

"You know," she looked down at their joined hands, "if you really wanted to try the whole date thing, there are some nice places to eat at the port and I'm sure some hidden places are in and around the village. I'm sorry I shut you down so quickly before. It was mean of me."

"I'm going to disappoint you, I'm going to piss you off and you're going to want me to fucking leave," Kyle admitted. "I'm half expecting it. I'm going to fuck this up a million times before I get it right."

"Kyle, that's not going to happen." Jennifer looked at him, shaking her head. "I mean what I said. I'm sorry I shut you down. Truth is, I'm just as useless at it as you are. So, we can fuck up together."

And fuck it up, they did.

Their first month together was littered with bickering and annoyances. Fights and frustrations infiltrated their relationship at least once a week if not twice over and a few times there were slamming of doors and sleeping separately. But they were working the kinks out.

Kyle was the hardest. He knew it, but his spoiled tendencies would pop in every once in a while, and Jennifer would snap. On more than one occasion, she reminded him she wasn't his mother, whore, slave or maid and that Mrs. Renley wasn't his personal chef, assistant or keeper.

At one point, he stormed from the house and headed down to the village. By the time he reached there, he was full of a shame and guilt he couldn't ever remember having felt before about the way he had spoken to someone. With a sigh, he beelined for a flower stall, bought a bunch and returned, handing them over to Mrs. Renley, along with an uncharacteristic apology.

After that, the kind woman made sure he was okay, and Kyle learned a valuable lesson; that treating people well got you further than treating them like shit.

It wasn't all him, though. Jennifer could be just as snappy and bitchy, and she learned fast that he didn't like being spoken to like a child. She was used to her own space, so was he, something neither of them really had the luxury of that now.

But it was Kyle, to her surprise, that solved that issue, bringing up his solution early one morning when neither could sleep.

"Fishing? You're serious?"

"Dad used to take me a lot when I was younger." He popped a shoulder, speaking of a fond memory of Dillan, "figured I could give it a whirl. I can even clean and gut."

"You can do all that?" Jennifer smirked. "You, Michael Kyle Hansberry, can fish?"

"Yes, I can!" He rolled his eyes, the use of his full name no longer bothering him, "we did a lot of outdoors shit. Before Layla and Jason packed me off to boarding school. Was never the same then."

"Okay."

"What? You don't believe me?" He arched a brow, an amused expression on his face.

"No, absolutely not. It's not that at all. I'm just a little surprised." Jennifer smirked. "Tell you what, if you gut and clean, descale and all, I will cook whatever it is you catch tonight for dinner."

"Deal."

That night they dined on red snapper with fresh boiled buttered potatoes and a salad with a light dressing. Kyle prepared the seven fish he'd caught, gave one to Mrs. Kyle, and the remaining four after they'd eaten were frozen for another day.

"I have to say, I'm impressed," Jennifer sighed with a full stomach.

"I found a nice spot," Kyle sat back with his crisp white wine in hand, "and got chatting to a few locals. There's more to be caught out to sea, so... maybe if I get to know them a bit better, I can hitch a ride."

"Well, you look the part," she chuckled as she took in his appearance.

His hair was still the same, swept back off his face in the style it had always been in since she'd known him, but his once clean-shaven face now sported a full, thick beard. His skin was slightly more than thanks to the warmer, early summer sun, but it was in his eyes she saw the biggest change.

They sparkled with a happiness she couldn't remember seeing before. It made him look younger, more carefree. The thought made her smile at him from across their small table. She looked at him with soft eyes, a glitter of happiness in her own stare.

"I love you," she said out of the blue.

Kyle swallowed his wine, a soft smile on his face. "I love you too"

"I have something for you," she scooted her chair back and left her napkin on the table, retreating to a drawer in the end table next to the couch. With a bashful smile, Jennifer returned with a brown paper wrapped gift and handed it to Kyle.

He looked a little surprised, but took it with a thanks and unwrapped it.

"For your thoughts or that book you want to write," Jennifer said as she stood next to him.

"Jen, it's great." He smiled, looking up at her. "Thank you, sweetheart."

He placed the leather-bound journal on the table and, with an athletic arm round her waist; he pulled her onto his lap.

"You're welcome." She whispered as she ran her fingers through his beard. "I know it's not a laptop, but..."

"It doesn't matter," he shook his head, kissing her. "It's perfect."

"There's a big summer storm coming in tomorrow. They're pretty impressive to watch from here, I'm told. What shall we do?"

"Wine, popcorn and watch the show." He shrugged, his large hand rubbing up and down her back.

"I like that plan. I told Mrs. Renley not to come tomorrow, and to wait until it passes. No one will be here. It's not particularly safe."

"But we're okay here... right?"

"Yeah, it's just heavy rain, thunder, lightning, crazy winds. Inside we're just fine, handsome."

"I love it when you call me that. It boosts my little ego."

"Oh baby, I don't. Your ego has ever been small."

He chuckled, his eyes looking out over the ocean. "Thank you."

Her hand scratched at the back of his neck, his hair falling between her fingers. "For?"

"My life."

"Oh, Kyle."

He looked up at Jen and let out a deep breath. "I mean it. I'd be rotting in a cell now if it wasn't for you, deservedly I may add. I don't deserve any of this. I see that now."

Jennifer leaned forward and kissed him long and soft. She bumped her nose against his. "I can't change what you did or what happened. But what I know is that you deserved to be loved, Kyle. To know what that's like. I believe that."

"I know." He whispered, his lips brushing hers. "You've shown me."

With nothing she could say left, she pressed a kiss to his lips again and slid off his lap. "I'll clean up real quick and we can finish the night by the fire, huh?"

"Do you want me to help?"

"No, handsome," she smirked.

Kyle chuckled as she stood and collected the plates, watching her pad back into the kitchen, his eyes roving up her bare legs to the point her denim shorts hit her thighs. Her skin had been kissed by the sun, freckles on display, and he enjoyed mapping them out like early astronomers mapped the constellations in the night sky. She kept her hair dark, and he was getting used to it.

Kyle Hansberry was in love, and it no longer scared the crap out of him.

* * *

Their routine changed a little over the rest of the summer, from spending days in the sun to morning walks with their coffee along the road into the village. Time ticked by, and soon they were at the end of the season and into a genuine relationship with full-fledged commitment and wonderful routines.

They learned each other's likes and dislikes, that didn't just revolve around the bedroom. He knew what made her tick and what made her flutter. She knew how to twist his ego and make him feel and push him to think. Kyle even started writing.

Sometimes the pages were filled with ideas or lists, other times it was filled with memories as he painfully worked through a traumatic moment, journaling his feelings down. A time or two, he even tore pages out with little notes left for Jennifer and sometimes a love letter or two.

It was about as good as anything could be, and as Thanksgiving rolled round, they found themselves preparing a special meal to celebrate the season in their new home.

Jennifer found two thick steaks for her and Kyle, a surprise he'd yet to know about while soft jazz played through the house. Roasted potatoes and vegetables sat cooking in the oven and a fresh apple pie cooked on the counter.

It wasn't quite Turkey, but it differed from their usual meals, and Jen knew he would appreciate it.

"Kyle, can you set the table, handsome?"

"Yeah, sure..." he strolled into the kitchen and pecked her cheek before he headed to gather what he needed from the drawer.

"You want wine with dinner?" He offered.

"Yeah, I found us a nice red. It's in the bar."

"Red?" He wondered, "with fish?"

"We're not having fish."

"What? It's not that weird dish Mrs. Renley made, is it?"

"No," she chuckled, "we have fillet steak with mushroom and pepper sauce, potatoes, roasted veggies, and an apple pie."

"Oh, sweetheart." Kyle looked like he could cry.

Jen chuckled, "it's Thanksgiving."

He set the table, poured their wine, and after Jennifer dished up their food, they sat with the fire in the living room and candlelight at the table.

Kyle had been quite morose the last few days, no doubt everything of the past year or two weighing on his mind. Jennifer noticed and treaded lightly around him lately, careful not to push too hard or press the wrong button.

"How is it?" She asked him as he stuck another piece of steak in his mouth.

"So fucking good," he purred. "Thank you, sweetheart."

Jen smiled as he continued eating, and then to her

surprise he looked at her and asked a question she never thought she would hear from him.

"Think we can get a Christmas tree round here?"

She blinked hard. "Uh, we can try."

He merely nodded and fell silent again.

She reached for his hand as it toyed with the stem of his glass. "Handsome...."

"Sorry, I was...miles away."

"Want to talk about it?"

He sighed, "just thinking, that's all. About how if I hadn't done what I did, things would be different. We'd be home now, maybe. Snow... a fire... how I'd be able to do the thing I want now more than anything."

Ignoring the topic of 'home', Jennifer wondered what he wanted. "What do you want to do, Kyle?"

"Marry you." His reply was instant, his eyes unwavering as they locked onto hers."

"W.. What?" Jennifer gasped.

Kyle shrugged, "I want to marry you. I know, I know-" he held his hand up to stop her from speaking, "it's not possible, but I just wanted to be honest."

"I.... Why don't you think it's possible?"

"How can it be?" He popped a shoulder.

"Uh, last I checked, I'm sitting right here." She gave a snort.

Kyle blinked, "but... how... I mean, we're hiding..."

"I think I'm trying to wrap my head around the fact that Kyle Hansberry wants to marry someone."

He groaned. "Don't, Jen..."

"Don't what," she smirked. "I'm sorry, Kyle, I.... Why don't you think we can?"

"We're hiding, like how can we legally do anything? Not to mention the fact I have nothing to buy you a ring with... although if I could get you one, it would be better than that monstrosity that bird dicked prick of an ADA gave you."

Jennifer sighed, "oh, Kyle." She stood and stepped to his side. Her soft hands cupped his thick beard, "if this were a proposal, I'm saying yes. I don't think it matters how legal it is. And I don't need a ring. Far as I'm concerned, I'm yours. I always have been."

Kyle smiled, his arm curling round her waist, "suppose that'll have to do. Nice idea, huh?"

"Well..." Jen moved to perch on his lap, "there's no reason why Vanessa and William couldn't tie the knot. Might not be exactly the same, but it would mean something to us..."

"To me." He whispered.

"And me."

"Marry me, Jennifer." He stated against her lips as he cupped her face, his forehead pressed into hers.

"Yes, Kyle," she smiled, her lips brushing his, "I will."

* * *

It happened a week after he asked, at sunset among candlelight.

It was as intimate of a wedding as one could get. Just the two of them. The only witness was the priest in the Spanish church near their home. She wore a white dress she found in the tourist shop in Porto Novo, khaki slacks and a white button-down shirt.

They'd picked their rings together, again from a jeweler in Porto Novo. A simple diamond solitaire 'engagement' ring for Jen, with matching platinum wedding bands for them both. The weight had felt odd on his hand, but Kyle welcomed it.

He was no longer that man he was when they first met, nor was he the same man who committed the worst of sins.

They didn't have a honeymoon of such, but dismissed their staff bar the bare minimum of security for two weeks and spent their days wearing as few clothes as possible, whilst their nights they dined in the restaurants they'd now come to know very well, taking long walks on the beach, toes digging into the sand.

Nearing the end of their honey-stay-moon, while laying in bed after their most recent copulation, Kyle sighed deeply. It broke the silence of their relaxation, his hand tracing up and down her shoulder and arm while Jennifer's head rested against his chest.

"Are you happy? Do I make you happy, Jennifer?" He soon asked.

"I wouldn't have married you if you didn't, Kyle." Her hand gently threaded through the hair on his chest, a thing he'd let grow back since coming to the island.

"Is Mrs. Jackson happy?"

"No, but Mrs. Hansberry is."

He chuckled and rolled over, caging her between his arms. "Fuck, I love you. You make me want to be a better person, Jen. I hope I am."

"You're an amazing man, Kyle. And you're going to be a brilliant father."

At that he snorted, "very funny."

"Kyle..." She softly smiled.

He froze, his eyes locked onto hers, "you... no, you can't be..."

"Yep," Jennifer nodded.

"I can't... I can't be a father," he shook his head, fear in his baby blues "I'm... I'm a fuckup!"

Her heart broke hearing him. "Okay. I'll uh, I'll get an appointment on the main island and take care of it."

"Jen... I... shit. I'm... no, that's..." he shook his head, "I don't..."

She pressed on his chest for space before slipping out from beneath the covers. Jennifer pulled her robe from the chair in their room and left him in bed.

Kyle led back, his hands running through his hair.

"Fuck," he shot out of bed, pulled on a pair of boxers, and hurried after her. "Jen..." He found her in the kitchen starting a tea kettle.

"Jen, sweetheart, I'm sorry."

"It's not like we planned this, it's a surprise for me too, I... It is what it is. Now I know how you feel. So, I'll figure it out. I'm sorry I did that to you."

"No, I... I don't want that. I don't... fuck, I'm scared, okay?"

"Yeah, me too. I mean, I'm a newly married and now pregnant fugitive. What's not to be scared about, right?"

He sank onto the stool by the breakfast bar, his hands in his hair. "I'm... I'm a screwup. Look at us. Miles away from anyone because of what I did and... what if I screw them up as badly as I am?"

"We can't have his conversation right now. Forget it, okay."

"Damned it, Jen, I can't forget it! You're having my baby. Our baby..."

She didn't say anything for a minute, only picked at the wrapper to her tea bag and fought her wobbling lip with eyes cast to her hands. Then, with a sniff, she spoke softly, "You know, I thought I was pregnant after you came back. Turns out I was just overwhelmed and that made me late."

Kyle swallowed, her admission catching him off guard, "you did?"

"Yeah, I was a week late. I was terrified then because I

wasn't so sure you were staying. That you couldn't handle this life that I selfishly dragged you into."

"You didn't drag-"

She cut him off, shaking her head. "But you've changed so much, Kyle. I don't know even know who that person you used to be is anymore." Her eyes fell upon his. " I left everything behind because I believed in you, that you made a horribly blind mistake in what you'd done. I trusted you then, and I trust you now."

"You do? I mean, you would... trust me as a parent?"

Jennifer shrugged. "Maybe that's where we're still different. I trust you with my life because I believe in you. To me, that matters more than anything. I wouldn't have trusted the man you used to be. I was scared then, but I'm not scared anymore."

His eyes filled with tears as he looked down at his bare feet, sniffing slightly. And she barely caught his words. "Please don't."

"Don't what?"

"Get rid of it?"

"I don't want to."

He took a deep breath, his face turned upwards as he glanced at the ceiling. After what felt like an age he looked at Jen, his blue eyes swimming. "I'm going to be a dad?"

Jennifer nodded slowly. "I'm two weeks late. I tested positive this morning."

He nodded, his steps towards her slow and deliberate.

When he reached her, he stopped, taking her left hand. He pressed a kiss to the inside of her wrist, his nose running gently along the vein.

The gesture made her shudder. "Kyle...."

"I love you."

"I know."

* * *

Charley Renée Hansberry was born eight months later in their home, set within the cliffside of Sano Antao Island. Mrs. Renley was Jennifer's midwife and she'd helped Jennifer deliver the six-pound baby girl with no drugs and a lot of pain.

And when Kyle held the baby, he'd seen his wife carry and grow, he felt a surge of love like nothing he'd experienced before. In fact, it'd brought a broken sob to his throat as Mrs. Renley placed Charley in his arms.

"Hi, Charley.... You're a beautiful girl, aren't you? Your mom, she's amazing." He sniffed. "I'm your dad, sweetheart. I promise to take care of you both. I don't know how, but I will."

His newborn baby daughter lay in his arms, her tiny mouth pouting as an equally tiny fist balled by her face.

Jennifer watched from their bed as they paced in front of the large windows overlooking the sea. "Michael..."

He turned to face her, eyes bright, a dopey smile on his lips.

"How's it feel?"

"Like I have so much love in my heart, my chest is going to burst. And I'll kill the first boy who even looks at her."

Jennifer laughed, then winced just as Charley began to fuss.

"You okay?"

"Sore, tired. She's probably hungry, she looking for a boob?"

"Aren't we all?" He snorted.

Scoffing, Jennifer popped a shoulder. "Bring her here." She undid the buttons on her nightgown and waited for Kyle to bring the swaddled girl her way.

Kyle crossed to their bed and gently handed her over, his large hand cupping her head until he was sure she was safely in her mother's arms.

Jennifer waited for her baby to latch before she looked up at Kyle. "Michael Kyle Hansberry, I love you."

"I love you, both of you. So fucking much."

With a teasing smirk, Jen looked at him. "Why?"

Kyle smiled, "you know why."